JOURNEY
TO THE
WEST

WILLIAM HAUPTMAN

JOURNEY TO THE WEST

iUniverse books may be ordered through booksellers or by contacting:

iUniverse
1663 Liberty Drive
Bloomington, IN 47403
www.iuniverse.com
1-800-Authors (1-800-288-4677)

ISBN: 978-1-5320-2234-0 (sc)
ISBN: 978-1-5320-2235-7 (e)

Library of Congress Control Number: 2017909476

Print information available on the last page.

iUniverse rev. date: 10/14/2017

For my companion, TEA
(1942–2011)

Thanks to Jan Reid for reading this when it was a work in progress, to Steve Davis for his encouragement, to James Magnuson for his friendship, and to Carolyn See for being a great writer.

The whole of world history often seems to me nothing more than a picture book which portrays humanity's most powerful and senseless desire—the desire to forget.

—Hermann Hesse, *Journey to the East*

PROLOGUE

I⁣ᴛ ᴡᴀs ᴍʏ destiny to take part in a great experience. By this, I mean the 1960s, which my companion Danny Abrams would later come to call "the Journey." And it does seem like we were always on the move then, going somewhere by bus or car or even hitchhiking, like our hero Jack Kerouac. What were we seeking? What young people are always seeking: love and freedom and truth, of course—and what the Zen Buddhists called satori, or enlightenment.

Then a series of catastrophes began. First, there was the Cuban Missile Crisis, which was followed a year later by the assassination of President Kennedy. The country was thrown into political turmoil, the Vietnam War began, and the decade became a troubled and confusing time of constant change. Through it all, the notion persisted that the solution to all our problems could only be found in California. But it took Danny and me seven long years to finally reach San Francisco, and by the time we did, the world Kerouac described had disappeared. The beatniks had been replaced by hippies, and Zen enlightenment, by the clear white light of acid and the teachings of Timothy Leary. There the Journey ended in despair for me, as it did for so many.

In the years that followed, I went to New York, where I finally managed to achieve some of my ambitions for myself. But in doing so, I had to forget about the sixties, including what we had been searching for. I decided the Journey had been a mistake. We had headed not for the morning light of the East but for the light that had shone on the longest afternoons of our childhoods. We had sought not necessity but the endless possibilities of the old frontier. We had taken the right Journey but had gone in the wrong direction.

More than twenty years passed before my true memories of the sixties returned, but when they did, I began to see the decade for its real worth. True, many of the ideas we had thought were new were old ones rediscovered, and the Journey had actually been going on since the beginning of human history. But I had solved some family mysteries that had troubled me since childhood—and even found some of the secrets we had been looking for. Finally, I decided to finish the story I had started long ago, an account of the Journey and my companions from the earliest days, when we met at a Texas high school and sometimes called ourselves, as Kerouac called the Zen lunatics of San Francisco, the Dharma Bums.

DHARMA BUMS

1

ON A WARM May morning in 1960, the bell rang, and the halls of Nortex High filled with students on their way to their next class. My girl, Becky Stamos, and I walked among them, holding hands. This was one of the largest buildings in town, made of red brick and covering more than four blocks. The halls were wide, and from the top of the great stairwells, you could look down five floors to the dark basement below. To me it seemed to hold all the years of school going back to our childhoods, and in a way it did. Ahead lay only one more, brilliant and empty as the sky above—our last, our senior year.

Today, there was a hint of anxiety in the air. The Russians had shot down one of our spy planes and captured the pilot. I had once dreamed of becoming a pilot—of flying a rocket to the moon and being the first man to set foot on it. That dream had died at Zundelowitz Junior High, when a hood named Bobby Lee Cummins had beaten me up on the first day of gym class. But it had probably been a good dream to lose.

When I'd reached Nortex High, I had started acting in plays. Now my senior year lay before me, and I was sure to be chosen for the National Thespian Society, get the lead in the senior play, and go all the way with Becky, who was my first real girlfriend.

"What are you thinking about, Will?" Becky asked me.

"Frances Gary Powers," I lied, "drifting down in his parachute, somewhere in Russia. Can you imagine what he's going through right now? He should have killed himself when he had the chance, with the poison needle. Spies are supposed to do that." My father had told me this the night before.

"Oh, the notice is up," Becky cried out, meaning the notice on the bulletin board next to the auditorium, where Miss Mott posted the names of those she had chosen for the National Thespian Society. "I can't wait to see it."

"Suit yourself," I said, letting go of her hand, and she ran ahead.

There was only one thing that bothered me. Becky's and my relationship was purely platonic. At the end of our dates, I would give her a friendly kiss or two, and that was that. And who had decided it would be this way, her or me?

Becky was waiting for me by the bulletin board, her books held in arms folded across her breasts.

"I'm sorry, Will," she told me. "But you didn't make it."

My face went hot with shame and then numb. Sure enough, my name was not on the list. My great performances as Johnny Appleseed and Lord Rochester had been ignored.

"She only picks football stars and rich people," I told Becky. "I don't play football, and my parents don't belong to the country club."

"She chose me."

"That's different. Your mother's a teacher."

"Oh, Will, I just hate it when you're so *cynical*."

More than anything else, Becky hated people who were cynical. It was better to be a good loser. "Sorry," I said. "You really *do* deserve it. Congratulations."

I was bitterly disappointed. Not only was I a good actor; I was one of the most popular boys in school. And who cared if my parents didn't have any money? Suddenly, when I looked at Becky, we seemed mismatched. She was slim and dark and quick; I was tall and blond and slow. Now that I was not going to be in the Thespian Society, she would never let me go all the way with her. My senior year would be empty and boring, and I couldn't wait to get out of this town and go to the University of Texas at Austin, where I would never have to see any of these people again.

But I was wrong. I was about to meet my great companions, the Dharma Bums. And the Journey was about to begin—our search for the meaning of life, the great secret.

Danny Abrams stood at the front of the classroom. We both belonged to DeMolay, a junior Masonic order, but had never really spoken. He was a short, muscular boy with cropped black hair who had moved to Nortex from Chicago in the ninth grade.

"My report is on *A Coney Island of the Mind*," he said, "a book of poems by the beatnik author Lawrence Ferlinghetti."

For once, I was listening. We were all listening.

"I don't believe that book is on the reading list," our teacher, Miss Moran, said.

"It's poetry," Danny said. "And I liked it."

"Oh, all right then. Just finish your report."

"I'm going to read Ferlinghetti's best poem," Danny said, "the way it might be read in a beatnik coffeehouse in San Francisco."

Then Danny cleared his throat and read "Sometime During Eternity," about the Crucifixion of Jesus, which ended with these lines:

Only He don't come down

From his Tree

Him just hang there

Looking real cool

And also

Real dead.

Danny had read an atheistic beatnik poem. It was the most shocking thing we had ever heard, and some of the girls, including Becky, began to cry.

"That will be enough, young man," Miss Moran told Danny. "You can go to the principal's office right now."

He went without another word. Joe Hollis was in that class, a hood who mysteriously made good grades. I didn't know him at all, but as Danny walked out the door, Joe gave me a wondering look, as if to say, *What did you think of that?*

That night, while my father played the piano in the front room, I asked my mother for the keys to our second car, the Chevy. Looking up Danny's address in the school directory, I drove directly to his house. His mother answered the door and told me he was in his room.

I found Danny sitting on his bed. He was watching the baseball game on television and was in no way surprised to see me.

"What'd you get?" I asked him.

"Three days detention hall. But I took my licks."

In those days, you could trade your detention hall time for licks that were delivered by Mr. Siebert, the dean of boys, with a perforated wooden paddle that had been known to bring tears even to the eyes of football players. I was impressed.

On the wall was a photograph of Danny, wearing strange robes and holding a scroll. I asked him what it was. "My bar mitzvah photo," he said. "I'm Jewish. You know what that means, don't you?"

I didn't really but said I did.

We watched the game in silence for another twenty minutes until the inning was over. Then Danny stood, turned off the television, and said, "You got your car? If you've got your car, then let's get the fuck out of here."

Lightning was flashing to the west, and a storm was rolling in from the Panhandle, filling me with secret excitement. We got in my car, and I drove out toward the south edge of town with no particular destination in mind. In those days, when I had just gotten my driver's license, I was still exploring Nortex and somehow thought there might be another high school out there, where I might have played football and gotten laid. On the radio, Roy Orbison was singing "Only the Lonely," the best song of the year so far.

I was about to say something about how Danny could be more popular if he tried, but suddenly he was talking, saying *everything* I had always thought but never told anyone.

"Senior High is ruled by conformity," he said. "It's all about the class system. There are the football stars, who get to wear their cowboy boots and Stetson hats on Friday, the day of the big game. There are the beauties, who aren't always beautiful but are always rich. Then there are the hoods, who get to beat us up any time they want. The rest of us are invisible—just like the Negroes, who go to Booker T—and Jews are the most invisible of all."

"You're right," I said. "All anybody in our school cares about is popularity."

"You're one to talk," he said. "Popularity is all you think about."

For a moment, I could say nothing. Popularity meant nothing to me, and Danny didn't know the whole story.

It had all started before Danny had even come to Nortex—on my first day of Zundelowitz Junior High, when Bobby Lee Cummins hit me in the face and I couldn't hit him back, just stared at the red drops of blood falling to the polished pine floor of the gym.

Bobby Lee was a son of the lowest oilfield trash, filled with hatred for anyone who was smarter than he was. The coach did nothing to stop this—I think the coach enjoyed it. My father offered to teach me how to box and bought me a punching bag. I got very good at hitting a punching bag, but I didn't want to hit anyone in the face, and I didn't want my father's help. Somehow, I was afraid that if I hit anyone in the face, I would feel a pain in my own fist beyond all imagining.

The worst thing the blow did was to drive a split between my mind and body, a wound that could not be detected by a doctor. Perhaps it had always been there, waiting for the blow to strike. This split between my mind and my body, between myself and itself, has long been a human problem and has been called by various names—sin, despair, a religious crisis, the divided self, and the Sickness Unto Death. Today we think it is genetic, that some people have always suffered from this wound. But I thought then I was the first person in the history of the world to experience it, and a great shame fell upon me.

I became a miserable ghost of myself, hiding out at the Strand Theater and watching the latest bad science fiction movies, like Roger Corman's *The Day the World Ended*. Radioactive fallout after a nuclear war had turned almost everybody into monsters. The survivors hid in a house in the Hollywood Hills until rain finally fell, killing all the monsters. Then the lovers set out into the world, a new Adam and Eve. I began to hope for nuclear war—if it came and I survived, I might find a girl who would go all the way with me.

But the split between my mind and body had also changed my appearance. In elementary school, I'd had the clean, hopeful face of a boy. In my yearbook photo at Zundy, my eyes were dead, my lips swollen, and my face was closed like a fist in the anticipation of another blow. *Now,* I thought, *no girl will ever love me.*

I tried religion. First I joined the Indian Heights Methodist Church, where I walked down the aisle and declared my love for Jesus Christ as my personal savior. I spent two years in dreary Fellowship Hall, drinking Kool-Aid and discussing the scriptures, and in all that time felt not the slightest trace of Christian love.

Finally I reached Nortex High, where I took my first drama class, performed my first scene, and got my first laughs—a moment that changed my life again. After that, I played young men and old fools and learned how to be all things to all people. I joined every group that asked me to join, including the Order of DeMolay, and thought I had finally healed myself. But popularity had not gotten me into the National Thespian Society.

Now I looked at Danny and said, "You got something better than popularity?"

"Yes," he said. "Zen enlightenment."

"What's that?"

"Complete honesty."

"I thought it was some kind of mystical thing."

"If you think it's so easy, let me hear you say one completely honest thing."

"Just let me think about it for a minute."

"No, you've got to say it without thinking."

On and on we argued about what I didn't know, and I had no idea where I was now, except I was driving down an empty road, when suddenly Danny shouted, "Turn left!"

I did and drove through an open gate in a cyclone fence. Beyond was an area of little two-story redbrick houses that looked like the campus of a junior college. I parked behind one of the houses and turned off my headlights. It was a spooky night. The lightning was closer, but I still heard no thunder. Overhead, the full moon shone down, showing every stick and blade of grass in brilliant detail.

"That was an almost perfect example of Zen," Danny said quietly.

"What's Zen?"

"You took an action without thinking."

Then I noticed the wire screens over the windows of the little houses and asked, "Where are we?"

"The state hospital," he said.

Suddenly, I was terrified. "We shouldn't be here."

"Be cool," Danny said, "and let's just dig this place."

So we stared around, and after a while, I whispered, "Who *are* these people?"

"People just like you and me. Probably the smartest people in Texas. They might have become artists or writers or poets—but they could not give up the roles society forced on them. Now they have found their way here."

"But they're *insane*."

"So is this whole town. This is what's waiting for us if we don't find Zen enlightenment."

I was exhausted and rested my forehead on the steering wheel. After long years of trying to forget my shameful secret, I had finally found a girl and almost become popular. Now Danny was telling me I had done the wrong thing and had to find Zen enlightenment, whatever that was.

"On the other hand," he said, "I sometimes think these people are happy here."

"Why?"

"Maybe here they have found satori."

"What's that?"

"Another name for enlightenment. The thing we are always looking for, the solution to all problems, the secret of life. Maybe they found friends here." He looked at me. "Why not admit it? You and I are a little more like them than we are like the other people in our class."

Maybe Danny was right. Popularity hadn't worked out. Maybe it was time for me to try something different. And Zen enlightenment sounded exotic, mysterious, exciting.

Danny softly recited the first lines of Allen Ginsberg's poem *Howl*:

> I saw the best minds
> of my generation destroyed
> by madness,
> Starving, hysterical, naked,
> Dragging themselves through
> Negro streets at dawn,
> Looking for an angry fix.

When he finished, there was a long silence, broken by a preliminary rumble of thunder.

"You may be right," I said. "We may be a little like them."

"We're going to be," he said, "if we never get out of Nortex."

But why did he say that? There was no doubt we were to graduate and get out of this town, was there? When I looked at him, he was smiling; then he started laughing hysterically, louder and louder. I was laughing too, but I was suddenly frightened and started the car, stepped on the gas, and roared out through the gate—out of that place for what I hoped was forever.

2

DANNY HAD COME to Nortex when his father, Morrie, had started a store called Popular Furniture. Danny was Jewish and had always known he was different. I had too, although I was not religious. For a while I began to think I might have been better off if I had been born a Jew—in fact, I even thought about becoming one.

One Saturday morning, Danny took me to the synagogue, where we sat through the incomprehensible service and later spoke to the rabbi in his office.

"What do you want of me?" the Rabbi asked us.

"You're from New York, aren't you?" Danny said.

"Queens," he replied. "Do you have a question you want to ask me?"

"No," Danny said. "It's just that you wear tennis shoes, and we were thinking you might be hip. We were also wondering if you might know Allen Ginsberg or Jack Kerouac."

The rabbi looked at me. "What are *you* doing here?" he asked me. "You're not Jewish."

I was honestly surprised he could tell. "No," I said. "But I'm interested."

The rabbi's face darkened, and he stood. "I wear tennis shoes," he said, "because the Torah tells us you should not wear the skins of illegally slaughtered animals. Did your parents teach you nothing? Why has God sent me here? This is the worst town I've ever been in."

As we left, Danny said, "So you see, being Jewish isn't such a great thing."

"You're a Jew."

"Like I told you, I'm a Zen Buddhist."

Then Danny took me to Thomas's Newsstand, which was open all night and sold pornographic magazines and switchblade knives to airmen. But here you could also buy paperback editions of serious books, including some written by beatniks. I had read exactly one serious book, *The Web and the Rock* by Thomas Wolfe, which had filled me with dreams of becoming a famous writer and making love to wealthy women, but I had never confessed this to anyone. Danny told me to buy Kerouac's *On the Road*; his new novel, *The Dharma Bums*; and *The Way of Zen* by Alan Watts.

Buddhism said the meaning of life was suffering. But to some extent this suffering could be lessened by following *dharma*, which meant "the law." Zen was a particularly contentious branch of Buddhism. Its followers shouted what sounded like jokes and riddles at each other, like, "What is the sound of one hand clapping?" But Danny explained this was really a discipline, and you had to be completely honest at all times. At first, I was excited because this sounded to me like acting. Up there in the brilliant light of the stage, you didn't have time to think or hide anything. But Danny said playing a role where the lines were already written for you was entirely different from the spontaneous honesty of Zen.

If you practiced Zen for years, you might attain satori, or enlightenment. I recognized this as a mystical experience—the thing my father was always talking about, especially when he'd been drinking—but Danny said it was the only thing worth looking for. The ancient Chinese poet Han Shan had found it when he'd climbed Cold Mountain, and he'd described it as a clear white light shining down on him.

Neither Danny nor I knew then that Zen Buddhism was a real religion, with its own pantheon of reincarnated saints. He thought it was a theology of jokes, and I thought, especially after reading *The Dharma Bums*, that it might be a good method of talking girls into going all the way with me.

That summer, Danny got us jobs through his "Jewish connections," by which he meant his uncle Larry Kris, a fat guy who drove a Cadillac and called himself a professional gambler. Larry, who was always telling us we should get some *quim*, found us jobs lifeguarding at a new pool out by the air force base. This was a job ordinarily reserved for football players, but once I tried it, I knew I wanted to do it forever.

Danny took the morning shift, and I took the afternoon. For five hours I sat on my tall white tower, covered with Coppertone, enjoying the admiring stares of air force brats. When it got dark, Danny reappeared, bringing a six-pack. I shut down the pool and cleaned it—red dirt was always collecting on the bottom—and a couple of the bolder girls sometimes stayed and helped us drink the beer.

Then Danny and I set out to explore the Nortex night. First, we'd go see a movie at the Wichita Theater, which was the classiest in town. There were a lot of great movies that summer, like Elia Kazan's *Wild River*, starring Montgomery Clift and Lee Remick. He was a Jew who worked for the TVA, and she was a hillbilly woman with a child. After I saw this movie, I often dreamed of going to Lee Remick's home in the smoky, old Tennessee Valley and making love to her. Then Danny and I drove around Country Club, the wealthy neighborhood where beautiful girls lived in great homes whose lawns were covered with emerald grass, oak trees, and statuary. Soon we began stealing these statues for some unspecified purpose, hiding iron deer, plaster jockeys, and concrete frogs in the weeds of a vacant lot.

"Now you're a gonif," Danny told me as we lifted a statue of a sleeping Mexican into the trunk of my car.

"What's that?"

"The Hebrew word for *thief*."

Finally we went back to Danny's house, where we watched *The Million Dollar Movie*. Usually it was one of the science fiction or horror movies we had seen in our childhoods and adolescence—movies that were, as Danny put it, "so bad they're good." Once he showed me a notebook in which he had written his favorite lines:

> ➤ "Friend." —Boris Karloff, *The Bride of Frankenstein*
> ➤ "Our real strength is the size of our god." —Rex Reason, *This Island Earth*
> ➤ "Keep watching the skies." —Douglas Spencer, *The Thing from Another World*
> ➤ "Let me tell you the story of left hand, right hand, love and hate." —Robert Mitchum, *The Night of the Hunter*

If Danny couldn't be a poet, he told me, he wanted to be a great movie director someday, like John Ford, Elia Kazan, or Nicholas Ray.

Toward the end of that summer, Danny and I went to see a movie, *The Fugitive Kind,* which was based on a play by Tennessee Williams. It was my first art movie and starred Marlon Brando. Joe Hollis, the hood who had been in our class the day Danny had read the Ferlinghetti poem, was also there with his low-rent girl—a red-haired Trans-Texas stewardess who was two years older than us and had already graduated.

"Brando is god," Danny said to Joe as we walked up the aisle and out of the theater.

"You're right," Joe said. "Brando is god."

Joe looked a little like Brando himself. His black Indian hair was combed straight forward, like Brando's in the movie *Julius Caesar.*

After the movie, Danny and I went to the Pioneer Drive-In. He was driving his parents' Olds that night, and as we pulled in and circled the parking lot, I looked through the thick green-tinted windshield and went into a Kerouac monologue. "There they are," I said, "the beauties, the favorites, the hoods. There's Joe Hollis, the hood who makes good grades, and there's Bobby Lee Cummins, who beat me up in Zundy. Fuck you, Bobby," I said, thinking he couldn't possibly hear me.

We parked, ate our Frito-chili pies, and drank our cherry Dr. Peppers.

Suddenly Bobby Lee Cummins, my hood nemesis, was pulling me out of the car.

"I heard you say 'fuck you,'" he told me.

"You couldn't have."

"I read your lips," he said. "Now I'm going to beat the dog shit out of you and your Jew boy friend."

It was happening again, and there was nothing I could do to stop it.

Then Joe Hollis was there, pushing his way between us. "Walk on, Bobby Lee," he said. "I beat you up in Zundy, and can I do it again right now."

"Well, shit," Bobby Lee Cummins said but hobbled away. Like most hoods, he was short and wore motorcycle boots for stomping his victims.

"I heard him call Danny a Jew boy," Joe said. "That's fucking prejudice, and I won't stand for it."

Later, Joe dropped off his girl and took us downtown to the Denver Café—an old pool hall on Ohio Street where hoods and Mexican kids met. Larry Kris was there, talking about getting some *quim*, and Kelso, the legless pool shark who lived at the YMCA and rolled around on a wooden platform with roller skate wheels. We watched as Kelso lifted himself onto a chair and leaned over the table to make his shots—"Just like a character in a Nelson Algren novel," Danny said to me. "And would you just dig that?"

Joe Hollis became my second great companion of that year. He was a hood and drove a hood's car—a black 1949 Ford with a chrome bullet nose—but what made him different was that Joe was a math genius, perhaps the only hood in Texas who carried a slide rule on his belt. There were dark rumors about his origins. Some said his father was a wealthy oilman. Others claimed he was a bad cop who was doing time in Huntsville. Whoever his father had been, Joe's mother had married Bud, a refinery worker, and they lived down on Victory Street, in the oldest and poorest part of town.

Danny and I began dropping in on Joe to listen to his Miles Davis and Chet Baker albums. Here his stepfather, Bud, came home every night to eat roast beef and boiled potatoes, the food I secretly wanted to eat. Joe had grown up down here—running with the hoods, fighting them on grade school playgrounds, staying out all night, and slipping into the Taystee Bakery to eat himself sick on doughnuts. If only I had grown up down here, I thought, I might have learned how to fight and had a low-rent girl who loved me.

Joe was going to Rice University, where only the smartest kids in Texas went, to study philosophy and higher math. His favorite book was Nietzsche's *The Will to Power*, but he had read all of Kerouac. And when Danny told him we were looking for satori, he told us he had already found it.

"You guys aren't doing so bad," he said, "but you'll never find satori by reading. You've got to do the things *you're afraid of doing*—like fighting and fucking and drinking wine and shouting poetry at the moon. When was the last time you got drunk?"

Danny and I admitted we never had.

"I can get satori for you any time," Joe asserted. "It comes in a bottle, and my first experience with it was when I was twelve years old."

My father was an alcoholic and had made me promise I would never drink. But I had always known that someday I would break that promise.

So on the night of the first football game, when the Prairie Dogs had won and the moon sailed over the water tower behind the stadium, Joe and Danny and I walked through the parking lot, got in Joe's old Ford, and drove down to Colored Town. There, he parked in front of a liquor store and said to the first old guy who walked past, "Hey, man, I'll give you twenty dollars if you'll buy us three bottles of wine, and you can keep five for your trouble."

The old guy went into the liquor store, and we sat there looking around us. Danny said, "This is the place where white people go to do everything that is forbidden."

"Dig it," Joe said.

After a while, the old guy came back with three bottles of Gallo Thunderbird, and Joe paid him. Then he drove to a place behind the television station where the cops would never bother us. Leaving the car by the side of the road, we walked toward the river, through a mesquite thicket, to the top of a little caprock mesa. There we unrolled our sleeping bags, and Joe built a fire of mesquite twigs. Finally we opened the bottles and drank down mouthfuls of warm yellow wine.

Joe and Danny talked about football, girls, the sadness of it all. The moon had gone down, and the Milky Way was a moraine of diamond dust across the sky. I told myself this was how I would describe it when I wrote it all down tomorrow. A numbing warmth filled my mind, and time stood still. *I could listen to these guys talk forever,* I thought, and soon it began to seem that I *had* been listening to them talk forever. So this was drunkenness, the state my father was so fond of.

"What are you thinking, Will?" Joe asked me.

"'I think we are lost in America,'" I said. "'But I think we shall be found.'" This was a quote by Thomas Wolfe. I didn't really know what it meant but had been waiting to say it for a long time.

"Oh, man, that was great," Joe said. "Will here just found enlightenment."

"Yes," Danny said, a little ironically, "he has achieved satori."

They were right. When I opened my mouth, I spoke the truth effortlessly, without thinking. I was having a mild mystical experience of the sort produced by alcohol, which the philosopher William James describes in *The Varieties of Religious Experience*. It was nowhere near as powerful as my later mystical experiences, but it was my first experience of drunkenness, and I saw myself and my companions in an almost mythic light. Joe was another Neal Cassady, Danny was another Allen Ginsberg, and I might be another Jack Kerouac, who would someday set down all our exploits on an endless roll of Teletype paper.

At this moment, I decided that, someday, I would become not an actor but a writer—or maybe both.

"So now you know what true satori is," Joe said. "To be drunk all the time. And now I'll tell you why this is going to be a great year for us. Because we are not like the others. We are superior. And this year, we're going to show everybody in this school that we don't believe in their bourgeois values—we believe in kicks and truth."

"We shall perform acts of Zen lunacy," Danny said, "and, if possible, get into serious trouble."

"Get laid," I put in.

"Yes, he is right, we shall all get laid. And at the end of this year, we shall all go out to San Francisco in my old Ford. There we shall drink wine, climb mountains, write poetry, and practice yab-yum—ancient Tibetan sex rituals—with beatnik girls. And there, I say, we shall finally become true Dharma Bums."

Then we gave ourselves up to Dionysius and ran around the top of the mesa. I heard Danny yelling at me for a long time, and then I fell down onto the dirt and stared up at the stars, which began to wheel around the pole star, until I lost consciousness.

To me, that was the first night of the Sixties.

At sunrise, my companions brought me home. When I opened the front door, I saw my father was playing the piano in the front room. He had been up all night, teaching himself the scores of the great composers, and there was a fifth of bourbon on top of the piano.

"Been drinking, haven't you, Sonny?" he said. "I knew you would, sooner or later. Sit down and talk to me for a while. I read your book—your Jack Kerouac."

It came to me that my father was doing an impersonation of Percy Dovetonsils, the beatnik poet as played by Ernie Kovacs on the *Ernie Kovacs Show*. "Some parts of it were good. In fact, I was moved. But I've got to say, man … that I just didn't *dig* it."

"Don't talk to me that way," I said.

"Now your friends have taught you how to drink. You've been getting Off the Beam for a long time, Sonny."

This was a reference to the On the Beam Society, the cult that had encouraged his mystical ideas and was a great embarrassment to both me and my mother. I turned away.

"Don't go," he said. "I'm just getting started."

But I went to my room, which I shared with my little brother, Ray. There I fell on my bed and instantly passed out, and my father resumed playing the piano again.

3

My FATHER WAS the original Dharma Bum, the first to go in search of the secret of life. He was a soldier, a geologist, a gifted musician. In the early fifties, he'd had a mystical experience, which he never forgot. But then he began drinking heavily, and worse, began telling everybody about his experience. For this reason I was reluctant for my companions to meet him.

He was born on a farm near Julien, Nebraska, and his parents named him Harmon Langner. I have a sepia photograph of him as a naked cherub with tinted red hair, clinging to his mother, Belle. She stares at the camera serenely, a beautiful woman. Another photograph shows him standing in a cornfield, holding his father, Raymond's, hand. But Ray's eyes avoid the camera, as if he already knows his destiny and is trying to hide it.

Ray was one of those mechanical geniuses who started out repairing bicycles and then moved on to cars and airplanes. When World War I came along, he joined the army, became an aircraft mechanic, and was sent to France. After the war, he divorced Belle and ended up as an aeronautical engineer at Wright Field in Dayton, Ohio. Ray belonged to the Rosicrucians, a reincarnational cult, and believed he had a talent for engineering because he had worked on the machinery of Atlantis in a past life.

Belle remarried a neighboring farmer, Thorn Ellis, and they moved to Lincoln. My father disliked his stepfather and consoled himself by learning how to play the piano. By the time he was a senior at Lincoln High, he was playing the organ for silent movies at the Capitol Theater. One was *The Lost World*, based on a novel by Sir Arthur Conan Doyle, about an expedition that found a lost plateau in the Amazon where dinosaurs still existed. When my father went to the University of Nebraska, he decided to study geology.

He was playing the piano at a fraternity party when he met my mother, Aline Vanderwaal, a pretty sorority girl from the small Nebraska town of Nemaha. He had just performed the role of the Melancholy Jaques in Shakespeare's *As You Like It*—a performance I will forever wish I had seen—and at the party got drunk for the first time and had what sounds like a mystical experience.

"My head was filled with light, Sonny," he later told me. "I heard music and could make up poetry like Shakespeare wrote. But by the next day, I'd forgotten it all."

For what it's worth, I have also heard the music. I am not talking about the theme music from the movie of my life—the story of a boy who grew up in Texas and went on to do great things—which all boys hear. I mean the faint, crystalline music, my special gift and my father's, which came to me only at the most important moments of my life. But like my father, I always managed to forget it.

Harmon and Aline were married after graduation, and he went to work for Shell. The company sent him to Nortex, a town on the Red River, where there had been a big oil boom in the twenties. His job was to make surface maps of old leases, finding overlooked deposits of oil. Harmon rented a house, bought a piano, and played it all night long, even until the neighbors complained.

He joined the army just after Pearl Harbor and was sent to Fort Sill in Lawton, Oklahoma, where I was born at the end of 1942. Later my father went to Staff and Command School at Fort Leavenworth and became a captain. He fought in the Ardennes and returned with a Bronze Star for valor, a box of lead soldiers he found in Germany, and a certain nervousness around the Fourth of July—he hated the sound of fireworks.

My brother, Ray, who was born ten years after I was, often argued with me about my father's greatest war story. He said it was the time my father shot a German officer who had surrendered his pistol but not his arrogance right between the eyes. But my father had never told me this story, and I hoped it was not true. He had told me that when his division was crossing Germany, they'd passed near Bayreuth, the site of Wagner's opera house. My father drove his Jeep there and was the first American to arrive. All he wanted to see was Franz Lizst's rehearsal piano, which was sacred and never touched. An old man told him obligingly he could play it if he wished. So he sat down and played Johnny Mercer's "Accentuate the Positive."

> You've got to
> Accentuate the positive
> Latch on to the affirmative
> Eliminate the negative
> Don't mess with Mr. In-Between

To me, this was my father's greatest war story.

I grew up a lonely child on Cedar Street in Nortex, sitting like Narcissus and studying my reflection in the goldfish pond behind the rented garage apartment where we lived. My father often drove off to the country in his Jeep to look for oil and left my mother and I alone—which I enjoyed, because then I had her to myself. Once she took me to see Walt Disney's *Bambi*, which I loved so much I wanted to *be* Bambi and live forever as a cartoon animal in a pastel forest.

In the summer of 1949, Shell sent my father to Wyoming, and he took my mother and me along. There we lived on a sheep ranch with real cowboys who carried real pistols. My father found a dinosaur skeleton, saw a flying saucer—a chromium hubcap sailing over the badlands—and started buying a new magazine called *Fate: True Stories of the Strange, the Unusual, and the Unknown.* One evening while we were looking through the telescopic sight of his rifle at the moon, he told me, "You can be the first man to set foot on it, Sonny, if you want it badly enough."

I loved the ranch, but my mother hated it. There was no electricity, and my father was thirty years old and still working in the field, making maps. Toward the end of the summer, we drove home through Colorado and Nebraska and Kansas in a hard rain. I sat on a blanket in the back of the Jeep, my teeth slowly grinding a piece of rock candy to saliva, until finally my mother said, "Let's stop. Something bad is going to happen."

At Pryor, Oklahoma, we stopped at a motel. The next morning, my father and I walked a half a mile down the road and found that a bridge had been washed out, and two or three cars lay atop each other in the streambed.

"Your mother sensed this was going to happen," he told me. "One night when I was in combat, the Germans lit me up with flares, and she had a nightmare I was in danger. Your mother has premonitions—and we should always listen to her."

When we returned to Nortex, my father bought a home in a new suburb called Indian Heights. There he took his piano out of storage, and on weekends, he and my mother gave parties for their geologist friends, at which he played popular tunes. I liked the new house, where I had my own bedroom, very much. There were also other kids on the block, and for the first time in my life, I had playmates.

That fall, I started Crockett Elementary School, and at Christmas, there was a play. The teacher gave me the role of a shepherd boy who found the Baby Jesus in a manger, and I got all my lines right. That spring, my mother told me I was going to have a baby brother or sister, and that fall, I began the second grade, which was even better than the first.

Life published an article about the new science fiction movies. One, called *Destination Moon*, had a rocket like a chromium artillery shell, and my father and I both wanted to see it. The night we were coming back from the movie we turned onto our block and saw an ambulance in our driveway, its red lights flashing.

My mother had suffered a miscarriage, and the next day, my father told me that my baby sister had died. My mother grieved for months and, even years afterward, would hardly speak on the anniversary of her death.

Soon my father started disappearing for two and three days at a time. Later I learned he took a motel room, where he could drink as much as he wanted.

Not until that spring did he began to play the piano again. On warm nights when I sat on the front porch and watched the moon rise, it seemed that he played for me alone. Then one night, he asked me if I had ever heard of the theory of reincarnation. We had just seen a strange movie called *You Never Can Tell*, in which Dick Powell played a police dog that was poisoned by gangsters and reincarnated as a Hollywood private eye, who then set out to find the men who had killed his master.

"Will I come back as a dog?" I asked my father, hoping reincarnation meant you turned into an animal, an erotic idea for me ever since I had seen *Bambi*.

"No, Sonny," he told me. "You will always come back as a man, a higher soul."

My father was full of new ideas that year. His chiropractor had just introduced him to the On the Beam Society.

The society had been started by Dr. Truman Swift, a chiropractor who claimed to have been a Medal of Honor winner in the First World War. In the late forties, Dr. Truman, as my father always called him, had a "cosmic illumination," a mystical experience, and was confined to Brooke Army Hospital in San Antonio. There he wrote down the secrets of the universe on the walls of his room, in hieroglyphics, which later turned out to be Babylonian cuneiform. Dr. Truman then established the On the Beam Institute on a ranch he called Aum-Sat-Tat, near Boerne, Texas. There he taught the lessons he had learned, Phases One through Seven. The printed editions of these lessons had the symbol of the On the Beam Society on the cover—an airplane following a radio beam through a thunderstorm.

It was a cult of course, very much like the Rosicrucianism or the Theosophical Society—in fact the name Aum-Sat-Tat had been borrowed from the writings of the theosophist Madame Blavatsky. Later it was easy for me to see that my father had returned to the reincarnational beliefs that his father, Ray, had told him about. But there was something compelling, even sinister about the On the Beam Society. Every Beamer, as they called themselves, learned hypnosis. Deep trance states and even the cosmic illumination itself were promised to Beamers who studied long and hard enough.

It cost a lot of money, and when my father sent enough to take Phases One through Five down at "the Ranch," as Aum-Sat-Tat was called, I heard my mother tell him, "You're trying to turn a man called Dr. Truman into a God."

That fall, my father came back from the Ranch and told my mother and I that he'd had a cosmic illumination himself. I knew *something* had happened to my father down at Aum-Sat-Tat, but my mother was more skeptical than ever. My father won the argument when he found oil in Clay County, which he credited to the teachings of Dr. Truman. Suddenly we had a new car, my father had stopped drinking, and my mother was pregnant again. Then, in the spring of 1952, my father insisted my mother and I go with him down to Aum-Sat-Tat to learn its lessons.

We stayed in a little limestone cabin and every morning walked down the hill under the low, fast clouds of the hill country. Dr. Conrad Smith, an important Beamer, taught our first class. "You should have been here last year when Dr. Truman taught Phase One," he told us. "We were on the Etheric Plane most of the time. Dr. Truman stuck pins into my wife's arms, and she didn't even feel them. She was in a deep trance and remembered her first incarnation, when she had been a priestess in Lemuria, the lost continent of Mu. Dr. Truman performed miracles every night. 'You want to see the stars?' he said. Little stars shot out of his hand. 'You want to see flying saucers? I'll bring them here.' Four or five flying saucers flew down the valley."

After the class, Dr. Smith told my father, "Your son is like Jesus Christ at the temple. I can see his aura, and obviously this is not his first incarnation."

I liked Aum-Sat-Tat. I was still a child, and to me it was like a theme park. The library in the Big House had all the Dave Dawson books, including *Dave Dawson on Guadalcanal*. Peacocks and tame deer walked around the swimming pool all day. At night, the paths on the hill were lit by colored lights, and classical music played from hidden loudspeakers. Dr. Truman had named each class after an Indian tribe; you were a Husta, a Gusta, or a Pusta. There were sayings nailed to each tree. There was also a tree house called the Husta Roost in a huge oak, and a telephone booth at a crossroads with signs pointing in different directions—to Heaven, Hell, Phase Five.

On our last day there, my father and I walked up the hill together, and he described what had happened to him here. "Dr. Truman gave me a hypnotic suggestion that I would have a cosmic illumination and that it would be a good experience. That night I sat by the pool for the SLUMP—it stands for *Souls Live Upon Many Planes*. Beethoven's Ninth was playing on the loudspeakers, and I heard every note like never before. Then I left the pool and walked up the hill. It was dark, but somehow I could see everything, and the colors were brilliant. A deer came out of the woods and licked my hand. I had the answers to questions I'd been asking my whole life. Beethoven was deaf, you know, but his dying words were, 'I can hear in heaven.'"

This was my father's cosmic illumination, the first I'd ever heard described. It was his most profound mystical experience, but he never had another, although he hoped he would until the end of his days.

When we returned to Nortex, my father played the piano constantly. He was teaching himself *Clair de Lune*, his well in Clay County was making plenty of money, and he was On the Beam. I was sitting on the front porch one night when he came out and asked me, "Are you ready for a piano lesson, Sonny?"

Perhaps I was afraid music would carry me off, as it had my father. Or perhaps I smelled bourbon on his breath and knew he had been drinking again. But I said, "Not tonight."

After a while, my father went back inside the house and resumed playing the piano. *Something* had happened to my father down at Aum-Sat-Tat. I didn't know what—but somehow I could not get over the idea that my father had been made a fool of.

So my little brother, Ray, learned how to play the piano, but I never did. As the years went by, my father forgot the promises he had made to himself and drank heavily. Perhaps he hoped to recreate his cosmic illumination, although he must have known that alcoholism finally made the experience impossible.

After that night, my life changed as well. That year I began reading the science fiction of Robert A. Heinlein, whose stories about spaceflight were based on solid scientific theory. I told myself I would forget about cosmic illuminations and flying saucers and, when I grew up, become a pilot and fly rocket planes. This was my best chance to get to the moon, not the On the Beam Society. Holding out my arms, I stepped off the front porch and revolved slowly around my yard, staring up at the stars and down at the lightning bugs at my feet. I was pretending I was a spaceman lost in zero gravity—my dream of total freedom ever since I had seen it in my favorite science fiction movie, itself based on a Heinlein story, *Destination Moon*.

4

ON ALMOST EVERY night in the fall of 1960, the Dharma Bums drove around Nortex in Joe's car or Danny's or mine, wearing black sweatshirts and sunglasses even at night. On the back of my sweatshirt, I had printed in white paint *Cogito ergo sum*—the proposition of the philosopher Descartes: "I think, therefore I am." On Friday nights, if there was a home game, we went to the stadium and cheered the Nortex Prairie Dogs. On Saturday nights, we went to the Wichita Theater with the rest of our classmates to see the latest movie. But the Dharma Bums snuck in bottles of red wine, sat in the balcony, and shouted out drunken comments like the San Francisco beatniks in Hubert Selby's great short story "Double Feature."

Kennedy and Nixon had been nominated that summer, and their campaigns had begun, but we cared nothing for politics. This was our senior year. Everything was happening for both the first and last time, but only two things were important to me. The first was finding a girl who would go all the way with me. The second was football—the Dharma Bums might be beatniks, but we knew the Nortex Prairie

Dogs had to win the state championship this year, or the rest of our lives wouldn't be worth a shit.

In September, Danny and I were rehearsing the DeMolay initiation ceremony at Maskat Temple. Part of the ceremony was a play about the martyrdom of Jacques de Molay, our founder, who had been burned at the stake by the Catholic Inquisition. I played DeMolay, and Danny had the small role of a monk. When rehearsal was over, we walked to my car, and Danny said, "You told me acting was a kind of Zen, but you are terrible in that role, and I was not enlightened at all."

"I'm not saying I'm a great actor yet," I told him. "But some of my scenes are pretty good."

"I will give you a performance on Saturday night," Danny said, "that will produce more enlightenment than you can, without saying a single word."

"I'd like to see that," I said.

But I forgot all about this until Saturday night, when Joe came by with Danny, and we drove downtown, sharing a bottle of wine on the way. Joe found a parking place, and we walked to the Wichita Theater, where we bought tickets and sat up in the balcony. When the lights went down, Joe took another bottle of wine out of his jacket, and we started drinking it. Danny got up without a word and left.

The movie was *The Alamo*, with John Wayne and Laurence Harvey. It had just begun when I heard a commotion under the balcony, and Joe said, "What the hell is going on?"

Then we saw Danny shuffle into view below, wearing the brown monk's robe with a hood. He had stolen his costume after rehearsal, brought it to the movie theater tonight, and put it on in the restroom.

Our classmates and their dates began to laugh and applaud as Danny walked the aisles. Then he climbed the steps to the little stage under the screen and made grunting sounds at the enormous images of John Wayne and Laurence Harvey.

Danny later called this "An act of Zen that enlightened everyone." I don't know about that, but it did create a riot. The manager finally turned on the lights, and Joe turned to me, said, "We'd better get out of here," and we ran to his car. The whole audience followed Danny outside, but we came around the block and picked him up in front of the theater, just before the cops arrived.

The following Tuesday was the first senior class assembly, and I stood up and performed my own act of Zen—by nominating Harvey Lutz for our class president. This was the name of a nonexistent grind I had invented, but the faculty didn't know that.

Harvey Lutz won the election, and it took an hour for our teachers to realize there was no such person. Another election had to be held, and this time Pigs Garland, the captain of the football team, was elected senior class president, as he should have been in the first place. I was a little surprised when some people told me they had thought I was nominating Danny, but I thought that was the end of it.

Then the next night, at the DeMolay meeting, we learned that Danny had been suspended for six months for wearing his monk's costume at the movie theater. The charge was "betraying the secrets of the Order."

Danny was furious. "I'd like to know what some of those secrets are," he said. "For instance, DeMolay is the only club in high school that accepts Jews but not Catholics."

"What do you care?"

"I also think that, since they kicked me out, you should quit in protest."

But I refused. I was in line to become master councilor of DeMolay that year and thought that was more important.

It was the start of a long competition between us. Ten years later, I would go to the first Nortex High Reunion. Nobody remembered that I had been master councilor of DeMolay that year, but everyone remembered that Danny had been Harvey Lutz, the Zen lunatic, the holy fool of our senior class.

The Dharma Bums always ate lunch at the Pig Stand, a favorite hangout for hoods. We sat in Joe's old Ford, drinking coffee in which he had soaked tubes of Benzedrine from Valo inhalers, bought at the drugstore.

"This year, you will have girls," Joe told us. "They won't want to graduate without having *the great experience.*"

By this he meant sex, which he said was a form of enlightenment.

"I've never had the experience," Danny admitted. "What's it like?"

Joe described it.

"Thank you," Danny said. "I've been waiting a long time to hear that."

Joe looked over his shoulder at me. "And you will have to whip Bobby Lee Cummins's ass, which is not so hard—I know this because I've done it myself."

"I think I should get laid first," I said. "What if I lose?"

"You don't have to win the fight. Girls will be impressed if you just try."

"I refuse to put up the effort to get a girl," Danny said.

A long silence followed this. Then Joe said, "It doesn't take any effort. All you have to do is think like a hood."

"How is that?"

"Pretend you don't like them. Girls can't resist this."

"It's all a matter of losing control, isn't it?" I said.

Here I must explain my attitude toward girls at this time. I loved them all but trusted not a single one. Even a good girl, like Becky, might lose control and go all the way with a hood or a football player, as so many had.

"It's the erotic dream of both sexes," I continued. "Boys secretly hope girls will lose control and go all the way with them. Girls secretly hope their boyfriends will lose control and force them to go all the way."

"It will take you years to learn how to lose control," Danny told me. I let that go by.

"You can try bad girls or rich girls," Joe went on. "Bad girls have a secret liking for smart boys. Both have already done it, with hoods. But rich girls have had abortions."

"Don't hoods use rubbers?"

"Rich girls don't like rubbers. They think a rubber means you don't love them. Hoods have used this method for years—knocked up rich girls by telling them they loved them too much to use a rubber and then gotten their fathers to pay them off."

I found this hard to believe.

"But you are not a hood," Joe said, "so you should always use a rubber. I keep mine in that red satin Valentine candy box in the glove compartment."

"What kind of girl are you going to try for this year?" Danny asked Joe.

"I already have a girl," Joe said. "But I might try a rich girl this year—I've never had one before."

I closed my eyes and felt warm sunlight on my face. The Benzedrine was making my stomach rumble, and something *so good* was just about to happen to me.

"Oh, this is going to be a great year," Joe was saying. "You will make love to girls in the backseat of your car, you will make love at the drive-in movies, I say you will even make love to girls in the rain, like in *Lady Chatterley's Lover.*"

I began by dating Harla Hines, a rich girl—I didn't know any bad girls. I did my best to make our date into an act of Zen and tried to take her by surprise. Instead of going to the Pioneer Drive-In, I drove to the old Riverside Cemetery, which was like the cemetery where Joanne Woodward had taken Marlon Brando in the movie *The Fugitive Kind*, which she had called "the Bone Orchard."

There I parked, opened a bottle of wine, took Harla's hand, and asked her, "Do you know there's a little bird with no feet so it has to spend all its life in the sky?" This was a line from the movie.

"What in the *world* are you talking about?" Harla asked me.

When I admitted I didn't know, she said, "I like you, Will—you have a good sense of humor—but not in *that way*. And aren't you dating Becky Stamos?"

This was the last thing I wanted to hear, so I took Harla home, being polite and platonic, and that was the end of that.

Then Joe surprised everybody by doing what he had suggested—he dropped his Trans-Texas girl and started dating a rich girl, Candy Todd. The next weekend, she invited the Dharma Bums over to her house in Country Club for one of her Saturday-afternoon Coke parties, which was held in a little room off the carport with a jukebox and a dance floor. Candy also invited some of her girl friends and a group of guys who had clever nicknames, like Bones and Pud and Pigs, and were among the most popular boys in school. I had always wanted to be invited to a party like this. There we danced the dirty bop to Jimmy Reed records and drank Coke and Ron Bacardi Superior, the drink of that year.

"You guys are insane sons of bitches, just like us," I heard Pigs Garland say to Joe, socking him on the arm.

Strangest of all strange things, the Dharma Bums were becoming popular. But Danny didn't seem to care. He got drunk, but he didn't dance with any of the girls and spent the afternoon lying in the yard, pretending to talk to Candy's dog.

Of course, not everybody approved of the Dharma Bums. One night my father asked me, "Do you have go out with your friends every night?"

"Why don't you mind your own business," I told him.

"I'm just concerned about you, Sonny," he said thoughtfully. "I'm not sure you're hanging around with the right crowd. Did you know that Joe's father was a bad cop?"

I admitted that I'd heard something about that.

"He was a police detective, but he helped some burglars who were breaking into homes in Country Club. Thought he was the smartest guy in town, but look where he ended up—Huntsville."

"Just stop drinking so much, will you?"

"Then there's Danny. He's a Jew, you know—and there's nothing they'd rather do than get a Gentile in trouble."

"I honestly don't know what you're talking about."

"Everybody's got an enemy is what I mean. They decide they don't like you. Who knows the reason? It could be anything. They want to see you lose, want to turn people against you, want to steal your girl. That's when you find out who your friends are."

I shook my head, wondering how my father, who was an intelligent man, could say such things.

Becky was also disappointed in me. I called her up just to talk, and she said, "I've heard you're dating other girls, Will."

To calm her down, I took her to the Cardinal Inn, a club out by the air force base that Joe had discovered, where a Negro played cocktail piano.

There Becky asked me, "What are we doing here? I don't like drinking coffee. It keeps me awake all night. Why can't we go to the Pioneer, like everybody else? I'm worried about you, Will—you're getting as cynical as Maynard Krebs on *Dobie Gillis*."

I was nothing like Maynard Krebs, a thoroughly harmless beatnik as played by Bob Denver. Couldn't Becky see the Dharma Bums were *dangerous*? And what was this compulsion of hers to be as *normal* as possible?

"Worst than that," Becky said, "you seem to think you're smarter than the rest of us."

"Maybe I am."

I went home feeling low. But that Sunday night, I went to Methodist Youth Fellowship, where I met Marilyn Donahue, who was a bad girl: redheaded, freckle-faced, two years younger than I was, and the sometime girl of Bobby Lee Cummins. I offered to take her home, and we got as far as my car in the church parking lot, where she slid into my arms, and we made out for an hour. Joe had been right; bad girls had a certain liking for smart boys. Marilyn let me do almost everything that first night, even touch the damp silk triangle between her legs. "If Bobby Lee knew I was with you," she said, "he would kill me."

He was more likely to kill me. But the car was filled with a springtime fragrance of honeysuckle and pollen that was not at all unpleasant, and suddenly I was closer than I had ever been to *the great experience*.

In November, John Kennedy was elected president, but it made little impression on me. Like everyone else, I was caught up in the fortunes of the Nortex Prairie Dogs. They had won every game and might even win the State Championship this year. I was taking Journalism and often stayed after school to work on the paper. As I left one Thursday afternoon, I saw a dummy of an Ysleta Indian hanging from a homeroom door, part of a spirit display—we were playing El Paso Ysleta on Friday—and on an impulse took it home.

That night, I called Danny and said, "I feel like climbing a mountain, and tonight's the night."

The mountain I had in mind was Senior High. I had no idea how I was going to do it yet, but I put the dummy, a length of clothesline, and an aluminum stepladder in the trunk of the Chevy. My father, who was watching television, never knew when I left. Picking up Danny, I drove to Senior High, which was a dark ziggurat in the moonlight. It looked, Danny said, like the Roof of the World in the Alexander Korda movie, *The Thief of Baghdad*. I parked in the lot behind the cafeteria and started giving Danny directions.

First, we climbed the aluminum ladder to the roof of the cafeteria and then to the roof of the girls' gym. Then we went up to the roof of the third floor, pulling up the ladder and the dummy of the Ysleta Indian from floor to floor on the length of clothesline. As I climbed, a voice coming from somewhere behind my left shoulder told me what to do next.

When we faced the last wall before the roof of the school, I turned to Danny and said, "What's going on with you? You've been pissed off at me every since that first night we got drunk with Joe."

"You're the one who's pissed off," Danny said, "and you're trying to copy my act of Zen. Why don't you stop showing off, and let's just get it over with."

It was true: I felt the righteous power of Zen that night—it was my turn to do something daring and unpredictable. So I told Danny to hold the stepladder while I climbed to the top. But when I jumped for the coping, I missed and fell eight feet back down on top of Danny, knocking him out for a minute.

"What are you doing to me?" he asked, when he came back to his senses.

On my second try, I got my fingers on the coping and pulled myself up to the roof. The full moon shone down with a cold, green light, and the brickwork looked black. I hung the dummy over the front door and tied the clothesline rope to a chimney. Then I lay on my back on the gravel roof for an endless time. Not too many people had been up here. I felt like Han Shan climbing Cold Mountain—I was high as I'd ever been in my life, and I hadn't even been drinking. It also seemed to me that I heard faint, crystalline music, perhaps coming from the stars.

The next morning, when people came to school and saw the dummy hanging over the front door, they said, "You and Lutz did that, didn't you?"

I wouldn't say—didn't like to think about the argument we'd had. Then I forgot about it for several years, which makes me think it may have been a natural mystical experience of the sort I will describe later.

On Saturday morning, Joe came for me early. Danny was already sitting in the front seat, and I sat in the back. We were on our way to the state game with Corpus Christi Rey, which was being held at Baylor Stadium in Waco that afternoon. It was still dark, but the eastern sky was filled with the same cold, green radiance I had seen from the roof of the school and in my dreams. We passed the Speedrome, a stock car track, and headed south on Highway 281. A norther had blown in the night before, and there was snow in the blue shadows of the fence posts. The sun rose in molten gold as we stopped in Windthorst for coffee.

Joe, wearing his gray longshoreman's jacket and smoking Camels, drove on down through the live oak country around Mineral Wells. Fog lay over the Brazos River, and we caught up with the band bus as we crossed the bridge. The band kids were waving and Joe was pounding his horn. He turned off beyond the bridge, drove up through the limestone hills to Glen Rose, and then headed east toward Waco. I stared out the window, seeing the great metaphysical knife of my childhood—which Kerouac had imagined in *On the Road*—that cut through everything, hills, houses, trees, and telephone poles.

I think my first premonition of disaster came when I saw Baylor Stadium. The student body of Nortex High, everybody I had ever known, filled only a small area of seats in the big stadium. This was neutral ground, a no place, and we did not belong here. Corpus Christi scored the first touchdown, and somehow I knew we were going to lose. At halftime, we gathered under the stands, drinking Ron Bacardi Superior and vowing to beat those sons of bitches—as if we had anything to do with it. The second half began, and Nortex scored a touchdown but didn't make the extra point. Then the seconds ticked off, the final gun sounded, and the Prairie Dogs had lost the state championship.

We ran onto the field where the Corpus Christi Rey students were pulling down the goalposts. I heard the sickening sound of fists hitting flesh: Bobby Lee Cummins was pounding a boy in the face over and over, taking his revenge the Nortex way. Becky stood before me, tears running down her face. "Can you believe it?" she asked me, clutching my hands.

"It's just a football game."

"Oh, Will," she wailed. *"You've lost your school spirit."* And she turned away, unable to face me.

It couldn't have happened, but it had. I felt the weight of it sink through me like lead. But I was a Dharma Bum, supposedly beyond earthly affairs, and so had to pretend it didn't matter.

On the way back, we stopped at a restaurant in Mineral Wells. Danny said he would pay the bill, but as we walked out, he pocketed the tips left on the other tables. The seniors were supposed to go to the Linda Lou Club in Fort Worth to see Ray Sharpe that night, but we all went home instead. When we reached Nortex, the whole town was dark, as if in mourning, and remained that way through Christmas.

Three weeks later, Danny and I were stuck on a muddy road behind the Continental Refinery. It was the night of the Frosted Fantasy Ball at the Women's Forum. Danny and I had gone without dates, taping half-pints of Ron Bacardi Superior to our legs. Joe had taken Candy Todd. Danny pissed under our table, too drunk to get up. Now we were stuck somewhere out near Lake Caddo. Drunken despair overtook me, and I groaned at the hopelessness of my life in this North Texas oil town. The stars looked like roofing nails driven into the black tarpaper of the sky, and the moon wore an idiot grin.

Danny and I finally got the car unstuck. He murmured the names of churches as we passed them: "Church of the Nazarene, Bethel Baptist Church, Starlite Baptist Church, Church of Christ, Church of Christ." I pulled into the Fat Boy, the only drive-in still open. I noticed Bobby Lee Cummins was there with his buddy Wayne Follet, but I ignored them.

Then Bobby pulled my door open and said, "Try to screw my girl, will you? Well, this time, your friend Joe's not here to protect you—and tonight I'm gon' beat the dog shit out of you."

So Bobby Lee Cummins knew I was seeing his girl, Marilyn Donahue. She must have told him. This was not the time I would have chosen to fight, but I was drunk and full of the righteous power of Zen, as I had been that night we had climbed to the roof of the school. This was the fight Joe said I had to have.

I got out of the car, and so did Danny, muttering, "Why the fuck are we doing this?"

I threw off my suit coat, and Bobby Lee and I began circling each other. For the longest time we circled each other in silence, until his fist shot out, so fast I couldn't see it, striking me on the side of the head, and the spell was broken. Ears ringing like bells, I forced myself to take several swings before I finally managed to hit him on the face. To my surprise, no pain shot back through my hand. Then Bobby Lee hit me back, but that didn't hurt either, and I thought, *I can go on like this all night.*

Wayne joined in, hitting me from behind. Danny stepped into his path to try to stop him, but Wayne threw him down and kicked him— his boot made a sickening sound when it struck Danny's ribs—and when Danny got up and ran away, I couldn't blame him. Then Wayne joined Bobby Lee, and they both started in on me. I lost heart and covered my head with my arms.

They're going to kill me, I finally decided and ran to a nearby house, where I threw open the door and shouted at the two old people watching television, "Call the cops!"

"Get out of here," they screamed back.

Bobby burst in, pulled me back outside, and knocked me through the porch railing into the front yard. *This is just like a movie,* I thought as I flew through the air. Then they pounded on me forever, teaching me the old Paleolithic lesson, until my head was numb as a stone.

When I woke in the emergency room, my hair was stiff with dried blood as if it had been dipped in red paint. The doctor was stitching up my scalp and scolding me. "Next time you start a fight, you'd better be able to finish it."

It was almost daylight when my father picked me up at the hospital, and I could see he had been crying. "I told you your friends would never help you," he said to me sadly.

5

WHEN I WOKE the next morning, everyone was gone, and the house was empty. I called Danny and mentioned that I could have used a little help. He laughed and said, "I am the Buddha known as the coward."

"I've been going out with his girlfriend," I told him, "and he found out."

"Does that make it all worth it?" he asked me and hung up.

I thought about this for a while. It seemed to me that he was trying to tell me something about Zen and himself. He was right, of course. I hadn't really expected him to help me fight. It was my thing, not his.

I went to the bathroom and stared at my reflection in the mirror. I had gotten beat up again, just like at Zundy; even the same guy had done it. My face was bruised, my lips were swollen, and I could see the split between mind and body in my eyes. The shame was unbearable.

I put on my gray corduroy car coat and a sweater. In a surplus army shoulder pack, I put a can of chili, a can opener, a spoon, a spiral notebook, and a ballpoint pen. In my pocket, I put a pack of Lucky Strikes, and in my billfold, fifty dollars. Then I walked down to Seymour Road and started hitchhiking, heading west toward the Panhandle.

Most of the people who picked me up that day were cowboys. I said little to them and stared straight ahead. Once I saw a coyote crossing an empty field. I spent the first night, which was Christmas Eve, in a motel in Post with a linoleum floor and a little gas heater, eating cold chili. *I am a lonesome traveler,* I wrote in my notebook, but that was all I could think of to write.

The next morning, my first ride took me as far as Floydada. It was cold up there on the caprock, but hitchhiking was easier than I had thought it would be. Some of the people who gave me rides that day were boring, some were interesting, and I suspected a few were dangerous.

I waited for two hours by a cotton gin, and the ham smell made me hungry. Finally, two cowboys picked me up. I had just gotten in the backseat when I looked up and saw one of them pointing a rifle at me. It seemed like my whole life had led to this moment, and I could clearly see the newspaper article about my death.

The cowboy grinned to show it was a joke, tipped up the rifle, and put it away. "Just let me out of the car," I said quietly.

They drove away laughing. I ate a hamburger in Tahoka, so sleepy I could barely keep my eyes open, and found a motel room very much like the first. That night, I thought about Bobby Lee Cummins. This would never be over until I fought him again and won—or fucked his girlfriend. Either way, I had to let go and lose control. My father was right: I had made an enemy for life.

The third day found me at a crossroads in Lamesa. One of the roads led west, and for the first time I thought, *Why not just go on to California?* So I started walking west. The road sloped downhill through a little oil patch, where pumping jacks nodded in the cotton fields. There were no cars to be seen, and I slept for two hours on the sandy floor of a corrugated iron drainage pipe. Then I stood for another two hours by the road, but not a single car showed. By that time, the sun was going down in a somehow cheap western sky. The horizon glowed red as neon gas, and a few stars hung above it like rhinestones. Nothing moved as far as I could see. I had achieved the satori of hitchhiking—was no longer going anywhere and no longer cared.

I stood there until it was completely dark, and then, without thinking about it too much, I crossed the road and started hitchhiking home.

Headlights appeared on the prairie behind me. It was a little green Nash Metropolitan. When it got closer, I stuck my thumb out, and it pulled over and picked me up. The driver was a Mexican American, and the dashboard was covered with plastic statues of John the Baptist, the Angel Gabriel, and Christo Rey himself. We drove on across the caprock, and as the moon rose, I wrote in my notebook:

> Riding back to Nortex
> Going past cotton gins
> With their oily ham smell
> Little guy who's taking me home
> Doesn't even realize he's a Buddha.

It wasn't much, but I had written my first poem.

When I got back to Nortex on the day after that, I looked at my reflection in the bathroom mirror. My face was still bruised, but I could no longer see the split between mind and body in my eyes, and I felt good, like I had out there on the road. Now I would have to go back to school, though, and that would be hard. In fact I never told anyone where I had gone, not even my parents.

The next day, I got a letter from Marilyn Donahue, saying she had heard about the fight and was sorry. She and Bobby Lee Cummins were dating again. "I see now you never really loved me," she wrote, "but maybe now Bobby sees he really does." I wrote her back, wishing her the best.

On New Year's Eve, my parents went to a party, and my little brother, Ray, went over to a friend's house. I was watching television when someone knocked on the front door. It was Joe. He'd heard that I'd gotten beaten up and wanted to know if I had learned anything by it.

"I always thought if I hit somebody in the face, I'd feel a pain in my own fist," I said. "But I learned it doesn't hurt to hit somebody or to get hit. Not at first."

"Then you have been enlightened," Joe said.

"I'm glad you think so."

"Now, do you want me to help you beat up Bobby Lee Cummings— or Lutz, for not helping you out?"

I thought about this.

"No," I said. "Danny and I were drunk, and I made the mistake of trying to fight them both when I wasn't ready. I'll do better the next time."

Joe was silent for a moment and then asked me if I'd ever heard anything about his father. I told him yes, I had.

"I guess everybody knows that story by now," Joe said. "My father was a police detective who got arrested and sent to Huntsville. He's gotten out now and lives in Houston. When he was in prison, he learned all about rare seashells, and all he has to do now is walk the Galveston beach and pick them up. Sometimes he finds a really rare one and sells it for thousands of dollars. So he turned prison into a good thing. Candy's father found out about him, and now he doesn't want her to date me anymore. But I still want to be just like my father."

"That's great, Joe. I hope you will be."

Years later, a psychiatrist told me that Joe was a sociopath who had no idea of right or wrong and made up his own rules. To the psychiatrist, this was a shortcoming. To me, it still seems like Joe's greatest strength.

That night, he also told me he'd found a new girl, Jayne Harper, and asked me if I'd like to out go out with them. I already knew Jayne a little. She was short and dark, and I had always thought she might be a Mexican since she spoke fluent Spanish and was president of the Spanish Club. But as it turned out, Jayne wasn't a Mexican. She had moved here from New Orleans, and Joe said she was smarter than either of us, because she'd read *The Catcher in the Rye* and we hadn't. Also, her mother was the only white member of the local chapter of the NAACP.

That night, Joe and Jayne and I drove through Colored Town, and I remember him saying, a little theatrically, "I can't believe the way these poor people have to live down here. We have to do something to help them."

Jayne ran her hands through his hair and kissed him.

So Joe had changed himself again, taking up two political causes at once—integration and dating a homely girl because he loved her mind more than her body. And although they were very affectionate with each other, I began to wonder if somehow their relationship wasn't a contradiction of everything I had thought Joe stood for; wasn't, in fact, platonic.

Going back to school was even harder than I'd thought it would be. My face was still bruised, and I couldn't look anyone in the eye. But I was all right as long as I didn't have to talk or think. When someone asked me if I'd been in a fight, I just grinned and kept walking. Once I saw Marilyn Donahue and Bobby Lee Cummins walking together, but they didn't see me.

Danny and I had some of the same classes, like Journalism, but I didn't speak to him at all. I began to wonder if my father could be right. Not that Jews secretly hated Gentiles. But could Danny have somehow become my enemy? Did he envy my friendship with Joe and think I was still too concerned with popularity?

He *had* run away that night, and gradually this came to seem like a betrayal of some sort.

I hung out with Joe and Jayne and went out only to Wednesday-night meetings of the Order of DeMolay. For the next three months, I was master councilor. The chapter was short of money, so I talked a junkyard into letting us have an old car for nothing, which we parked at the Pioneer Drive-In and sold tickets—for a dollar, you could take a swing at it with a sledgehammer. In this way, we made a surprising amount. I also played the role of Jacques DeMolay at an initiation and sent in my application to the University of Texas at Austin.

Sometimes I dreamed about the fight and felt the shame of it again even in my sleep. But it never came back to me as strong as it had at Zundelowitz. Someday I would have another fight—and that one I would have to win. Even then I knew you became the person you wanted to be by repeating the past until you *got it right*. But the possibility of this happening before I graduated became remote.

In March, Joe called me and asked if I'd like to go with them to a beatnik coffeehouse that had opened downtown called the Alley Opus. I was curious and agreed to meet them there on Friday night. The entrance to the Alley Opus was in an alley, of course—a black door with a single light burning over it. Inside, you found yourself in a large room hung with black curtains and sat on black cushions around low, circular black tables.

Joe and Jayne were already there. I sat down with them, a waitress served us espresso, and we listened to a quartet—of airmen, I think—play Dave Brubeck's "Count Five." They weren't bad, but Joe and Jayne agreed with me that when you had a coffeehouse in Nortex, the beatnik thing was over.

Then Danny came in, smiling a little hesitantly, and sat down at our table.

"We thought it was time you guys made up," Jayne said, and Joe smiled and nodded.

I shook hands with Danny and told him I wasn't really angry; I just hadn't felt like talking to him.

"There wouldn't have been much point to me staying with you that night," he said. "And getting the shit beaten out of me."

"No," I said. "But I'm not sorry I stayed."

Danny nodded, still not looking at me, and said, "But we're still friends, aren't we?"

"We'll always be friends," I said. And I thought, *This, at least, is true.*

Suddenly it was spring, the best time of the year. There were thunderstorms almost every night, and the grass turned green. My parents gave up on keeping me home. One Friday night, Joe picked me up, and we went to the movies, then to the American Trust Life Insurance Company—an old Greek Revival mansion in the suburbs with an enormous green neon sign on the roof. There we unrolled our sleeping bags under the hedge and the noses of the cops, who parked there to sleep with their radios on, and drank beer until daylight—feeling like

Robin Hood hiding from the Sheriff of Nottingham in old Sherwood Forest.

The next morning we ate breakfast at the Toddle House, then went over to Jayne's house and hung out. Like Joe, she lived in an older part of town, and her home was shabby but comfortable. The refrigerator was full of beer, and anybody could have one whenever they liked. Mrs. Harper and Joe sat in the kitchen, discussing race and Catholicism, while Mr. Harper, a retired mailman, listened to them and said not a word. Later Danny came by and sat with Jayne and me in the front room, where we played her great collection of records by Mary Wells, Smoky Robinson, and the Shirelles. Later we all went to a movie, and it was so late when we got out that Joe and I slept over at the Harper house.

When I finally went home on Sunday afternoon, I realized that we had reached the final spring, the last weeks of our senior year. For us, all the rules were suspended.

The senior play that year was *Huckleberry Finn*—a strange version of the novel in which the slave Jim did not appear, and instead of floating down the Mississippi, Huck spent most of his time hanging out with Tom Sawyer. But I had decided I wanted the part, and when Miss Mott held open auditions, I read for it. The role went to Bones, who was in the National Thespian Society, but I was not that sorry. Like Huckleberry Finn, Bones was simple and honest, a friend to everyone, and his performance was much better than mine would have been.

Becky was also cast—as Becky Thatcher, of course—and told Miss Mott she wanted me to play her father, Mr. Thatcher. Finally I agreed. So once again, I whitened my hair with Esquire Lan-O-White shoe polish, penciled brown lines around my eyes, and played the old fool for my classmates.

When dress rehearsals began, I sat in the house with Becky. On the proscenium above the stage was a wonderful pastel mural, painted sometime during the Great Depression, which depicted the gods and goddesses—Zeus, Dionysius, and Athena—sitting on their thrones in the Elysian Fields. Behind them, a great thunderhead was blowing up from the Aegean Sea, and waves broke on the rocks of the shore. It was a perfect landscape that contained all sorts of terrain, all kinds of weather, all degrees of light. On the stage below, the gods and goddesses of the senior class, the football stars and the beauties, tried to remember their lines.

"I can't wait until we get old, Will," Becky whispered, touching my hair. "You'll look so handsome when your hair turns white. Then we'll look back on this as the best year of our life."

"Be quiet, will you?" I said. "I want to hear this part."

Bones, as Huckleberry Finn, stepped downstage and spoke to the audience:

> It's time to slide out of here one of these nights, get an outfit, and go to the West for some howling adventures over in the Territories, and I says that's all right with me ...

As he finished, the lights faded and the curtain whispered down. Then the lights came back up again, and we were in the same old auditorium, with the flags of the United States and Texas on either side of the stage.

Becky was looking at me and said, "You're crying, Will."

"This has been the best year of my life," I told her. "And I never want to leave."

The Dharma Bums were hanging out at the Harper house one Saturday when Jayne said we should have a party and invite only the coolest people. So Jayne called some of her Negro friends who went to Booker T. A guy named Ty and two girls named Cindy and Georgia showed up. They were shy at first but awfully funny, and soon the Dharma Bums were dancing the dirty bop with Negro girls at Jayne Harper's house.

Everybody was talking and smoking cigarettes and drinking beer, and the house was so warm I had to step out on the front porch to clear my head. The day before, I had received my acceptance from the University of Texas. Danny had already been accepted by the University of Oklahoma, and Joe had already been accepted by Rice. In a week, we would graduate from Nortex High and head out for San Francisco together in Joe's old Ford, which would be the trip of a lifetime.

As I was thinking about this, Danny joined me on the porch and told me his parents were moving to Dallas next year and so was he.

"I can't believe it," I said.

"Oh, we'll still see each other," he said. "Come to Dallas, and we'll have some kicks. This town is dead."

But I saw the end of our time here everywhere I looked—in the setting sun, in the long shadows, in the empty streets—and felt a strange despair. Soon the Dharma Bums would be scattered across the dark earth.

Night fell, and we were all lying around in Jayne's front yard when suddenly I had an idea, jumped to my feet, and said, "Let's go to the Bone Orchard." So we all got in Joe's car and mine and drove to Riverside Cemetery, which was just down the road. The iron gates were wide open, and we drove through and parked at the top of the hill, by the marble mausoleums of the wealthy that overlooked the river. Then Danny took off all his clothes and swam naked in the reflecting pool.

I was especially fond of Georgia and led her away from the others, to a distant place where the graves of Mexican children were marked with chips of blue bottle glass and tiny, oval photographic portraits.

"That's so sad," she said, looking at the graves. "But you're sweet, aren't you?"

For the first time in my life, I sensed the true gentleness of Negro girls and found myself kissing her. As I did, I remembered the other high school I had once dreamed of, where my life would be perfect. Suddenly it came to me that there really was another high school out there—Booker T—and I thought, *I should have been born a Negro.*

The next instant, the sky turned a sickening green, so bright the stars disappeared, and a big meteor fell. It was seen all over Texas and Oklahoma that night. I thought it was a Russian missile coming in, that thermonuclear war had finally begun, and tears filled my eyes. It took me forever to get over it. Georgia had to keep telling me that everything was all right.

Finally, we returned to the reflecting pool. Danny was nowhere in sight, but Joe and Jayne and Ty and Cindy were all sitting on the marble rim.

"Never met folks like you before," Ty was saying to Joe.

"Really glad we got together," Joe said, shaking his hand.

Jayne said, "Isn't this just the greatest night?"

Then I saw flashing red lights through the trees and headlights coming up the hill. Danny was running toward us up the road, completely naked, a police cruiser right behind him. It hit the brakes, and a cop emerged from the blinding headlights, caught Danny, and threw him to the ground. Joe was on his feet and running downhill with his arms up, yelling for the cops to stop. I was right behind him. More cops were appearing with their billy clubs out, and as Joe reached them, one hit him in the stomach, and he went down.

I stopped and threw up my hands, and a cop with a flashlight grabbed me and spun me around. Sensing his anger, just barely held back, I let him handcuff me. Then Joe and Danny and I were all lying handcuffed on the gravel road together as more cop cars arrived, their flashers going.

They belted us into the backs of the cars and drove us down to the station. Joe was still trying to explain, and I heard Jayne sobbing as they took the girls away to another part of the jail.

"Cogito ergo sum," the cop who took my mug shot said. "That the name of your gang?"

Ty was also taken away. Then Joe and Danny and I were put in a cell with perforated metal walls and light bulbs in cages on the ceiling. The cops had given Danny a pair of Jockey shorts, but he was still almost naked and laughing hysterically.

Suddenly, Joe slammed him up against the wall. "You think this is funny?" he shouted.

"Take it easy, will you?" Danny said, still laughing. "I was just mooning cars; that's all."

But I understood why Joe was so angry. Danny hadn't just been mooning cars. He had been totally naked when I had first seen him running toward us, and suddenly everything had fallen into place—his disdain for girls, his compulsion to get naked, and now this.

Danny was a flasher.

Joe grabbed Danny's shoulders and banged him hard against the metal wall, three or four times.

"Just *stop it*," I cried.

Joe turned to me and said, "You want a shot at this cocksucker?"

"No," I said. "I want you to leave him alone."

I took Danny by the arm and pulled him to the other end of the cell. Joe turned away, shaking his head, and sat down on the floor.

"I was just following the way of Zen," Danny told me. "Anyway, we always said we'd get in serious trouble someday, didn't we? Now we have."

On the walls were the scribbled names of the Great Hoods of Nortex—Bobby Lee Cummins, Wayne Follet, Joe Joyner, and others. I found a pencil in my pocket and gave it to Danny, who added our names to theirs, quoting the movie *The Fugitive Kind* as he did. "Yes," he said, "now our names are written on the stars also."

Joe said nothing to us for the rest of the night.

We were in more trouble than we knew. White kids had been caught drinking beer with Negros, and the cops had long been watching Mrs. Harper, whom they suspected of buying alcohol for minors. But in the end none of these things could be proven, and we were allowed to graduate, with the understanding that we were never to see Ty or Cindy or Georgia again. Then Danny called me and said Joe was so angry with him that he was canceling our trip to San Francisco. I went over to Jayne's house to talk him out of it and knocked on the screen door. I could hear Jayne inside; then Joe appeared.

"Just get the fuck out of here, will you?" he shouted. "I never want to see you around here again!"

Then he slammed the door in my face, and I was left standing there on the porch, alone. It was the end of the Dharma Bums.

THE A-BAR HOTEL

6

I HAVE ALWAYS LOVED Austin. My earliest memory is of lying on my stomach under a cedar tree in the front yard of my grandparents' home on Alice Avenue, staring down into a world of fascinating detail. There are little blue berries, the transparent shells of snails and pill bugs, and the tiny inverted cones of ant lion dens in the soft dust. Knobs of limestone, porous as bone, protrude from the ground, and the sky is a luminous gray. As I grew older, I came to love the parks, the streambeds full of fossils, the dinosaur footprints in the glass case behind the Texas History Museum, and my grandfather's fishing cabin out on Lake Travis.

But when I entered the University of Texas, in September of 1961, I took a room at the A-Bar Hotel, a four-story private dormitory made of limestone bricks on Guadalupe Street, which students called "the Drag." The building was beginning to show its age. It was infested with cockroaches and had a stale smell, despite the Mexican maids who came to the rooms and changed the sheets once a week.

To the north, Guadalupe Street ran out past pool halls and hamburger stands toward the pleasant suburbs of Austin, where there were parks and public swimming pools. To the west were the hills and

Lake Travis. South along Guadalupe were clothing stores, restaurants, and movie theaters. To the east was the great campus, the largest of any school in Texas, with its neoclassical buildings; its fountains; and the tall, white sandstone shaft of the University Tower. But I had no car—my parents had decided they couldn't afford the insurance—and could only travel as far as I could walk.

I put my Smith Corona portable electric typewriter, a graduation present from my parents, on the desk and hung my clothes in the closet. Then I lay down on one of the two beds and waited for my roommate to arrive.

In walked Buddy Cossey, a tall, slightly nearsighted former football player from Wharton, Texas, who had a car and high hopes for the future. I watched as he unpacked a complete frat guy wardrobe of madras shirts, wheat jeans of white denim, and Cole Haan penny loafers.

"Once I get into a good fraternity," he promised me, "I'm gonna get more ass than a toilet seat."

Cossey would be disappointed. He had bought a complete wardrobe of madras shirts, wheat jeans of white denim, and penny loafers; subscribed to *Playboy* and had all the Kingston Trio albums. But no fraternity would pledge him because he hadn't been much of a football player and his family had no money.

I thought I would find my freedom here. But getting out of Nortex would prove harder than I expected. Each summer I would find myself back home, unable to put the town behind me. Somehow I had lost the power to change my life, and this would go on until that morning in November, two years later, when history came to a dead stop.

But my freshman year got off to a good start, when Gabe and Phil, two guys I had known in Nortex, showed up later that day. They had just pledged Sigma Nu and said I could go with them and their pledge brothers on a "Big Trip to Mex," if I could pay for my share of the gas. I instantly agreed. A few minutes later, their pledge brothers drove up, we got in the back of their car, and we all headed for Nuevo Laredo. On the way, I did what I thought I was supposed to do—drank so much beer that when I got out of the car to piss, I fainted and fell backward into the ditch, my piss rising above me in a whale spout. Everybody laughed and then picked me up and threw me back into the car. When we reached Nuevo Laredo, we went to the Cadillac Bar, where we drank Ramos gin fizzes, and then to a whorehouse called Pappagallo's. There we had more drinks, and I technically performed the act of love with a prostitute in a small bedroom cubicle.

I told myself I had finally had *the great experience*. But by the time we got back to Austin, I realized it had not meant much—the girl had been a Mexican prostitute, not a *real* girl. A real girl was a sorority girl, and to find one you had to belong to a fraternity like Sigma Nu.

Still, when anyone asked me after that if I'd ever had a girl, I just nodded my head and said nothing more.

Gabe and Phil asked me to a couple of pledge parties, where I drank beer and did my best to fit in. They told me their brothers liked me, and I should pledge Sigma Nu. But they were wrong. The pledges liked me, but I knew the actives thought I was uninvolved somehow—keeping my distance, secretly watching them—and they were right.

I registered at Gregory Gym, and a few days later classes began. Thinking I was going to be a writer, I declared myself an English major, but every freshman had to take English Composition. Our first assignment was to write an essay on our summer vacation. I turned in a Kerouac monologue. My teacher, a young woman who obviously knew nothing about writing, read aloud to the class and pointed out my sentence fragments.

After the class, I went to her office and told her the fragments had been conscious choices. She explained the point of the assignment had not been to show off, but to write a simple, grammatically correct paper, and I saw the sense of this. Our next assignment was to read and write about *The Red Badge of Courage*, by Stephen Crane, which was a very good book. I wrote a grammatically correct paper about it, and the teacher and I became friends.

I had no more trouble with English Composition. My other courses—History, Algebra, Government, and Introduction to Philosophy—which required memorizing dates and facts—did not interest me at all. But Phil had a car, and in late September, we drove down to Port Arthur, where he had gone to junior high school, so he could see his old girlfriend again. On this trip I got to know Gabe again, which was one of the pleasures of that year.

Actually, we had first met back in grade school, at Crockett Elementary, when his father was the director of the YMCA. Gabe and I had ridden the Hayes Street bus down there for gym and swim on Saturday mornings, and later we had gone to the Wichita Theater to see movies like *Twenty Thousand Leagues Under the Sea*, starring Kirk Douglas. Later still, his father had forced him to work in the school cafeteria. When I turned in my tray at the little window, Gabe was there, wearing an apron and a paper hat, waiting to scrape the food off. But he wouldn't look at me, and after a while we stopped speaking.

Gabe, like me, had endless trouble with his father. At Nortex High he stole the family car and drove it to Florida, where the police caught him sleeping on a golf course. For a time, it looked like he was going to be sent to reform school, but somehow he got off. In our senior year, he managed to stay out of trouble and made good grades.

When the three of us reached Port Arthur, we stayed at a motel. Phil's girl couldn't get us dates that night, so Gabe and I got drunk on Bacardi and went for a walk. Ahead we saw the Orange Bridge—the highest non–suspension bridge in the world—rising out of the fog like a concrete hill and decided to walk across it. At the top, we climbed down onto the girders beneath and, from there, looked down hundreds of feet to the shipping channel below, where shrimp boats chugged out into the Gulf. Gabe was fascinated with the Holocaust, which I also knew a little about, and we talked all night about the gas chambers and concentration camps. Later he would become one of my companions on the Journey.

Jayne Harper, who was also going to the university that year, lived not far from me in Scottish Rite Dormitory, which was famous for its homely girls. I hadn't seen her since the night we had all gotten thrown in jail and was a little nervous, but she seemed glad to see me. She talked mostly about Joe.

"He really helped my mother and I when we were in trouble last summer," she said. "I've been writing him letters every day, but I haven't heard from him for a month."

We both agreed Joe must be busy with his studies down there at Rice. Then Jayne and I went to see a showing of *The Long, Hot Summer* at the student union.

Several Longhorn football players came in before the movie started and sat down in the row ahead of us. Then a beatnik boy and a Negro girl came in and sat in the row in front of them. When the lights went down, the football players started chanting, "Nigger pussy, nigger pussy." I felt the same fear I had felt at Zundy; there was going to be violence here.

"Let's go," I said to Jayne.

We walked out into the October dusk.

"Why didn't you stop them?" she wanted to know.

"Because I'm a coward."

"I don't believe that."

"I am though."

We walked back to Scottish Rite, where Jayne introduced me to some of her folksinger friends who were sitting on the front steps. One was Janis Joplin, who in the course of the sixties would become famous and was already notorious. The fraternities had just named her "Campus Ugly Woman."

Was Janis ugly? Not at all. It was just that she wore jeans, no makeup, and wasn't trying to look like a sorority girl. But she was easy to talk to.

When Jayne said she had to study, Janis and I walked down into the park behind the dormitory and lay down under a Moon Tower—the city of Austin had batteries of mercury-vapor lights on towers in public parks and dark areas—and there she told me stories about growing up in Port Arthur. Janis said she and her friends had sometimes gotten drunk and walked across the Orange Bridge, as Gabe and I had just the week before.

"Man," she said, "when you get to the top ..."

"I know. It's a long way down."

"You got that right."

Janis was a true Dharma Bum, and I wished I had met her earlier, in Nortex. Jayne later told me that Janis liked me and I should ask her out, but I didn't—I had no car, and I couldn't play the guitar, which was very important to the beatnik thing here.

In October, Gabe and I rode with Phil up to Dallas for the Texas-Oklahoma football game. A great river of people had flowed to Dallas from all over both states to rain down empty beer bottles from the windows of their hotel rooms to the street below. On a street corner, we met Danny Abrams, who had pledged Sigma Alpha Mu, or "Sammy," the Jewish fraternity. He was already known to his fraternity brothers as Lutz.

That Danny had so totally become Lutz, a character I had created, made me feel a little jealous and somehow responsible. He was drinking Bacardi from a bottle and seemed deliriously happy.

"It's great how we just ran into you," I said. "It proves there's something to the Way of Zen."

"This *is* the Way of Zen," Danny said, indicating the anarchy all around us.

Then he took us to the Sammy party at the Adolphus Hotel, where Gabe drank every drink that was offered to him, fell down the lobby steps, and threw up green bile on the carpet. I spent that night at a motel room, where a Sigma Nu came in and had sex with his date on the bed while I pretended to be passed out on the carpet. But I could hear everything and was humiliated.

The next day, I went to Fair Park, where the Texas-Oklahoma game was played at Cotton Bowl Stadium. Danny and I met, as we had agreed the night before, under the statue of Big Tex, the giant cowboy who presided over it all. I had often come here with my father when I was a boy, not to see a football game but to go to the Hall of Science and the Auto Show and ride the rides on the Midway. Now Danny and I sat on a bench and talked as UT and Oklahoma students hurried past us on their way to the stadium.

"You mean what you said last night?" I asked him.

"What's that?"

"You really think this is the Way of Zen?"

"It's one way."

Danny took a half-pint of Bacardi from his pocket, drank from it, and offered the bottle to me, which I refused.

"Maybe I'm just doing what you were doing back in high school," he said, "seeking popularity. They think I'm Lutz, so that's who I'm going to be."

"You told me once you weren't a Jew—you were a Zen Buddhist. Now you're saying you're a fraternity guy. How're you going to find satori if you're drunk all the time?"

"The Zen poets got drunk."

"People join fraternities because they want to get laid. What I don't understand is why *you're* doing it."

He took another drink and threw the bottle away.

"I take it by now you've had a girl."

"A prostitute."

"Was it so meaningful?"

"No," I had to admit.

"Come on then," he said. "Let's go to the game."

I don't remember who won the football game. By the end of it, I had started drinking too.

Gabe and Danny and I stuck together that night, and Danny took us to The Cellar, which was a Sammy hangout. There I glimpsed a stripper's black triangle of pubic hair—the second vagina I had seen in two months. But nobody seemed to think this was important. As Phil drove us back to Austin the next day, I wondered why the Sammies had accepted Danny, but the Sigma Nus were reluctant to accept me. Then I realized it was Lutz, not Danny, who the Sammies liked—and Lutz was always drunk.

We took our midterm exams, and a week later, it was Thanksgiving. My parents and my brother, Ray, came down to Austin to eat turkey with my grandparents, and I joined them. But by this time, my grandparents had moved out on old Highway 183. They still sold used cars and raised police dogs, but their house was much smaller, and it felt lonely out there in the country. *If only I had a car,* I thought. Without a car, nobody could get a girl. Of all the freedoms I had lost, this was the most important.

When I returned to the A-Bar, I tried to write all this down but couldn't finish a single sentence. By now, I had read everything Kerouac and Thomas Wolfe had ever written and was looking around for someone to replace them. For a while, I had been fascinated by Lawrence Durrel's *Alexandria Quartet* and tried to write like him but had only produced endless paragraphs of description. The most popular book at school that year was *Franny and Zooey,* by J. D. Salinger. Everybody was reading it—even Cossey—and wondering if Franny had fainted at the end of the book because she was pregnant. Since I had never made love to a *real* girl, this question was of no interest to me at all.

I picked up Faulkner's *Absolam, Absolam!* and tried to read a few pages. Cossey came in, looked over my shoulder, and said, "Don't let your friends in Sigma Nu see you reading that."

"Why not?"

"It looks too intellectual. You should read *The Temple of Gold*," he said, mentioning another popular paperback. "They say it's the greatest novel of our generation."

"Have you read it?"

"No, but I'm going to."

"I'll take a look at it," I said.

I did but barely got past the cover.

Cossey claimed he was romantically involved with several girls here, but I began to notice he was going home to Wharton every weekend in his '55 Chevy, his freshly pressed clothes hanging from an aluminum pipe across the backseat. Cossey talked about joining a fraternity and dating a sorority girl, but obviously he was still seeing his high school girlfriend. I vowed again never to join a fraternity. I was going to be a writer!

At Christmas, I returned to Nortex with Gabe and Phil. High school was still in session, so I dropped in on my old Radio-TV class. Becky Stamos, who had also taken the class, was there. She was studying drama at Midwestern but had little to say to me. My teacher, Mr. Yeager, said, "Will has turned into a real Joe College. He's letting his hair grow, so he'll look like President Kennedy." I denied this—although I was letting my hair grow and wouldn't have minded looking like Kennedy.

Lutz was at a Sammy party in Dallas, so Gabe and Phil and I got drunk and went to the Frosted Fantasy Ball at the Woman's Forum. There I kissed the girl I was dancing with, whose name I have forgotten, at midnight. Everyone was invited, but many of my classmates did not show up—the new senior class had somehow won the state football championship, which meant they would forever be happier than us—and I went home early.

Opening Christmas presents with my family was not so different, except our home seemed small now, and when I reached up, I found I could touch the ceiling. On New Year's Eve, Gabe and Phil and I went to a drinking party at the Pioneer Number Two downtown, which was the oldest drive-in in Nortex. Perhaps for that reason, it had always seemed like it was for adults, and I felt that was what we were, now that we had graduated from Nortex High. I drove home, and as I passed Jayne's house, I noticed that Joe's old Ford was parked in front, but I was afraid to knock on the door.

The next morning, I went to Sunday school at Indian Heights Methodist Church. Marilyn Donahue and Bobby Lee Cummins were there together, and someone said they were married now. At the end of the class, everybody stood up and said where they were going to school—Midwestern, Texas Christian, Southern Methodist, Baylor, and the University of Texas. Last of all was Ray Franklin, a slightly handicapped boy who wore a green uniform and said proudly, "Ray Franklin, US Army." All the boys looked at the floor. The army was already something to be avoided.

I returned to Austin to study for finals. By now, Cossey had passed through four years of college in one semester—in his first month, he had been hopeful, in his second sophomoric, in his third cynical. Now he had grown mellow. Sometimes he looked up from his books and said, "Will, we shall remember these days forever."

Cossey failed all his courses and drove back to Wharton, where I hope he married his girlfriend and was happy forever. Gabe moved in with me at the A-Bar Hotel.

In my second semester at the University of Texas, I began to realize how long I was going to have to go to college to get a degree. My days and nights were empty, and it seemed I was always alone. Food and cigarettes were part of the problem. I always ate at Dirty's, a classic hamburger joint in Guadalupe, where I got the special, a "Cum-Back Burger." The name made me slightly sick. Once I had dreamed of eating nothing but hamburgers and smoking a pack of Marlboros a day. Now I did, and it was not as pleasant as I had thought it would be.

There was also something going around called the Great Sleep. Several students at the A-Bar Hotel began sleeping through their morning classes—sleeping all day, in fact, until sunset, when they got up, ate breakfast, then stayed up all night trying to study. It was Kid Spudnut who first explained this to me.

A new café called the Spudnut Shoppe had just opened next door to the A-Bar Hotel, which I liked because it had a pinball machine and a television set hanging from the ceiling, on which I could watch *Combat*. Kid Spudnut was one of the ancient grad students who hung out there. I never knew his real name—he called me Kid, so I called him Kid Spudnut.

"Oh yeah, I know all about that," he told me. "The Great Sleep, the Long Night; there's a lot of names for it. It's not really so much a compulsion to sleep as it is a compulsion to stay up all night. I call it the Great Boredom, because that's what it's all about, kid."

When I asked him what he meant, he said, "Day is boring. Night is not."

The Great Boredom, he explained, had been happening since the fifties. It was a form of depression that flourished on every college campus in America, especially in dormitories. At first it was a mild illness, like a cold you couldn't get rid of. There was no anxiety, just a lethargy that meant you slept through all your morning classes and suffered from an inability to study for an exam until the night before. Only seldom did it lead to suicide—although there were a few students who died of the Great Boredom every year, leaping from the top of the University Tower and crashing through a skylight into the library below. When Kid Spudnut told me this, I realized that I often went up to the top of the Tower myself—surely this was just because I enjoyed heights.

"Boredom has always been the root of all evil," Kid Spudnut said. "But this is the worst time and place for it in human history. All the factors that create it are here—dull courses, the impossibility of finding a *real* girl. Then there's the Cold War, and the draft—the certain knowledge that if you fail and drop out of school, you'll be drafted. But even if you graduate with honors, you'll still be drafted. So in the end, you have to enlist."

"But not a single frat guy ever suffers from it," I protested.

"Why should they? Your frat guy's got a girl. He never doubts himself. And if he starts to feel bored, he can just get drunk."

Kid Spudnut was, of course, a philosophy major. He added that boredom already been described by the great Danish philosopher Søren Kierkegaard in a book called *Either/Or.*

> The history of this can be traced from the very beginning of the world. The gods were bored, so they created men. Adam was bored alone; then Adam and Eve were bored together. Then the people of the world were bored ... and to divert themselves they conceived the idea of constructing a tower high enough to reach the heavens. The idea is as boring as the tower was high, and constitutes the idea of how boredom reached the upper hand ...

But I went on telling myself that the Great Boredom would never get me. I had survived getting beaten up at Zundy, being turned into a ghost, even getting beaten up again by the same guy in my senior year. I was a Dharma Bum, and I swore I would never be like Kid Spudnut—at least thirty years old and still a student of obscure European philosophies.

There was a warm week when the nights were foggy and drops of moisture appeared on the bronze statues of the mustangs in front of the State History Museum. Then spring break came along, and Lutz appeared, driving down to Austin in a little red Chevy Nova his parents had bought for him.

Gabe and Phil were spending Hell Week in the basement of the fraternity house, being initiated into Sigma Nu. So there was nothing for Lutz and I to do but get drunk and hear Lightning Hopkins play. I tried to tell him about Kid Spudnut and the Great Boredom, but he wasn't interested. We ended up standing in the parking lot of a joint on Guadalupe at closing time, trying to think of something to say to each other.

"Your brothers gotten you laid yet?" I asked him.

"Fuck girls," he said. "Larry Kris was right. They talk about love, but money's all they care about. All girls can be bought."

"That's just false. You don't know any more about girls than you ever did."

"No," he said, laughing.

"Trouble is, I still believe in everything we talked about in high school."

"Oh, fuck all that," he said. "You believe in unhappiness, that's all."

"I don't know what you're talking about."

"You think it's so meaningful, but it's not. Happiness is better. You don't have to go to a monastery to find it. You don't even have to go to California. It's right here, in this very moment—but you keep missing it."

"And you found it in the Sammy fraternity?"

"Oh yeah, someday I'm going serious, like you. Hit the road and write it all down. That's what you want to do, isn't it? But right now, I think I'll have another drink."

He took out his bottle of Bacardi and drank. At that moment, I realized I had never talked to Danny about becoming Lutz, or about him getting us busted that night in Nortex when he had exposed himself to passing cars, and probably never would.

"You," Danny said, "are like that guy you were telling me about, Kid Eternity or whatever his name is—the one who knows all about the Great Boredom. The truth is, you're the one who's boring and always will be—because you make yourself so fucking unhappy."

He drained the bottle, threw it away, and I heard it shatter on the blacktop parking lot.

Gabe and Phil invited me to their graduation keg party at the Sigma Nu Lodge on Lake Austin. I accepted, although I already knew I could not abandon myself to hell-raising—the more I drank, the more sober I got. Still, I tried once more.

The pledges were glad to see me, but the actives were still suspicious, still thought I was standing off and watching them. One kept frowning at me over the top of the keg, until I asked him, in what I thought was the right voice, "How you doin'?"

Then he gave me a tremendous shove, and I fell backward off the pier into the lake. When I surfaced, I swam to shore and watched the pledges and the actives pushing each other into the water for a while. So I walked back to the A-Bar Hotel and was never asked to party with the Sigma Nus again.

Gabe was now an active, but he still stopped by sometimes, and we went to the pool hall and played nine-ball together. It was the metaphysical game of those years, made famous by *The Hustler*, a movie starring Paul Newman and Jackie Gleason. We also went to art movies at the Texas Theater on Guadalupe. They were directed by Bergman, Fellini, and Antonioni; most were in Italian, and all were in black and white. First the title "Janus Films" appeared, in a silence that deepened as the movies went on, and we read the subtitles. Everyone went to these movies, but no one could agree on what they were about. Sometimes we heard a grad student behind us whispering about the symbolism, which was a big concern with grad students at that time—particularly phallic symbols. Once, when we were watching *Phaedra* (a miserable movie by Jules Dassin, starring Sophia Loren, who was inexplicably in love with her stepson, Tony Perkins) we saw Raf Vallone knock over an Erector Set tower his son had built for him. "Did you see that?" a grad student behind me whispered. "He toppled the erection."

Gabe and I weren't interested in symbolism at all. But we thought we could learn *something* from these films that we could not learn from our classes, and we were partly right. What we were learning about was boredom.

7

WHEN MY FRESHMAN year at the University of Texas was over, my parents brought me back to Nortex, and once again, I slept in the bed of my childhood. Gabe's parents had moved to Longview, so he went there to work on an oil rig. Danny's parents had moved to Dallas, but instead of going to see him, I stayed in Nortex. My parents tried to talk me into getting a job, but somehow I couldn't get out of bed long enough to look for one. The Great Sleep or the Great Boredom, whichever you wanted to call it, was waiting for me even here.

With my little brother, Ray, I went to the Wichita Theater to see *Lawrence of Arabia*, which was a great movie. But downtown Nortex seemed deserted now, and when we came out, we could smell the Great Plains, thousands of empty miles of grass under the full moon. As we walked back to my car—my parents let me drive in Nortex—we went past Thomas's Newsstand, and I showed Ray some books he should read, but he wasn't very interested.

As I drove past Jayne Harper's house one day, I noticed Joe's old black Ford parked out in front. So Joe was in town, back from Rice. We hadn't spoken for a year, and I was afraid he would still be angry with me, but I pulled in behind his Ford and knocked on the screen door.

"Come on in, Langner," I heard Joe say—a slight formality, which was the only sign we hadn't spoken for a year.

Soon we were talking easily. When I asked Joe what he was doing, he told me he was working for the Texas Highway Department, breaking up pavement on a stretch of road out toward the river. "I work from daybreak to noon," he said. "Then it's too hot to go on, so they send us home, and I come back here and sleep on the couch for a couple of hours."

I was wondering why Joe was working so hard—breaking up pavement was the toughest job you could do—but he told me he needed the money. Then I asked him what he had been reading.

"Kant, Hegel, Spinoza," he said, and I thought, *I'll never catch up.* "Right now, I can't decide whether to major in mathematics, physics, philosophy, or logic. Plus, I've got to learn another language this summer. I may be the smartest son of a bitch in Nortex, but I'm not the smartest one at Rice, and I've got to study my ass off just to keep up."

Jayne, he told me, was working at the telephone company. When she came home, she seemed glad enough to see me and asked me to stay for supper. The whole family ate together at the table in the kitchen, and then Joe went back out in the front room and started studying.

Jayne and I sat on the back porch and talked for a while about the University of Texas, Scottish Rite Dorm, and Janis Joplin. "We're three of a kind," she said, "You, me, and Janis—we're all homely. But Joe is smart *and* good-looking. He's a lucky guy, isn't he?"

I thought this was a strange thing to say, but maybe she was just trying to tell me how much she loved Joe. We talked for a little longer while her mother did the dishes, her father read the paper, and Joe studied on the couch in the front room. He was so completely absorbed in his books that when I left, he didn't notice.

At home, I picked up the hardest book I could find—*A Reader's Guide to William Butler Yeats*, by John Unterecker—and tried to read it, but I kept falling asleep. Boredom enclosed me like a thick, cottony cloud. This went on for a couple of weeks. Once, I talked Joe and Jayne into going to a movie, but most of the time, he studied. Neither Danny nor the Dharma Bums were ever mentioned.

Finally, I remembered that, back in high school, Joe had once promised that we should go fishing and mentioned this to him. To my surprise, he agreed to go.

On Sunday morning before daybreak, Joe picked me up and drove out to Lake Caddo. There we picked out a cove, baited our hooks, and fished for a while but caught nothing. I thought I felt the beginning of boredom. There was a sandbar about three hundred yards offshore, and I suggested we swim out there for the hell of it. So we started swimming, fully dressed except for our shoes, carrying our cigarettes and lighters in plastic bags. The situation changed when the wind came up, and muddy lake water started splashing in our faces.

Suddenly I realized we might not make it.

Then I remembered an article in *National Geographic* with photographs showing how navy aviators turned their dungarees into flotation bags. Taking off my jeans and tying knots into the legs, I pulled them over my head. The wet jeans held plenty of air. Joe did the same, and we floated the rest of the way, finally staggering ashore on the sandbar, our feet sinking into the soft, red mud. There was nothing on it but the skeletal remains of a few catfish and a water moccasin.

For a while, we sat in the mud and smoked. The boredom was gone, and everything looked incredibly valuable, like it had just been made.

"I got to hand it to you," Joe said. "That was pretty smart."

Like me, he was shocked by what had almost happened—something out of his control.

"Look," I said finally. "Why don't we get out of here this summer? Take a car trip, like we were going to do after our senior year. Jayne can come if she wants. Let's just *go* someplace."

"I have August off," he said. "But Jayne's got to work for the phone company, and I don't think my old Ford'll get very far. Let me think about it."

Strangely enough, it was my father who came through for me. My family was going to Nebraska that summer, like we always did, and I proposed we take Joe along. Suddenly, my father remembered a great trip he had taken to Colorado with his fraternity brothers and decided Joe and I should have such a trip. He even let me take the Chevy, our second car.

So at the beginning of August, Joe and I followed my parents to Nemaha, the small Nebraska town where my mother had been born. We stayed there a couple of days and then started out one morning for Colorado in the Chevy. I didn't even look at the map—just roared across the plains on dirt roads, shouting to Joe over the roar of the wind, my life finally in motion again.

The first night, we spent at a hotel in western Nebraska that was full of bedbugs. The second day, we reached Colorado Springs and climbed the great red rocks in the Garden of the Gods. The third day, we drove to Estes Park, where the Colorado air was thin and cool. That night, we went to a club called Jax Snax, where the patrons did a new dance where they never touched, just stood apart and made cool moves. A waitress told us, "It's called 'the Nigger Twist.'" This was disappointing: because she was pretty, we had hoped she was smart.

At first, I thought Joe was having as good a time as I was. But when I asked him about Kant, Hegel, and Spinoza, he told me, "You wouldn't understand them anyway." He began to seem distracted, and his silences got longer and longer. On the fourth and best day, I drove up Corona Pass Road on a little, narrow-gauge railroad I had explored with my father in a previous summer. The rails and ties had been removed, leaving a dirt road that curved high above a perfectly circular lake. At the top, we drove through a tunnel and emerged into the sunlight on the Continental Divide, where Joe and I explored the redbrick ruins of an old hotel and climbed up to a glacier on the side of a nearby mountain. In a pink dusk, I drove back down below the timberline, where we crawled into our sleeping bags and instantly fell asleep.

On the fifth morning, Joe and I walked down a trail through the sunlit woods.

"Look there," I said, pointing to a big pile of sticks in a tree. "That's an Eagle's nest."

"Well, I guess we'd better be heading home today," Joe said.

For a moment, I couldn't believe I'd heard him right and asked him what he meant.

"I mean I love Jayne, and I've got to get back to her."

"But we've got a car," I said. "We don't have to be back until the end of the month. In three days, we could be in San Francisco."

"Look, man," he said. "You're one of my best friends. But I'm a little beyond this endless road shit. You really think that you or any city, even San Francisco, can compare with a woman like Jayne? You ask me, it's about time you grew up."

My face burned with shame and anger, but he was right—also, I was getting a little tired of his silences myself.

"Anything else you want to tell me?"

"Yeah, your friend Lutz really fucked everything up for Jayne and her mother," Joe said. "There's something wrong with that guy. Is there something wrong with you?"

"Probably a lot," I said finally. "But I hope to get over it."

"Sorry," Joe told me. Then he sat down on a rock by the side of the trail, picked up a stick, and began drawing diagrams in the dust. "This is my plan for the future," he said. I sat on the rock beside him and watched as he laid it all out like a logical formula. Joe intended to marry Jayne in another year. There would be two more years of school and then grad school. Joe planned to be a full professor by the time he was thirty and married to Jayne, with tenure and two kids.

"Playing it safe," I said.

"Playing it smart. Mathematical logic has military applications— it's used to program computing gun sights and listening devices. But you've got to work hard if you work for the military," he added. "And there can't be anything wrong with you. You've got to be a dependable person, you know what I mean?"

I saw what he was getting at. Joe was all right. He was the first one of us to grow up; that was all.

So we started back for Texas that day, drove through the night, and arrived in Nortex the following afternoon. I was home days before my parents and had to break into my house when I got there. My room was very small and hot, and for a long time I lay on my bed, staring at the ceiling, wondering what I was going to do now. I would not see Joe again for several years.

One other thing happened that summer. I met Becky Stamos in the bookstore out at the shopping mall. She was buying new clothes for school and was in a good mood, easy to get along with. There seemed to be no harm in taking her out for a Coke. So we went to the Pioneer, and later I parked by the American Trust Life Insurance building and talked about how often we thought of our senior year.

Finally she asked me. "Will, do you think you really *know* me?"

"How do you mean?"

"I'm Greek. My last name is Stamos. Have you ever stopped to think that's a Greek name?"

I had, of course, a thousand times, but asked, "What does that mean to you?"

"A million good things," she said. "And some bad. My parents don't mind me studying drama, because the Greeks invented it. But we're Orthodox, and my family is very traditional. My mother wants me to marry a nice Greek boy."

"I see," I said, thinking this explained Becky's passion for all things *normal*—but why she was telling me this now?

"I have impulses just like everybody else, Will. And I'll tell you, there are times when I think I'd almost *do* it—"

Do it? I wondered. Was she talking about what I was thinking about?

"I mean get married," she added, as if reading my mind, "just to get out of that house!"

Suddenly I was kissing her, and she was kissing me back, even letting me touch her breasts through her clothing—the first time I had ever touched a *real* girl's breasts. When I did, she gave a little gasp that I thought was a gasp of erotic excitement. I see now it was just a gasp of surprise, but at the time, I thought it was the most wonderful sound I had ever heard.

8

BUT THE NEXT day, I was so confused by what had happened and let my parents take me back down to Austin without saying goodbye to Becky. There, I moved back into the same room at the A-Bar Hotel.

Gabe had returned from Longview with enough money to live at the Sigma Nu house. Jayne also was back, living at Scottish Rite Dormitory, but I didn't feel like seeing her. My roommate at the A-Bar was now Manuel Rios, a Mexican American from El Paso. He was a good guy in many ways but also that worst of roommates, a poker player. He and his friends set up a table in our room and played continuously. I started sleeping in an empty bed in the suite next door.

On a cloudy morning in October, I stood on the observation deck of the Tower. The noon bells rang, and a tide of students poured out of the buildings and began crossing the mall below. This was the second month of my sophomore year, and it was not going well for me.

The life of a Joe College was definitely beginning to wear thin. My courses were dull. This year I was taking English Literature, European History, Chemistry, and German. The chemistry class had more than a hundred people in it and was held in an old auditorium with hard wooden seats that had put generations of students to sleep. My English

Literature teacher, who was from Amarillo, read *Beowulf* aloud in the original Olde English, but with a groaning Panhandle accent. The month before, *Esquire* had published its first "Back-to-College" issue, with an article by Benton and Newman, which asked, "Why go back to college when you can learn more by hitchhiking around the country?"

How I wished I had done this. I tried not to think about Becky Stamos and avoided Kid Spudnut because I had started sleeping through my morning classes and was afraid I was contracting a case of the Great Boredom.

I left the top of the Tower and walked back to the A-Bar Hotel. And that was when I first heard about the Cuban Missile Crisis—the week that should have changed everything.

That night President Kennedy gave a speech on national television. The next day, my chemistry professor advised us, "Drive into the hills. Take canned food. You'll probably be all right." None of us, of course, had a car. My adolescent dread of thermonuclear war—a mixture of fear and longing—returned. The night after that, Russian ships approached the American blockade, and I walked the halls of the A-Bar, waiting for the flash and the shock wave. I was also studying the fossil impressions of prehistoric seashells on the limestone bricks and finding them very interesting. The Great Boredom had disappeared. Every moment was important, and for once I felt *alert*.

When I returned to my room, Manuel was saying to his poker-playing buddies, "I'll tell you guys, I don't really give a big shit about world events. When the sirens blow, I'm going to go downstairs and fuck the first girl I meet." I knew this was an absurd idea.

Just then, we heard the noise of a great crowd coming down Guadalupe Street, shouting at the top of their lungs. *This is it,* I thought. But when they got closer, we understood the crowd was shouting, "Panties, panties, panties."

So began the Great Panty Raid of 1962. We joined the crowd and went to Kinsolving Dormitory, where the girls threw down their panties. The next day, we learned the Russian ships had turned around, and shortly after that, things were back to normal. Somehow this made me feel worse than ever.

Two weeks later, I took a Benzedrine tablet to study for my chemistry midterm. For a while I felt *alert* and wished I had started studying before now. I stayed up all night and, when I entered the classroom the next morning, glimpsed for a moment the poetry of the periodic table. Then the teacher rolled up the chart, and the exam began.

When it was over I knew I had failed. That night, I went to Dirty's, ate a Cum-Back Burger, and smoked half a pack of Marlboros. My fingers were yellow with nicotine. I knew I was going on scholastic probation—the first step toward dropping out of school and being drafted—but somehow couldn't bring myself to care.

I was saved by mononucleosis, a disease I still think was brought on by the Great Boredom. The symptoms were almost the same—lethargy and an inability to study, go to class, or take exams. After a week, I rode back to Nortex on the bus, where I fell into the bed of my childhood and slept for three days. Sometimes my father stood in the door and watched me sleep, saying nothing. Fortunately, our family doctor was only too glad to diagnose me with mononucleosis, which meant I could drop chemistry and would not have to go on scholastic probation.

By the fourth day, I felt good enough to go with my mother to Hamal's grocery store, where I found the first Fantastic Four comic book, and a paperback of *Catch-22*, a novel by Joseph Heller that was so good I read it in two days.

On the fifth day, I felt so much better that I called Becky Stamos. Her mother answered the phone and told me she had moved out and was living with two other girls. When I finally got hold of Becky, she said she was very busy but agreed to have coffee at the Cardinal Inn.

Becky was doing very well at the Midwestern University Drama Department, playing small roles but getting good notices. She seemed to think I was doing just as well at the University of Texas, and I let her think so. My hair was now much longer—although nowhere near as long as it would be—but instead of asking me if I was trying to look like Kennedy, she ran her hand through it and said, "I like it. You look very grown up."

After coffee at the Cardinal Inn, I drove her to a new parking spot on the hill above the Continental Refinery, where Becky finally said, "What's the big idea of not calling me before this?"

I admitted it had been the wrong thing to do.

"Oh, well," she said. "I guess it doesn't matter, because I've finally moved out. I lived at home for twenty years, Will, just like that girl in *The Glass Menagerie*—it's a play about the very same thing, and I did a scene from it in my acting class at Midwestern."

"It's a great play."

"But now I'm living with these two girls, the most wonderful girls I've ever met in my whole life. We stay up all night and talk about boys—I've always wanted to do that. Not Greek boys, but boys like you, and I've learned so much."

"I can tell."

"From now on I'm going to be free, Will. I'm going to walk in the rain, read poetry, find myself, and I'm not going to feel sorry for myself a single minute! There's this boy in the drama department who always says, 'I'd rather be sorry for the things I did than the things I didn't.' That's the way it's going to be with me."

I leaned forward and kissed her.

"I thought you had the kissing sickness," she said.

"I don't think it's contagious anymore."

For the second time, Becky let me touch the soft contours of her breasts through her clothing. We had broken through some sort of wall, and I think we both felt great happiness.

It may seem strange now, but by Christmas, I knew that I wanted to marry Becky Stamos and live with her at the Married Student Housing Project on Town Lake in Austin. It was the only way I could gain control over my life, a control I had somehow lost in the grip of the Great Boredom.

When I told my mother I was getting serious about Becky, she cried tears of joy and let me give a party at our house at Christmas, while my parents went to their own party at a hotel downtown. Becky and I invited some of our friends over, and everybody drank Ron Bacardi Superior and danced the twist to the music of Jimmy Reed. Several people told me that Becky was the girl for me. I had many friends who were getting married then. Some are married still. Marriage was the only way to change your life—it would soon be the only way to keep from getting drafted. It was also one of the few times in my life that girls found talk of marriage sexually exciting.

Even then I knew Becky and I would not be in love forever. But I thought we might marry for a few years and be happy together. All I had to do was make the Big Decision. Girls often talked then about how important it was for boys to make the Big Decision. If they did, it meant they had finally grown up.

After the party, Becky and I drove out to the hill above the

Continental Refinery, where I finally spoke the formula, the magic spell, the three words that would change our lives forever: "*I love you*—and I think we should get married someday."

"I'll always love you, Will," she said seriously and let me touch her even more intimately. It had been just the right thing for me to say. I noticed that the moment I told her I loved her, it became true—and going all the way became a real possibility. It was so simple, once you learned this was the way things were done.

Finals were easy when you had a girl back home. Manuel Rios dropped out of school, just as Buddy Cossey had, and went back to El Paso where he had come from. Gabe ran out of money and could no longer stay at the frat house, so he moved back in with me at the A-Bar Hotel. Ahead lay the long second semester. It would be almost three months until spring break, when I would see Becky again.

Sometimes the Great Boredom threatened to return, but Gabe and I fought it off in various ways. In February, we went to San Marcos to make a parachute jump, but it got too dark for the plane to take off, so the pilot told us to return next week. We went back to Austin and never returned.

When I told Kid Spudnut I was going to marry my high school girlfriend, he said, "Typical."

"Of what?"

"Kierkegaardian repetition or rotation. This is the way of life for those who are in unconscious despair—the strategy of those who think they have found a way to defeat boredom."

"I don't get you."

"You will repeat your senior year over and over," he said, "always with the idea of sleeping with the girl you really loved."

Kierkegaard had a name for everything—and *repetition* did sound a little like my own idea of doing things until you finally *got them right*.

But what I was doing was different! I would be getting married for the first time, making the Big Decision, changing my life.

In early April, Gabe and I went to see an art movie called *Lilith*, written and directed by Robert Rossen and starring Jean Seberg as a schizophrenic girl who was confined to an asylum. Warren Beatty, who had taken a job there as an orderly, was gradually drawn into her world and finally asked to be committed himself so he could be with her forever. This movie had an electrifying effect on me.

Of course Jean Seberg was far too beautiful to be a schizophrenic—later I learned the first thing they lost were their looks—but the idea of the movie was that insane girls were the most attractive of all. Suddenly I found myself wondering why I wanted to marry Becky and live at the Married Student Housing Project. I should be looking for a girl who was at least disturbed—she might be able to teach me the meaning of life, *the secret of becoming a writer.*

There was also a scene in the movie where spiders on LSD spun crooked but beautiful webs. I had read Aldous Huxley's *The Doors of Perception*, and as we walked back to the A-Bar, I said to Gabe, "I'd like to try that LSD."

"Let's talk to Foss," Gabe said. "He can get us peyote."

Foss was a Sigma Nu from Laredo, a town on the Mexican border, and he had taken peyote several times. "It's the worst shit you've ever tasted," he said, "and you'll get sick as a dog—but you'll see hallucinations like you won't believe."

Peyote was easy enough to get. He took us out to a cactus farm out near Lake Travis, where we bought a burlap bag full of peyote buttons. But Foss was busy the night we decided to trip, so we asked the Chief—a Native American we had met at the pool hall—to be our guide.

The Chief was a morphine addict and loved to talk about his sorrows. "Peyote is the sacred cactus," he told us. "It will teach you how to live." We spread the dirty buttons on my desk. They did not look edible in the least. I bit into one, tasted the sickening alkaloidal taste.

"How is it?" Gabe asked me.

"Horrible."

The Chief picked up the biggest button and began chewing it. "This is good medicine," he said. Suddenly he stood up and cried, "The Lord God is speaking to me. I have betrayed Mary, the Mother of Jesus." Then the Chief—no Don Juan—staggered out, and we no longer had a guide.

"I still don't feel anything," Gabe said. "Let's go to the Sigma Nu House."

There was a party that night, and the Hot Nuts were playing. The noise was intolerable, so Gabe and I went upstairs and fell on Foss's bed. Then the hallucinations began. Still nauseated but feeling a strange freedom, we crawled through the upper floor of the Sigma Nu house, which throbbed with the sound of the Hot Nuts. The many holes burned into the carpet by cigarettes looked miles deep. Gabe's frat brothers had to step over us to get into the bathroom.

Suddenly we were frightened and fled back to the A-Bar Hotel. There we threw my mattress on the floor and lay on it for the rest of the night, describing to each other the intense hallucinations that began to appear—exotic flowers, jeweled spiderwebs, the whole pre-Columbian world of canine gods and geometric pyramids. I heard voices speaking Indian tongues and heard flute music. *So this is artificial schizophrenia*, I thought.

Toward morning, the hallucinations faded away, and Gabe and I found ourselves in another state—a mystical state where we could hear each other's thoughts and finish each other's sentences—a state where there was nothing but absolute truth. Or at least a state where it was impossible to lie.

Then I rode the bus back to Nortex to see Becky, who had the small role of a nun in *Cyrano de Bergerac*. When I told her I had taken peyote, she seemed frightened. And all she could talk about was Bain Conley, who played the leading role of Cyrano and was the best actor in Nortex.

I had looked forward to playing the role myself someday. Cyrano was a supremely intelligent swordsman and poet who had one defect— an enormous nose. The play was not about everything but about one intolerable thing that the French had noticed; some brilliant men were not handsome, and most young women—like most young men— preferred looks over brains.

When I saw the show that night, I thought Bain was miscast. He had Cherokee blood and was far too handsome to play Cyrano, even with a long, putty nose. I decided his parents must have sensed his destiny when he was born and given him his dramatic name so he would not have to change it later.

But when I watched Becky and Bain talking after the show, I noticed they were standing very close together. Becky was constantly touching her hair and face, and when she put her hand on Bain's arm, I could tell it was not the first time she had done this. They were falling in love with each other!

I refused to go to the cast party that night and instead took Becky to our parking spot on the hill overlooking the Continental

Refinery. "I love you," I said. "And I think we should set a date for our marriage."

But this time she asked me, "Have you gotten a ring?"

"No, but I can."

"I don't know if you're ready to make a decision like that, Will," she said thoughtfully.

What was going on here? Suddenly we were back to talking about the Big Decision, the one I had made long ago. I wasn't sure if she knew she was in love with Bain or not, but I wanted to get what I had coming to me—so I kissed her again and again, trying to remind her that she had loved me first. And when she still would not understand, I finally said, "I thought we would go to a motel tonight."

"Not yet, Will."

I rode back to Austin, and three days later got a letter from Becky.

By the time you read this, I will be married to Bain. As you know, for years, I have thought of nothing but getting away from my mother and finding my freedom. I hoped you would join me on this adventure because you were the one who first put this idea into my head. But when I finally accomplished it, Bain was here for me, and you were not. So I have given my heart to him. I think if you knew him, you would like him—he is so like you in so many ways.

Becky

Oh sure, I thought. *If I knew him, I'd like him. He's just like me—except he's better.*

I don't believe I was, by any means, the first person in history to get such a letter. But when I did, my life blew out like a candle, and the pain did not leave me for months. Never again, I promised myself, would I tell a girl that I loved her and ask her me to marry me—because, when you did, she always married somebody else.

Becky and Bain lived in Nortex for a while. Then they moved to the Crow Indian reservation near Missoula, Montana, where they lived in a trailer and taught drama to Indian kids for several years before they got divorced. They never had any children.

On the last day before finals, I woke as the sun was setting. The Great Boredom had finally struck us both down. Now Gabe and I stayed up all night and slept all day. We stopped using ashtrays and threw our cigarette butts on the floor, creating an interesting mosaic of burns. When the maids came, we shouted at them to leave us alone.

I got up, went to my desk, and wrote a fan letter to Mr. Stan Lee, the editor of Marvel Comics (instead of studying, I read comic books) praising his new superhero, the Incredible Hulk. When it was dark, Gabe woke, and we went down to the Spudnut Shoppe and ate breakfast. Kid Spudnut was there. I had told him about Becky, and he gave me his copy of Kierkegaard's *Either/Or.* One passage was underlined:

> Marry a girl, and you will regret it. Do not marry her,
> and you will still regret it. Either way, you will regret it.

"It's all happened before, kid," he said.

This was no consolation. When Gabe and I had finished breakfast, we walked to the Texas Theater to see Antonioni's *La Notte,* which was the greatest art movie yet. Monica Vitti wandered through the world, looking for love, but never found it. The film ended with a montage of empty streets, a rain barrel filling with water, and finally a glaring streetlight.

And when we came out of the movie theater, what did we see? The University of Texas was undergoing a big building boom, and the campus looked just like Rome in the movie. So we walked past floodlit construction sites topped by cranes and finally stopped by the fountain on the Main Mall and sat on the rim until it hissed off into silence at midnight.

"What happened with you and that girl, anyway?" Gabe finally asked.

"I'm not sure," I said. "*Somebody* wanted to get married. I guess it just wasn't me."

The long night loomed ahead. Gabe went back to our room to study, and I walked on through what seemed like the ruins of a great civilization. Down long staircases and past marble statues I walked, sometimes meeting another solitary student like myself, but we never spoke. The illuminated sandstone shaft of the Tower shone down on a silence. Sunrise found me behind the Texas History Museum, staring into a glass case that held a loaf of sandstone covered with dinosaur footprints, which my father had once shown me. My attempt to grow up had failed and left me drifting in time and space. Face pressed against the thick plate glass, I stared into the world of my childhood, which I could never enter again.

9

WHEN MY PARENTS brought me home that summer, in June 1963, they told me I had to get a job. So I went to work at White's Auto Stores warehouse, a big galvanized tin shed on the west side of town. Every day I took order forms, found goods on the shelves, and put them into the chain of grocery carts that circled the warehouse. At noon I drove home for lunch—two Swiss cheese sandwiches on white bread and ten minutes of watching *You Bet Your Life* with Groucho Marx—and then drove back to work. The interior of the warehouse was very hot, and in three months, I lost fifteen pounds.

At night, my brother, Ray, and I went downtown to the movies. *The Great Escape* was the best—we sat through it twice—but when we came out, the abandoned brick buildings of downtown Nortex looked as desolate as the ruins of Ancient Egypt. It was one of those summers when the June bugs hatched out, and hard brown beetles clung to the screens and covered the pavement under the streetlights.

I tried to avoid the house where Becky and Bain lived, but one Sunday morning, I drove past it, and of course they were standing in the front yard. Becky's eyes were downcast, and they were dressed for church. I sped up and drove on, hoping they hadn't seen me.

Jayne Harper was also home that summer, and one day she called me and said that she and Joe had broken up. "He's going to marry an older woman," she said, "the nurse at his college at Rice. And my parents have run out of money, so I have to quit school and join the army."

I was surprised but somehow blamed Joe. He had told me of his detailed plans for the future when we were in Colorado, but now he had changed his mind, decided to marry somebody else, and never said a word about it.

A couple of weeks later, I took Jayne down to the bus station so she could catch a bus to Fort Polk, Louisiana, for basic training. The old station still had separate restrooms and water fountains—one for white, the other for colored—and was empty even in broad daylight. I got two sodas out of a machine, and we drank them and talked for a while.

"I thought you and Joe were meant for each other," I said.

"We thought so too."

"You had a lot of good times together."

She looked at me. "Truth is, I may not be meant for any man," she said.

We talked a little longer about nothing at all. When her bus came, I loaded her suitcases into the baggage compartment, and we said goodbye. As I watched the bus pull out for Fort Polk, I decided she had been trying to tell me something about herself but still wasn't sure what it was.

When Jayne finally got out of the army, she went to the University of the Americas in Mexico City to study Spanish. She was there during the riots, when the Halcones fought the student demonstrators, and the government called in the helicopter gunships. Years later, someone told me she was gay—a word that was finally in general use by then—and living with another woman.

That summer, my father taught himself Chopin's *Kinderszenen* (*Scenes from Early Childhood*). I must have heard him play it a thousand times. Sometimes when he was finished practicing he went out into the backyard, and one night I found him out there staring at the full moon, which was yellow as brass and just rising.

We stood beside each other in silence for a while, and finally he asked, "Do you remember the Beamer convention in Kansas City?"

I remembered it well. The On the Beam Society had met there at a big hotel, and my father had taken the whole family. It had been the summer after the fifth grade when I was twelve years old. "That's when I bought the E-meter," my father said, "and the tape recorder. But you never used them, did you?"

A salesman at the convention had shown my father a device he called the E-meter—a galvanic skin response meter, a sort of lie detector, which is used today by the Church of Scientology to determine if members are "clear." First the salesman had told me to hold the electrodes in my hands; then he'd asked me what I thought of school, subject by subject. Once the needle dipped, and he'd told me, "You seem to have a problem with math." My father already knew I had a problem with math, but he'd accepted this as a revelation and bought one, along with a tape recorder for sleep-learning.

"I tried them a few times," I told him. "But I didn't know how to make them work."

After the convention, my father had put my mother and my little brother, Ray, on the train to Lincoln, and we'd driven back to Nemaha together. On the car radio, we heard Dinah Washington singing a strange song called "The Day that the Rain Came Down," whose lyrics mentioned fields of corn. At that moment we were passing a cornfield, and my father said, "See? When you're On the Beam, everything's in tune."

When we reached Nemaha, my father played the piano in the front room of my grandfather's house all day long and told anyone who would listen about the wonderful things we had experienced in Kansas City. At age twelve, I was thoroughly tired of the On the Beam Society but for some reason felt I had to defend him. Once I even passed my father a note while he was playing, telling him that I could see his "aura"—a golden radiance surrounding his body—and at the time it seemed that perhaps I could. One night we were all lying on the grass in the front yard, while my father tried to explain the ideas of Dr. Truman to my Aunt Edith, when suddenly two pale blue crescents streaked across the sky.

"Flying saucers," my father said. "I've seen them before."

My heart was pounding, and I felt a sudden pride. Here at last was proof of my father's beliefs—I had seen them myself. And even today, I cannot explain those two blue crescents in the sky. *But it made no difference!* Aunt Edith just said, "Well, how do you like that?" Then she went inside as if nothing had happened.

My father and I sat on the front porch, and he said, "Dr. Truman showed me how to put out a star. Just keep staring at that star there, over the trees."

I did, and as I watched, the star went out.

"My mind bent the light waves," he explained. "This is something you can do when you achieve the higher powers."

Years later, I learned there is a blind spot in the center of your field of vision. Stare at a star long enough, and it will disappear. It had just been more Beamer magic—but I fervently hoped my father had not known this at the time.

Now, standing in our backyard in Texas, I heard my father saying, "I've always thought you were one of the new children predicted in Arthur C. Clarke's *Childhood's End*. Dr. Truman and I often talked about that. He said, if there was a nuclear war, that he and some of the old Beamers and the new children like you would get together and stop it."

There had almost been a nuclear war during the Cuban Missile Crisis, and I wondered if my father thought Dr. Truman had stopped that one. Suddenly I remembered taking peyote and asked my father, "Do you remember your cosmic illumination?"

"Oh, yes," he said. "How could I forget that?"

For a moment, I almost told him that I'd had a mystical experience myself on peyote and had reached a state of absolute truth where it was impossible to lie. But then I'd taken a drug, and my father's cosmic illumination had happened after he had taken Phase Five. Still, they sounded very much alike. Could my father somehow have been given peyote at Aum-Sat-Tat?

No, I told myself, *that was impossible.* Peyote had been around then— the Indians had taken it for hundreds of years—but if my father had taken peyote, he would certainly have known it.

In fact, peyote was not the only way to have a mystical experience. There was another drug, lysergic acid diethylamide, which was much easier to take. You might not even know you had been given it. The schizophrenics in the movie *Lilith* had been given LSD, and Timothy Leary was handing it out to college kids that very summer. In a few years everybody, myself included, would be off to San Francisco to take acid, as LSD came to be called, and see the pure white light.

"Is there something you want to tell me?" my father asked me, somehow reading my mind.

"You're playing very well," I told him.

"Thank you, Sonny. The Chopin piece is difficult, but I'm learning."

"I'm going for a walk."

So I took another walk. This time, it was my old erotic moonlit journey through the alleys and streets of my childhood, but somehow it was not as stimulating as it had been before. My second year at the university was over, but the lethargy of the Great Boredom went on. There was nothing I wanted to do more than write, but a strange pressure kept me from touching the keys of my Smith Corona portable electric typewriter. Why had I lost Becky? Why was it so hard to stay in school? And why couldn't I change my life?

Something was going to happen soon—I could feel it like a storm just below the horizon—but there was nothing I could do to make it happen now. My life was at a standstill. At the end of the alley, a streetlight cast a strange, billowing shadow on the pavement. Looking up, I saw a giant black and gold garden spider had spun a web around it, and the shells of dead June bugs covered the pavement below. Danny had been right: This whole town was one big insane asylum. I should never have come back here.

10

I woke on a November morning in the A-Bar Hotel and heard the poker players in the next room saying, "Shot him in the head, huh? I hope that son of a bitch dies."

I dressed quickly and walked from the A-Bar to the Nueces, another dormitory a block away. It was a beautiful, sunlit day, but people were stopping their cars and listening to their radios. I went into the Nueces and woke up Richard, a guy from Nortex, by pounding on his door and shouting, "Turn on the television."

He did, just in time for us to see Walter Cronkite take off his glasses and say, "This just in from Dallas ..." Tears were running down his face. "The president is dead."

Tears were also running down Richard's face, but not mine. Some sense of dread or history had alerted me even in my sleep, and I had been among the first to know.

Classes were canceled. For the next three days, we watched the funeral on television and saw Jack Ruby shoot Oswald—almost as great a shock as the assassination. The coffin lay in state under the Capitol dome, and the next day was the funeral. Kennedy was buried at Arlington Cemetery, and Jackie Kennedy lit the Eternal Flame, all of it on somber, black-and-white television. Still, I felt no sadness—but I was extremely *alert*.

Then I rode the bus home for Thanksgiving and, while I was there, celebrated my twenty-first birthday. My parents agreed it was a dreadful time, but my mother thought Pearl Harbor had been a little worse, and my father wasn't sure he'd liked Kennedy all that much anyway. My alertness began to fade away.

The night I returned to the A-Bar, Gabe, who had been living at the frat house since September, came over to see me. I lay on my bed, listening while he walked around the room, talking endlessly.

"My father got me a job working for the Forest Service last summer," he said. "I thought I was pretty lucky until I found out I was supposed to stay up alone in a tower for three months. I couldn't even take it for a week. So I hitchhiked down to Estes Park and drank beer for the rest of the summer. Now I can never have that job again, because I left without giving notice. Well, it doesn't matter because you know what I'm going to do? I'm going to San Francisco and start a new life."

I sat up, instantly *alert* again.

"Kennedy was shot by a nobody. He was this country's last hope, and now everything is going to end. The beatniks are right—everybody can be an artist if they want to be, and living for the moment is the only thing that counts. You've always wanted to go to San Francisco, haven't you? Then let's go together. We'll get motorcycles, grow beards, find girls, and take peyote."

"How are we going to get there?"

"Hitchhike to Norman and talk your friend Lutz into going with us. He's got a car, doesn't he?"

"What if he doesn't want to go?"

"Are you kidding?" Gabe said. "The world as we know it is over. There *is* no other place to go."

The next day, I went to the registrar's office and dropped all my courses. This was my third year of school, and I hadn't even earned two years worth of credits. Then I took all my money out of the bank, about $300, called my parents, and told them what I was going to do. Gabe also called his. Like mine, they were very disappointed. "Maybe it's better if we don't tell Lutz we're coming and surprise him," Gabe said.

The following day, Gabe and I packed our suitcases and hitchhiked up to Norman. It was cold and rainy, and the truck drivers who picked us up said they were glad Kennedy had been shot. When we arrived that night, I found Norman was smaller than I had expected. Lutz lived on the second floor of an apartment complex arranged around an empty swimming pool.

"What the fuck are you guys doing here?" he said incredulously when he opened the door.

"We're going to San Francisco," Gabe said. "And you're going with us. You must be sick of this bourgeois fraternity life."

"Let's talk about that," Lutz said. He put on an album by the Four Seasons, a group that was a big Sammy favorite. Lutz had let his hair grow and looked a little like Jerry Lewis as Buddy Love in the movie *The Nutty Professor*. "You guys have gone insane," he said, snapping his fingers. "You got any money? What are you gonna do for money out there?"

I told him we would get jobs. Lutz reminded me that he hadn't worked since we were lifeguards and wasn't about to start now.

"Look, you can take us, and we'll pay you for the gas," Gabe said.

"I've got to think about it," Lutz said. "I'm in a little trouble with my frat brothers—I'll explain later. But you guys can stick around here for a couple of days. Maybe you can convince me."

"We're hungry," Gabe said.

"There's a bowl of onion dip in the refrigerator and a bag of Fritos. And I've got some pills here I stole from my psychiatrist."

"You're seeing a psychiatrist?" I asked him.

"That's part of the trouble. But look—there's going to be a poker game here on Friday night. Maybe you guys'll get lucky and win big."

The next morning we sat around the apartment and tried to convince Lutz to go to California. But mostly he told us about his troubles. Just before the assassination, he had gone to the Carousel Club, Jack Ruby's strip club in Dallas, where he'd stood on a table and shown everybody his cock. Jack Ruby had had him arrested, and the Sammies had put him on probation and insisted he see the school psychiatrist.

"So I've got to be careful," he said. "There's some kind of conspiracy going on, and I'm under suspicion. Ruby was part of it—everybody knows that. You hear what he said when he shot Oswald? 'I did it to prove a Jew had guts.' That was my defense for hanging my cock out at the Carousel Club. But now my brothers think I'm part of the conspiracy."

"All the more reason to quit school," Gabe said.

"You guys want some pills?" Lutz asked, changing the subject. Opening a bottle, he offered it to Gabe and me—he seemed to have hundreds of pills—and told us his psychiatrist had left the office during one of their sessions, and Lutz had cleaned out his desk drawer. Gabe and I took the pills—probably Valiums—and sat around in a fog of mild astonishment. Outside, it had started to snow.

"I don't like the idea of hitchhiking to San Francisco in this weather," I said.

"Know why you're depressed?" Gabe said. "You need protein. How about a big steak for dinner?"

I told him I couldn't afford it, but Gabe said it wouldn't cost a thing; we would steal our dinner from the Safeway. "When I was a pledge, the Sigma Nus used to send me out to steal steaks," he told me, "and I *never* got caught."

Then Gabe got Lutz to take us to the Safeway. He said he operated better alone, so Lutz and I bought baked potatoes and salad greens, while Gabe went to the back of the store by himself. When we returned to the apartment, Gabe pulled a huge steak wrapped in plastic out of his pants and cooked it for us. I had to admit, it was a great meal.

"Glad you liked it," Gabe said, "because, from now on, you've got to steal your own."

"I'm not much of a thief."

"Take another pill. You won't feel a thing."

That night I lay awake for hours. It was clear that Lutz's fraternity brothers were upset because he was a flasher. That didn't bother me, but the idea of going to San Francisco was becoming unreal, and we seemed to be falling into dangerous habits. In the last three years, I had gotten drunk, had sex with a prostitute, and eaten peyote—but I had never stolen a single thing. I knew the moment I did, I would get caught and thrown in jail.

The next day was sunny. The big poker game was that night, and Gabe was feeling so lucky he said he thought he would steal two steaks today. Before we went to the Safeway, I took two Valiums and began feeling so good I decided my fears of getting caught were illusory. Lutz drove us there and waited in his car while we went in. Gabe took two steaks out of the bin, and I took one. Nobody seemed to be watching us and I felt invulnerable, until the frozen rib eye I had shoved down the front of my jeans began to melt, staining them with blood. As we left I saw an older man who had to be the manager staring right at me while he talked on the phone.

The streets were icy, and as Lutz drove away in his little red Chevy Nova, he hit another car. A cop pulled over and gave him a ticket. As Lutz signed it, his hand shaking, another cop car drove by with its siren going, headed for the grocery store. I sat there with Gabe in the backseat, my jeans bloody, trying to remain invisible.

Gabe made a little money at the poker game that night. The other players were all Sammies, and Lutz watched but didn't take part. I stayed in the back bedroom, reading Norman Mailer's *An American Dream* in *Esquire*, thinking that I had completely lost all desire to go to California.

When Gabe came in, counting his money, I admitted that I was afraid we were going to get caught shoplifting. He asked me who I was reading, and I told him Norman Mailer.

"He went to jail for stabbing his wife, didn't he?" Gabe asked me.

"Yeah, but what does that have to do with it?"

"You'll have plenty of time to write in jail."

The next morning, I woke and found Gabe sitting at the kitchen table, reading an article in the *Daily Oklahoman*, the student newspaper. He handed it to me without a word.

> Police are investigating a rash of shoplifting incidents
> by students at local grocery stores and expect to make
> an arrest soon.

"Time to get out of town," Gabe said.

We repacked our suitcases, and Lutz agreed to drive us out to the western edge of Oklahoma City. There he pulled off the highway onto the access road, and said, "End of the line."

Gabe started to get out of the car and then looked back at me and asked, "You coming or not?"

"Can't go for it," I said, unable to look at him.

He nodded and then walked to the edge of the highway and stuck out his thumb. The first two or three cars passed him by, but the third picked him up.

Gabe had done what he had said he was going to do! He had made a decision, had changed his life, was on his way to California—it could not have been more astonishing if he had vanished off the face of the earth.

Lutz took me to the bus station, where I bought a ticket to Nortex. For some reason, I was angry at him, and we barely spoke. The bus went first to Dallas, where I changed to another one for Nortex. On the way out of town, it drove through Dealey Plaza, where a single decoration, a little red electric Christmas wreath, stood on the grassy knoll.

ELMWOOD PLACE

11

WHEN I RETURNED to Nortex, I called my father from the bus station to pick me up.

"Back so soon, man?" he said. "Well that was a pretty goddamned short trip."

"Don't call me 'man.'"

"What's the matter? Didn't you *dig* it out there?"

He was right to be angry with me. This time I had dropped completely out of school, and if I went back, would be on scholastic probation. For days he tortured me by pretending I had actually gone with Gabe to California.

"Is it raining out there now? Didn't the climate agree with you? Couldn't you get a job?" When I begged him to stop, he said, "I have only one thing to say to you, *man*. From now on, you're on your own."

Finally, my father fell into an angry silence, drinking and playing the piano all night while I slept in the bedroom, which I shared with my little brother, who was no longer so little but seemed afraid of me. My mother said almost nothing during this time, but sometimes I found her crying while she did the dishes.

Then, the day after Christmas—a painful ordeal for us all—my father came to me and said he wanted to talk. He and my mother had decided that if I wanted to go back down to Austin and try school one more time, they could give me a little money.

I was surprised. "You told me from now on, I was on my own."

"To tell you the truth, I don't think we can stand having you around here much longer. You'll have to get a job, of course when you get back down to Austin. Just promise me one thing. This time you'll study something you enjoy, like drama."

My father had been in some plays at the University of Nebraska, but I could hardly believe he was saying this.

"I'm not telling you to major in it," he said. "I'm just asking you to do something that makes you happy for a change."

Of course, I had been certain since high school that I could be an actor. (I was sure I could be anyone I wanted to be, which was part of my problem.) And performing was suddenly appealing to me—at least I would get an immediate response, which was better than months of laboring over a few pages of prose that I never showed to anyone. Best of all, I could now pretend to be somebody else for a while instead of trying to find myself. No more honesty, no more trying to write. Life might be fun for a change.

My father even told me he would give me the Oldsmobile, our older car. When I asked him what had changed his mind, he told me, "Your mother showed me your shoes, and they're full of holes—you put cardboard in them to keep the water out. You could have bought some new shoes, but I guess it's easier for me to give you our car. No, don't thank me. I was going to have to buy another one pretty soon anyway."

He said this in his old, bitter, ironic army voice—the exact same voice George C. Scott later used in the movie *Patton*—but it was the biggest favor he ever did for me.

A few days later, I drove down to Austin in the Oldsmobile. My plan was to find a part-time job of some sort and enroll at the drama department when the second semester of school began. If this didn't work, I might as well give up and join the army before I was drafted. But I told myself that this time it would be different, because I had a car and wouldn't be living at the A-Bar Hotel.

Of course what I was really hoping to find was a girl. Here I was, twenty-one years old, the last young man in Texas and perhaps the whole world who had not yet made love to a *real* girl. For years I had been lying to everyone about this, and a great shame was beginning to descend on me. But somehow I was sure that this time I was going to find her. The drama department would be full of gays—for simplicity's sake, I am going to call them that, because it is better than what they called themselves at that time—but there were sure to be plenty of girls who were looking for a *real* man like me. (Only later did I learn that every actor ever born has said, "I took my first acting class so I could meet girls.")

As I drove through the hills around Lampasas, it began to rain. I spent that night with my grandparents and, the next morning, took a single room in an apartment house on Nueces Street and found a part-time job serving meals and washing dishes at Seton Hospital.

In a sense I am still looking for that room, where I stayed for a month. It had a bed, a couch, a gas heater, and the bathroom was down the hall, but I could concentrate there. When I got a postcard from Gabe saying he was living in North Beach with a stripper, I threw it away. I did not envy him.

Solitude proved to be a good thing for me. In the afternoons, I served meals to the patients at Seton Hospital and then washed dishes and was later given my own supper in the cafeteria. Every night I returned to the room and read Mary Renault's *The King Must Die* and *The Bull From the Sea*, two beautifully written novels I had found at the co-op. In them, she retold the myth of Theseus as someone who had actually existed. Her version of archaic Greece was a real country, and her Theseus was a person of flesh and blood, not a marble statue.

That year, I would go on to read the plays of Aeschylus, Sophocles, and Euripides; the philosophy of Socrates and Heraclitus; and the poetry of Archilochus. They were the first works that had really excited me since the novels of Jack Kerouac and Thomas Wolfe. I can't explain their power over me, but I know I am not the first to fall under their spell. Every morning, I woke with my head still full of dreams about the ancient world.

At the end of January, I walked across the campus to register. Warm, moist air was blowing up from the Gulf, and the campus was lost in a fog so thick the buildings looked like photographic transparencies. I remembered just such a morning when my Grandpa Thorn had shown my father and me his fishing cabin on Lake Travis and thought, *This is my fortunate day.*

The drama department had just relocated to a new, modern building on the east side of the campus that still smelled of fresh paint. It was situated on Waller Creek, shaded by ancient oaks, and pleasantly remote from the rest of the university. At the center of the building was the Theater Room, where on Fridays we gathered to watch acting class scenes performed in Demonstration Lab. Five major productions a year were still staged across the campus in Hogg Auditorium, which was as big as many Broadway houses.

In the last decade, the school had graduated several actors who had become movie stars, like Rip Torn, Pat Hingle, and Jayne Mansfield, but our teachers never mentioned them. The emphasis was on turning out drama education majors, and any dreams we might have had of becoming professional actors were always discouraged.

When I registered, I was told that I would have to declare myself a drama major. But by this time, it didn't even bother me. I took acting, theater history, scene design, dance, and shop, where I was put to work for two hours every weekday building flats for *The Cherry Orchard*. There I learned stage carpentry and made friends with three guys, Larry, Mike, and Shan, who were straight (or heterosexual) and asked me if I wanted to take a room in their apartment. Like me, they wanted to act. But the casting for each major production was done by a faculty director, and a coterie of gays got all the leading roles. There was a good reason for this. Most of them were far better actors and had spent far more time onstage than we had.

I tried to get along with everybody, gay or straight. After all, I shared many gay fascinations, like getting a good haircut and wearing the right clothes—I had a whole collection of favorite blue jeans that I had worn since high school. Sometimes I was told, "You're gay, but you don't know it." I refused to believe this and kept trying to talk to gays about plays and acting. As for the girls, they were not at all what I expected—many of them seemed to prefer the company of gays to that of straights.

Nobody had seen me act yet, and I knew I had to get a couple of good roles under my belt to establish my reputation. Then I did get a good role. In my first appearance in Demonstration Lab, I played a sexually frustrated husband in a scene from *The Dark at the Top of the Stairs* by William Inge. This was a role I should have been perfect for— but my performance was met with complete indifference.

Afterward, I went to see Mr. Moller, the head of the acting department, who was also disappointed in me. "You might have been very good in high school," he said, "but you haven't had much experience since. Or it could be that the role you played was a lead, and you are a character actor. In fact, the more I see of you, the more I'm convinced that's what you are."

I didn't really understand the difference between character actors and leading men, and I asked him what they were.

"Character actors," he told me, "usually play supporting roles."

"Are we talking about looks?" I said, thinking about the time Bobby Lee Cummins had hit me at Zundy, split my mind from my body, and ruined both.

"It's not just a matter of looks," Mr. Moller said. "It's more a matter of your approach to your work."

"How do you mean?"

"For instance, leading men are usually method actors. They play themselves and fall under a kind of spell, where they believe their role and the world of the stage are *real*. This gives them a certain unpredictability, a certain *danger*."

"I see."

"Character actors are usually technical actors. They achieve complete control over their voice and body and give you a detailed portrait of a character. But they are *not playing themselves*, and they almost always get supporting roles. Yes, in my opinion, you are definitely a character actor."

Both of these approaches, method and technical, sounded a little insane to me (who could think the stage was real?) and I didn't want to take either approach—I just wanted people to *like* me.

"Is there anything else?"

"Yes," he said. "You lack a certain polish."

I nodded, thinking that "polish" meant gay sexual attractiveness, which was partly right and partly wrong.

"Only a few of us are lucky enough to make a living in the professional theater," Mr. Moller went on. "In all honesty, I think you should consider changing your major to drama education."

"Thank you for telling me the truth," I said and walked out of his office—still strangely certain I was going to play big roles someday, even if I was a character actor and not handsome enough for a leading man.

But since I wasn't going to get a big role anytime soon, I had to create one for myself to play offstage. So I decided to be Steve McQueen—an ordinary guy who at that time was not yet a star. He was tough when he had to be but always had a good sense of humor.

After every major production, there were cast parties, where the first records of the Beatles and the Rolling Stones were played, and I threw myself into Beatlemania. There was a real happiness in abandoning yourself to a teenage fad, and it also had the advantage of canceling out the Kennedy assassination and my wasted years at the A-Bar Hotel, making me years younger. So I drank a lot of beer and danced until I got good at it. Probably I was a pain in the ass, but at least I was not an onlooker—I was *involved* as I had never been at fraternity parties. And there was a method to my madness—the old Zen solution of complete behavioral freedom.

So I went about the serious business of having fun, with the secret conviction that someday I was going to get big roles. Mr. Moller had also said one thing that was definitely right. Good actors (and this included character actors) were unpredictable, they were *dangerous* in some way, and danger was sexual. Soon I would make a move on a girl, which was what I had come to the drama department for in the first place, and that girl and I would become lovers.

Now that I had a car, I started driving out into the hills around Lake Travis on Sundays. I was looking for something but didn't know what. One day, I came to a hilltop called Comanche Pass and saw a lake below. Suddenly I recognized it as Lake Travis, where my grandfather had his fishing cabin, and remembered the morning he had brought my father and me out here, not long after the war. The fog had parted, and I had seen the waters of the lake far below. To me it had looked as big as an inland sea.

Finally, I found a side road—it had been caliche then but was blacktop now—and followed it down through the cedars until I came to the place where Grandpa Thorn had parked his car. There we had walked down a flight of cinderblock steps so steep I had been afraid I would lose my footing and roll downhill.

I found the old cinderblock steps and followed them down to a clearing in the cedars where the cabin had once stood. Now it had collapsed. There were only a few logs in the grass and broken bits of bottle glass turned violet by the sun. Through the cedars I could see the blue waters of the lake.

Then I heard the music.

It was faint, crystalline, and somehow familiar to me—although at first I thought it was the wind in the cedar trees. Slowly, memory by memory, that first day came back to me. I had seen the waters of the lake on that day too, but it had been black and cold through the fog. Grandpa Thorn had unlocked the door of the cabin and built a fire in the cast-iron stove. On the table was a copy of *The Iliad* that my father had left the summer before the war and forgotten. I sat in the halo of warmth around the stove and looked at an old *Popular Mechanics* that I had found under the bed, while Thorn and my father talked.

And on that day I had also heard the music, and *time had stopped*—or somehow I *had known where I was in time*.

In the *Popular Mechanics* issue, there was an article about the New York World's Fair of 1939 and an illustration of a city where helicopters flew above tall buildings connected by elevated roads. When I asked my father about it, he said, "That's the world of tomorrow." I could not read the article, but as I studied the illustration, I began to understand that time had moved on, and we were now living in the world depicted on that page. The war was finally over; my father had come safely home; and from now on, things were going to be better.

The feeling lasted for about an hour, and when we left, I saw the lake with new eyes. The dripping cedars looked black, and the white caliche road ran off to the vanishing point. It looked almost exactly like the India ink illustration of the path the Cat Who Walked By Herself had taken, through the Wild Wet Woods by her Wild Lone, in a book my father had just read to me called *Just So Stories*.

Someday, I thought, *I will come back to this place where time stops*.

Now I had. I could remember that day with such perfect clarity it seemed like a clear white light was shining on me—and I sensed there had been other such moments back there in my childhood, when I had also heard the faint, crystalline sound of the music—which now gradually faded away and was gone.

As I drove back to Austin, I noticed that my vision was still slightly altered, and I saw the terrain of the Hill Country was almost the same as that of Greece—cedars, oaks, limestone, and blue water. The university, with its neoclassical buildings, was Athens. Lake Travis was the wine-dark sea. A few days earlier, I had gone to the library and had taken out some illustrated books on the architecture of ancient Greece. Now my mind was full of images—kings wearing bronze ceremonial helmets in the shape of bull's heads, Minoan priestesses holding their prophetic snakes, the beehive tombs of Mycenae, archaic marble statues carved with the dolphin smile of Apollo.

I had just had what my father was always talking about—a mystical experience. But I told no one about this because I had no one to tell. There was also the faint feeling that, if I did, it might not come to me again. It would remain my secret.

12

Finally I made a move on Jody Brown. She was a beatnik girl from Houston with red hair and green eyes who always wore a green skirt and a black leotard. I can't really describe her—since I still love her, I can't picture her face. Sometimes she looked as sad as Julie Harris, and at other times, as beautiful as Lee Remick. She had a theatrical way of talking and called many people "darling," but I loved her low, controlled voice. In dreams, I have noticed that a woman's face may be invisible, but her voice carries a strong erotic charge. Jody's voice was like that.

She had performed Sartre's *No Exit* in Demonstration Lab, where she had kissed Kate, a tall dark girl in our class who kept to herself and was rumored to be gay. I thought Jody was a good actress and felt her talent, like mine, had been overlooked. My roommate, Shan, had dated her and warned me, "She'll pretend she likes you, and then she gets cold. She's got a split personality." Today I think Jody was what would later be called a borderline personality, a term that had not been invented yet. But this quality only increased my determination. Like Jean Seberg in the movie *Lilith*, she was a dangerous girl, but the only one for me.

Still I held off until old Dr. Payne, the director of the annual

Shakespeare production, which was staged at Hogg Auditorium, cast us together in *As You Like It*. The Duke Senior and his men had fled to the Forest of Arden and there fleeted the time carelessly, as men did in the golden world. This was the same play in which my father, at the University of Nebraska, had played the Melancholy Jaques—a wonderful role, and I wanted to play either Jaques or the Duke Senior, who in the forest had found "tongues in trees, books in the running brooks / Sermons in stones, and good in everything." But Dr. Payne cast me as William. This character was a "natural"—the village idiot— and in love with Audrey, a shepherd girl, who was played by Jody.

On opening night, I got laughter and exit applause, and as we left the stage, I asked Jody for a date. "Meet me tomorrow morning at Eastwoods Park," I said.

"What will we do?"

"I thought we would play catch."

She laughed and said, "That sounds original."

On Saturday, I went to the park as Steve McQueen in *The Great Escape*, wearing my old blue sweatshirt with cut-off sleeves and wheat jeans. Fortunately, she had never seen this movie and did not know who I was pretending to be. I also brought two baseball gloves and a hardball and found Jody waiting for me in a glade.

Eastwoods Park was one of those little Austin neighborhood parks with a swimming pool, tennis courts, and ancient oaks. Some were state landmarks, so old their trunks had split apart and were nailed back together with iron spikes. It was a fine April morning, and for an hour, we played catch, until Eastwoods Park began to feel like the Forest of Arden. I felt Jody was having good time.

"This is fun," she said. "It's nice to do something normal for a change."

Then she suggested that we go back to her apartment, and I agreed.

Jody lived with two gay guys, Punky and Dwayne. I sat on a red velvet sofa that smelled of cat piss, and she disappeared into her bedroom. She reappeared wearing a beige slip—the sexiest female garment of that time—and carrying a pitcher of White Russians. It was not even noon, but the four of us began to drink.

For a few minutes, I felt great and even kissed Jody when we were alone in the kitchen. But the alcohol was too strong for me. And the next thing I knew I was lying on the floor with my eyes closed while Dwayne and Punky talked about me. "He's drunk," they were saying.

"I'm not," I protested, my eyes still closed.

"Then *do* something," Jody said.

I got up and said, "Let's go back to the park."

It was a beautiful day, she was a splendid girl, and I thought we should be enjoying the healthy, normal pastime of playing catch. But Jody told me to go home and get some sleep, which I did. That night, I performed our scene with a terrible headache.

This was not the end of my relationship with Jody, but after that day, it went downhill. One night, I took her to the bus station, where we had our picture taken in the twenty-five-cent photo booth—pictures I have still—and later to the Longhorn Drive-In to see *West Side Story*. When I brought her home at midnight, she put her tongue into my mouth and rubbed her pelvis against mine. But the next morning she said coldly, "I don't think we should see each other anymore."

A few days after that, I found a note on the call-board from Mr. Charles Caldwell, director of the Victoria, Texas, Shakespeare Festival:

> I am offering you two roles for this summer: Snout in
> *A Midsummer Night's Dream* and Grumio in *The Taming of
> the Shrew*. You will get your food and lodging, and there
> is every possibility you will receive your Equity Card.

They were character roles, mechanicals, not really good enough for me. But Equity Cards, the actor's union card, were all we dreamed of. They were hard to come by because they were protected by a double bind: You couldn't get your Equity Card until you had worked in a professional production, and you couldn't work in a professional production until you had gotten your Equity Card.

So I accepted this job and when school was over drove down to Victoria. I could have stayed in Austin, gone to summer school, and perhaps played a small part, as Jody did, in *My Fair Lady*, which was being performed on the main stage in Hogg Auditorium. But I was still following the advice of Joe Hollis—*pretend you don't like the girls you like*. And so a long period of waiting began, while I pursued Jody by ignoring her.

Victoria was the perfect South Texas small town. It had a courthouse square, a big movie theater that could show Cinerama—*How the West Was Won* played all summer—and a wealthy neighborhood of large Greek revival homes. The artistic director, Mr. Caldwell, lived in such a house. In fact, he had been born here and had played one of the three Hamlets in Paul Baker's famous production at Baylor. But after a disappointing year in Hollywood, he had returned to Victoria to do quality Shakespeare.

We ate lunch at his home, and then he showed me the theater—a movie theater at an abandoned Naval Air Station—and my lodging, a room in an empty barracks with a broken window.

"The lights aren't working yet," Mr. Caldwell said, "but they will be soon. The electricians are coming, and I'll bring you a mattress. Here's a padlock for the door. Your meals will be free, of course, at the cafeteria of the state school just across the highway." The state school was a reform school for disturbed teenagers who had committed violent crimes.

I should have left, but I told myself I had nothing better to do—and I wanted that Equity Card.

So began my first summer theater experience. Mr. Caldwell played Oberon, King of the Fairies. Friends of his from Baylor played various roles. Others were played by wealthy locals like Ennis, who was on the board of the festival, and the fairies were played by their daughters, none of whom were more than six years old.

My roommate was Bottoms, an alcoholic actor from Baylor, now in his thirties. I found his empties all over the barracks. He also played Bottom the Weaver, whom Oberon turned into a donkey. Bottoms became my hero early on, when we were eating lunch at the cafeteria of the state school. The largest of the disturbed teenagers walked up our table and said, "I'll fight either one of you sissies."

"Leave us alone, kid," Bottoms said quietly, "or I'll fuck you up." He meant it, and the kid walked away.

Bottoms couldn't remember his lines and carried his script around, shoving it down the seat of his trousers so his ass-crack showed, referring to it even on opening night. But he was the best actor in the company and got the best reviews in the local papers. He had also played baseball for Baylor, and we sometimes played catch between rehearsals and on Monday afternoons.

On opening night, Ennis took us to a galvanized tin shed on the edge of town where the real action was—a poker table, a roulette wheel, and mixed drinks. The local sheriff was there, along with Joe Billy Potter—a backer with big money and a lisp, a tough old Texas queen of the type portrayed by Tommy Lee Jones in the movie *JFK*; you used to meet them everywhere. I told myself that I had nothing in common with these people, but who was I kidding? I had joined the fabulous temporary family of a summer theater company and was having the time of my life.

I even had a girl, Leslie—a high school girl whose father taught drama at Southwest Texas State. Her hair was bleached blond, and she wore a thick coating of pink pancake makeup to cover her acne. Leslie was far too young for me, but I began dating her anyway. On Mondays, our day off. We drove as far north as New Braunfels, where we went to the big old Art Deco movie theater in this small town. Any movie depiction of the classical world interested me then, even *Jason and the Argonauts*, *Hercules in the Haunted World*, or *Cleopatra*, which we watched one rainy Sunday afternoon.

When Leslie and I got back to Victoria it was dark, and I drove directly to the wealthy neighborhood of old Greek Revival homes, where we made out on a blanket beneath a hedge, doing almost everything except the final thing—I had to remain true to Jody, in my fashion.

I returned to Austin once, in the middle of the summer. Jody was now living on Duval Street. She was not there when I arrived, but her roommate, Genise—a jolly but serious fat girl, who always played a barmaid in the annual Shakespearian productions—was. She told me that Jody had "acted like a slut" all summer; she'd played poker with the frat guys next door and put her legs up on the table so they could see her panties.

I lay in her bed and pretended to fall asleep. When Jody herself came home, she stood in the doorway and stared at me for a long time. I hoped she would join me, but instead she went back to the front room, sat down with the frat guys, and played poker. I left early the next morning and drove back to Victoria, my hopes dashed.

The second show—*The Taming of the Shrew*—opened and Mr. Caldwell played Petruchio as a cowboy with a gun belt and a Stetson hat. By now we had exchanged our Shakespearian diction for a Western drawl, which was more acceptable to local audiences. But this show was no more liked than *A Midsummer Night's Dream*, and it was clear that nobody was going to get their Equity Card—Mr. Caldwell didn't have enough pull with the union. I walked around the old naval air station all afternoon in the incredible heat. Finally I went to the theater. It was dark, but when I turned on the lights, I saw Bottoms sitting on the front row and asked him, "What are you doing here?"

"I don't know," he admitted. "This is how I went insane the first time; I kept going down to the theater and staring at the stage even when nothing was going on."

He was trying to tell me something about the theater, but I ignored him.

When the season was over, I returned to Austin and went directly to the house on Duval Street. Jody was no longer there. Genise told me she had moved out and was living alone in a little house on Elmwood Place.

"She always liked you Will," Genise said. "Then she got depressed, and started sleeping all the time--that's what she does when she feels bad. When I went over to her new apartment, she wouldn't even answer the door. But she told me once she really liked you, even if she won't admit it now. Why don't you go over and see her?"

But pretending I wasn't interested in Jody had gotten to be a habit. Then Mr. Moller gave me a big comic role in *Bartholomew Fair*. What with one thing and another, it was a November night just before Thanksgiving when I showed up at Jody's apartment on Elmwood Place.

It was in the front of a little California hobbit house of white stucco with green shingles and a live oak tree in the front yard. Jody had a cat for company but had not thought of a name for it yet. It was my twenty-second birthday, and we walked to Eastwoods Park, at the end of the block—the place where we had gone on our first date. The pool had been drained, and the ground was covered with live oak leaves, which had a bitter tannin smell. But to me, it was still the Forest of Arden.

"I heard you dated a high school girl this summer," Jody said.

"I heard you dated frat guys."

"I might have," she said, not exactly denying this.

"What are you going to do now?"

"Live alone," she said. "Graduate at the end of the year and get out of this town." Jody was a year older than I was and had only a year to go.

We lay on the dry leaves under an ancient oak and made out for a while.

"I probably would have slept with you before, if you'd just asked me," she said, and I began to tremble.

Lightning flashed in the distance. A storm was coming—the storm which was to come at so many important times in my life. "Do you mind if I lay on you?" I asked, quoting *Hamlet*. "Or do you think I mean country matters?"

"I don't care if you mean country matters," Jody said. "But if you'll come back to my apartment, I'll give you everything you want."

So we went back to her apartment. My heart was pounding as Jody lit a candle on the dresser, and we took off our clothes.

But when the moment came, I could do nothing.

"What's wrong?"

"I don't know," I said.

The truth was that I had kept myself under control for so long—been as detached as a Zen master—that now my body would no longer respond. Jody told me to take it easy, but I could not.

As the storm broke, I drove away in the Oldsmobile but got only three blocks. The car kept going slower and slower—the alternator was broken, and my battery was dead. Finally I coasted to a stop near Memorial Stadium and then walked back through the rain and knocked on Jody's door.

She let me in, and this time I was able to perform.

13

THERE IS NO doubt that falling in love with Jody inspired me to have more mystical experiences. I don't mean that she was the source of them. They began in my childhood, long before I met her. But when I was in love with her, I had several—including one so strong it changed my life.

I thought of these experiences as natural because they happened to me without drugs or alcohol. The psychiatrist I saw later never really believed in them, but they were not a kind of mental illness, as anyone who has ever had one can tell you. Compared to the chaotic world of drugs like alcohol, mescaline, or acid, they were moments of complete sanity.

The Western philosopher who has best described the mystical experience is William James, who attended Harvard medical school and became a doctor but never practiced. After a "revelation," he wrote two books, *The Will to Believe*, and *The Varieties of Religious Experience*. He also wrote about mystical experiences induced by nitrous oxide gas. To me these experiences are not natural, since they are produced by a gas. But to James, all mystical experiences were the same.

I did not read *The Varieties of Religious Experience* until after I had my mystical experiences with Jody, but I will describe them in his terms because they describe exactly what happened to me.

First, as James says, they were *noetic,* which means they were a state of knowledge. Time seemed to stop—or as I thought of it, *I knew where I was in time.* Somehow this allowed me to see a story to my life that I had not been able to see before. And a strong light seemed to shine on me from no visible source.

Second, most were *brief,* lasting no more than an hour at the most, and *passive.* I did nothing once the experience started, just let it happen to me, safe and serene as my mind became clearer and clearer. There was no feeling of strange chemistry at work, no hallucinations.

Third, I heard what I call *the music*—a simple, crystalline, resolving chord infinitely prolonged—and sometimes it seemed that everything I was thinking and feeling came to me through this music.

Fourth, these experiences were often *forgotten.* I sometimes had the feeling there had been a lot of them in my early childhood—perhaps they were all repetitions of a childhood state of mind or discovery. But it was if the adult mind could not contain these thoughts for very long, and the memory of them soon faded away. I'll try to describe this later on.

William James thought the mystical experience was similar, if not identical, to the states of satori, samādhi, and nirvana—in other words, the enlightenment the Dharma Bums were looking for. But to me, the mystical experience is a mirror of what the mind is concerned with at the time. I was interested in the ancient Greek religion and their gods, so I sometimes felt I was seeing the world as they had seen it. And because I had finally found Jody and finally experienced physical love, my idea of the great truth was not religious. It was eros, or love.

Jody and I always made perfect love. She was my first lover and told me I was her second, but when we made love, it always seemed like the first time. It also seemed to me that we were transformed into beautiful animals—lion and lioness, stallion and mare—as the gods and goddesses were transformed when they came to earth to make love. And in this transformation, all the erotic dreams of my childhood came true.

I became Jody as well as myself—learned how a woman's shoulders blushed with pleasure, tasted her secret honey. It took me a long time to come back to myself as I lay in her bed, staring at the reproduction of a Rosa Bonheur pastel of horses that hung on the wall, lit by the blue flames of the gas heater.

Jody had given me a great gift—had made me just like everyone else. She was not only my first love; she was my first sexual love. So began the happiest days of my life. I will describe only one.

I woke to the ongoing miracle of Jody lying asleep beside me, wearing the yellow panties she called her "dime-store panties." I got up, pulled on my jeans, and went into the kitchen, where I made some coffee and fried some eggs. Jody joined me, wearing her slip, and we ate them standing over the stove.

For seven days I had not left this apartment except to go to school, and she had not asked me to leave. Today was Saturday, and neither one of us had a rehearsal. "Why don't you just hang around today?" she said.

I put the rest of my clothes on, went to the living room, and opened the front door. Elmwood Place was strangely deserted. The leaves of the live oaks had turned orange but not yet fallen. A dove called in the brilliant silence and, after a moment, was answered by another.

Then I lay on the couch reading Robert Graves's *The Greek Myths*. Jody came in, still wearing her slip, and put on our favorite record—Rachmaninoff's *Rhapsody on a Theme of Paganini*—which for some reason my father had never played for me. Now it had become the theme of our love, although this was never mentioned.

There was a knock on the screen door. It was Kate, the girl Jody had kissed in *No Exit*, and Jody let her in.

"Aren't we going to the maharajah's lecture on Krishna consciousness today?" she asked.

Everyone knew the maharajah, a guest professor of Eastern philosophy at the university, was her lover.

"I don't think so," Jody said. "I didn't get much sleep last night."

I smiled, because Jody and I had made love all night. Both women looked at me briefly and then back at each other.

"You promised you would," Kate said.

But Jody still refused to go, and after a while Kate left.

"I can't deny I felt something when I kissed her in *No Exit*," Jody said. "But that's just kid stuff, isn't it? Today I want to stay here with you."

"Do you think she knows we're lovers now?"

"Yes, I think she knows."

"Poor Kate."

"Yes," she said, "poor Kate. Now she'll hate us forever."

We both felt sorry for Kate now that we were lovers, sorry for anyone who was not as fortunate as we were. Finally Jody said, "Can't we get something to eat? I'm so hungry."

When we went outside, Elmwood Place was still deserted. Then I heard a faint roar from Memorial Stadium—Texas was playing Arkansas today and everyone was at the football game. To me it was the old dream of lovers come true; everyone except us had disappeared.

We got in the Olds, and I drove to our favorite restaurant, the old Spanish Village on Red River Street. There we walked across the patio, past the oak in the courtyard, and through a series of rooms that got smaller and smaller. In the last room of all, which had a silver Aztec mask on the wall, we sat down and ordered our lunch from the waiter.

"You know, darling," Jody said as we ate, "I think I know why the birth rate in Mexico is so high."

"Why?"

"The food smells like sex. It's the *comino*. Every time I eat Mexican food, I'm thinking of making love to you."

"You're such a little trash mouth."

"Do you want me to stop talking?"

"No. I want you to eat more Mexican food."

"Oh, Lord," she said. "I love you so much."

"And I love you," I told her.

It was the first time we had told each other this—and she had said it first. This was a major step in our lives, but neither of us was going to make a big thing out of it.

"It's a little frightening, isn't it?" Jody added after a while. "Now I want to be with you all the time."

"Tell me about when you were a little girl."

Then we fell into our favorite conversation. First Jody told me about when she had been a little girl and dreamed of marrying a sailor, like her father. I told her about when my father had been a soldier, and my mother and I had followed him all over Kansas and Missouri. In this way, we confirmed the truth of our love, which began to seem destined, natural, inevitable—a state we had known in childhood and somehow forgotten.

When we walked out of the restaurant, it was still early afternoon. "Let's go out to the lake," I proposed.

Jody had never been to the lake before. I drove out Bull Creek Road to the top of Comanche Pass, where we looked down on Lake Travis. Now there are big houses out there, like those above Los Angeles, but then the hills were empty. We drove on down the road past the cliffs and out to a little headland called Windy Point.

At the very end was a floor of polished limestone running out into the water. There I parked by an oak mott, a circular grove, and we got out. Not a soul was in sight.

Then I started taking off my shirt, my jeans, everything.

"What are you doing?"

"Going for a swim."

I walked to the end of the marble floor and dove into the water naked. The top layer was still warm, but it got cold deeper down. I swam for a while and then got out, dried myself with a towel I carried in the trunk of the car, pulled my jeans back on, and lay beside Jody on a blanket.

"You know," I said, "this country is just like Greece. I mean it's all limestone, and this lake is the wine-dark sea."

Then I fell silent. A feeling of perfection was stealing over both of us. For a while we said nothing, just stared at the sky.

"Read to me from your book," Jody said.

So I read to her from *The Greek Myths*, by Robert Graves, which I had brought with us:

> The Greeks believed there were four ages: the Age of Gold, the Age of Silver, the Age of Bronze, and the Age of Iron. The race of Gold lived without care or labor, eating only acorns, wild fruit, and honey. Never growing old; laughing and singing much. To them, death was no more terrible than sleep. They are all gone

now, but they remain: spirits of happy music, retreats, good fortune, and upholders of freedom.

"This has been the most beautiful day," Jody said when I finished.

Beautiful it was, and it was becoming more beautiful. Later, my psychiatrist would tell me that Jody had found her father again in me, and I had found my mother again in her—but I was not consciously aware of any such thing. I also know now that our bodies were flooded with serotonin and each other's pheromones and that we were in love and ready to reproduce, but I didn't think about this either.

Something else was going on here. It was now evening, but the day seemed to grow brighter as the sun sank. At first I thought I was seeing Plato's Ideal World shining through the Real World, the ordinary one, as if it were as transparent as glass. And then I heard the crystalline sound of the music.

Again I had found the place where time stopped. The hills were touched with the last sunlight, and the oak mott was a sacred grove. This was the golden age, and I knew if I had the sense to say nothing, it would last forever. This time there was also a message: *If you have a child now, it will save the world.*

The sun finally set, the full moon rose, and we heard coyotes calling in the hills.

Then we drove back to Austin, where the Tower was iodine orange—Texas had won the game—but Elmwood Place was still strangely deserted. Hungry for each other, we fell together on the bed and made love.

Jody did not take birth control pills—few girls did then—and when I was spent, I waited for her to go to the bathroom and douche. But tonight she would not leave our bed, and instead told me, "Don't move, darling. I want to fall asleep with you still inside me."

So we did, but later woke and made love again. And Jody is still the only woman in my life that it has ever been that way with.

14

AROUND THIS TIME—the late fall of 1964—the Journey seemed to begin for me. The early years of the sixties, which had been so much like the fifties, were over. The Kennedy assassination had been a tragic shock, but it had also freed some of us from the fraternity/sorority system and the Great Boredom of the dormitories. Now we found ourselves in a new world, which demanded a new lifestyle. There was no name for it yet, but some of us were discovering we had more in common than we had thought.

I went home that Christmas and visited Crockett, my elementary school. The back door was unlocked, but the whole building was deserted, as if under a spell. I walked upstairs to the library on the second floor. There I found the favorite book of my childhood, *The Hobbit*, by J. R. R. Tolkien. My name was still written on the card—only five other children had checked it out since I had, in the fifth grade—so I shoved it down the front of my pants and walked out. Later I brought it back to Austin and gave it to Jody, who loved it so much she named her cat Bilbo.

Why did I do this? It was two more years before *The Hobbit* would become the necessary hippy book—by then I had to pretend I'd never read it. But suddenly we were all rereading old books and watching old movies along with the new ones, which were getting better. Everyone was interested in all the arts, particularly pop music, and buying the latest albums of the Beatles, Bob Dylan, and the Rolling Stones. And everybody was falling in love. The greatest proof of this was that Jody and I were living together like a couple of beatniks in Greenwich Village and felt no need to get married.

But the first and most intense part of our love lasted only a little more than a month—although when I went back to Nortex for a few days, it seemed like a long time had passed since I had last been there, and I had changed forever. When I returned to Austin, Jody and I went down to Mexico for New Year's Eve—drove to Nuevo Laredo, where we went to a nightclub across the river, and then came back and made love all night in a motel on the American side. The next day, we returned to Austin and, that night, made love one more time.

Then she got up and disappeared into the bathroom. I heard the red rubber bag and the hose being taken out and water running down the drain. When she came back, her sex was cold and dry.

"I'm sorry, darling," she said, "but we have to stop taking chances."

"I know," I said.

"I can't believe I've let myself do this. It's not fair to you either."

So we went through the choices—condoms, which I didn't want to wear, and birth control pills, which I'd heard sorority girls used.

"My sister told me when you start taking them, you stop getting your period. They don't seem natural."

"Then what are we going to do?"

It was up to her, of course. But for six weeks, we had made unprotected love, and it had been the most intense experience of my life.

The next time we made love, I compromised by spilling on her belly, which Jody said she liked almost as much as the completely natural way. "Just don't feel like you have to ask me to marry you so we can make love," she told me afterward.

"I won't."

"We have to stay free."

"Don't worry. I won't ask you to marry me. But I promise I'll love you forever."

"And I love you. Oh, I didn't know it could be this good," she said, holding me tightly.

How different this was from the year before, when I had promised I would marry Becky so she would let me make love to her. I was so much smarter now than I had been just a year ago—almost as smart as Jody.

But the first part of our love was over, and I noticed that making love became slightly different for us. There was almost as much pleasure, but it had lost some of its abandon.

People were also getting interested in drugs.

Shan came over with his beatnik girl, Toni, and said he wanted to try peyote, which he had heard I'd taken before. So one night not long after that, Jody, Shan, and I took peyote at Toni's apartment. She put a mattress on the floor and turned off the lights, and when the peyote came on, we rolled around for a couple of hours in an uncomfortable state.

"Don't look at me," Jody said. "I can't stand it. There's something I don't want you to see."

"What?"

"You can't trust me, that's what. Women are terrible. You don't know how easy it would be for me to destroy you."

I went into the kitchen for a while, and when I came back, Jody felt better. But in rolling around on the mattress, she had slipped out of her top, and her breasts were exposed. I pointed this out to her, and she said, "Oh my, when did that happen?"

"Hours ago," Toni said.

"You don't have to hide them," I told her. "They're biblical—you know, like clusters of ripe grapes."

"Well," she said. "I do love my breasts." She let us admire them for a while.

Then Toni asked us if we would like to go for a drive. Her car was parked in the alley, which was now a dry streambed full of the debris of past civilizations—I saw the acropolis, broken statues, bells, and violins all buried in the sand. Jody stared at Toni's car and asked her, "What kind is it?"

"An American Rambler."

"What do you mean," Jody asked suspiciously, "an *American Rambler*?"

Everyone laughed and got in. Toni drove us past the Capitol, and the glowing alabaster dome seemed as big as Jupiter. At the apogee was a statue of the goddess of the Texas Revolution, holding a torch. Jody said she was waving it at us, and I could see this for myself. The Holiday Inn looked like a stack of television sets, each screen showing a different picture. At various times, we found ourselves in every city we had ever lived in. Toni finally dropped us off in front of our apartment on Elmwood Place, the fabulous little hobbit house with the peaked roof.

Jody wanted to take a bath and, when we were together in the tub, asked me, "Do you think we can make love now, darling?"

"I'm willing to try."

At first it seemed impossible. Our bodies grew larger and larger until they met like two continents in a slow, tectonic event. Then magma erupted from the core, surprising us both.

In the first blue light of dawn, we found the state where it is impossible to lie. Jody and I had passed the test of peyote, and as we lay together, our bodies cool and smooth, she asked me to read her more of Robert Graves's *The Greek Myths*:

> In the beginning the Goddess of all Things rose naked from Chaos, but found nothing substantial for her feet to rest upon, therefore divided sky from sea, dancing on the waves. The great serpent Ophion, grown lustful, coiled about these divine limbs and was moved to couple with her. Next, she assumed the form of a dove, brooding on the waves, and in due process of time laid the Universal Egg. Out of it tumbled all things that exist, her children: sun, moon, planets, the stars, the earth with its mountains and rivers, its trees, herbs, and living creatures.

"That sounds lovely," Jody said. "I'd like to give birth to the whole world."

"Maybe you will," I said.

We cried silent, painless peyote tears.

Of course some of you are thinking, *It can't have been as great as he says it was. These were just two ordinary kids discovering sex and drugs.* And so we were ordinary—but at the same time, all of our imperfections were absorbed in the radiance of our love. I was certain that the whole world, or at least the whole drama department, was watching Jody and me and knew of our love for each other, and that it was only a matter of time before our perfection was recognized.

Sure enough, in February, Jody was asked by a film school director to star in his 16-millimeter short film called *A Texas Memory*, which was based on a short story by Fred Gypson, the local author of a book that had become a popular Disney movie.

Good things were happening to me too. After I played Matt Burke in a scene from O'Neill's *Anna Christie* in Demonstration Lab, Dr. Hodges asked me to audition for his main stage production of Ibsen's *The Lady from the Sea*. The role was that of a mysterious sailor, the lady's sexual fantasy. I looked at my face in Jody's mirror, and decided I was getting better looking, or people were changing their mind about my looks—it had to be our love that had made the difference. I didn't get the role, but being asked to audition meant I was being taken seriously by Dr. Hodges, who was the best director in the department.

One night Jody and I went to see the rushes of *A Texas Memory*. I held my breath as we watched them. It was a period movie, and the scenes were shot in Fredericksburg, a small German town not far away. Jody, wearing a homespun dress, walked across a gray field under a gray sky. I thought her small features were perfect for film, that her face was both mysterious and full of light.

"Do you know what the director told me, darling?" she said later. "He said the camera loves me."

"That's good. So do I."

On that night, I felt our love had transformed us—that we were both finally becoming the people we had always known we could be.

But the next day, we heard that old Mr. Gypson had suffered a heart attack and went to see him at Seton Hospital that night. He had taken a liking to Jody. "She's just the girl I was thinking about when I wrote the story," he said fondly. "She's my girl."

"I know," I said. "She's my girl too."

"Take good care of her. There's not many like her."

Mr. Gypson died a few days later, and the film was never completed. But we felt he had given us his blessing, and young lovers are always in need of blessings.

Before Christmas, Jody and I had gone to see the graduate directors' thesis plays. The first, *Waiting for Godot* by Samuel Beckett, had featured, among other actors, my roommate, Larry, who played Pozzo. The second was *Caligula* by Albert Camus. It had starred a new actor, Cal Hammer, who had gone to school with Jody at Lon Morris Junior College in Jacksonville, Texas, and transferred here this year.

They were both good shows, and Larry was great as Pozzo. But I was fascinated by *Caligula*, which was about an insane Roman emperor. Cal was not effeminate, like the movie stereotype of Caligula as played by Peter Ustinov, and was therefore more believable when he took any woman he wanted, including the wives of other men—which excited me more than I was willing to admit.

Cal Hammer was another person whose parents had obviously seen his destiny was to be a great actor and given him a theatrical name. His face was hard and handsome, and his head looked larger and denser than a normal human head. He was an authentic tough guy who had done time in a Houston reform school but was also rumored by his gay admirers to accept blow jobs. This may or may not have been true, but to me this made him the most mysterious, and therefore the most *dangerous*, guy in the drama. Mr. Mott thought he had polish and gave him leads, which, I will admit, he performed superbly.

But when I saw him talking to Jody in the lobby of the drama building one morning in February, I felt a sharp pang of jealousy—and remembered, for the first time in months, that she was a year older than I was and was going to graduate soon.

Every year most of the graduating seniors decided they were going to teach. But a few decided they were going to New York or California. New York City was the traditional destination, but everyone knew it was the hardest and dirtiest city in America. California meant Hollywood, which was pleasant enough, but no place for serious actors.

Both places frightened me. The actors who went to Hollywood and tried to make it in the movies always came back after a few months and said you had to be impossibly good-looking to make it.

The ones who went to New York City never came back. They vanished off the face of the earth.

Later that afternoon, Jody and I went to lunch at the Spanish Village, where she said, "Cal is thinking about going out to California this summer and trying his luck. Ever since I saw myself in that movie, I've thought I could make it out in California."

"I'm sure you could," I said. "But what's your hurry? Stay here for another year until I graduate. Then we'll both go to New York together."

"I'm sure we'll love each other forever," Jody said. "But I might want to try California this summer."

That night, after we made love, I found myself asking her, "Did you ever sleep with Cal?"

"Once," she admitted. "He was my first. But that was two years ago. You're not going to get jealous, are you?"

"No," I said. "There were other girls before you."

By this, I meant there had been one girl—the Mexican prostitute I had slept with years before—but I didn't tell Jody this, because a prostitute didn't count. Jody was my first *real* girl, and I was sure we would love each other forever.

I was cast in a directing project of three French farces and got the lead in one, *Bobouroche*. They were directed by Fred, a grad student who was considered talented, and my expectations were high. But when I went back to Jody's apartment to tell her, she seemed disappointed somehow.

It was cold and gray, the middle of winter, and we felt a need to get out of the house. So we started going to movies. First we went to see a new one, *Zorba the Greek*. Like one of the old art films, it was beautifully photographed in black and white, and it carried a lot of meaning for us. "I'm Irene Pappas," Jody said after we saw it, "and you're Alan Bates, an innocent boy I have to teach about love."

This bothered me a little—what more did Jody think she had to teach me?

The weather was cold and gray, and rehearsals for *Bobouroche* were disappointing. Try as I might, I couldn't make my role as funny as it should have been. Or maybe Fred's ideas—like the song I sang and the tap dance I did between shows—just weren't that good.

One night, I came home from rehearsal and found Jody sitting in the dark and smoking a cigarette, her eyes hard.

"I can't stand this anymore," she said. "Time is just going by, I'm going to graduate this spring, and I've never had a halfway decent role since I was in *No Exit*."

"I know," I said. "You're one of the best actresses in the department, and I can't understand why you're not working all the time."

"Do you really think that?"

"Of course I do."

Jody considered this and said, "I'm going to talk to Mr. Moller."

I suggested she just write him a letter, but she said, "No, I'm going to go see him—what have I got to lose?"

Then we went to the Longhorn Drive-In to see *Crack in the World*, a South African science fiction movie. Dana Andrews was a mad scientist who drilled a hole in the crust, which started a fissure through which lava erupted. But then the crack started circling back toward the drill hole. His wife, Janette Scott, and his assistant, Kieron Moore, became lovers. In the end, Dana Andrews sailed off into space on a spinning piece of the world, which became another moon. The lovers emerged into a red twilight, their clothes partly burned off, in time to see life returning in the form of baby birds hatching out of eggs buried in the hot ashes. It was like my old dream of the end of the world, when Jody and I might survive and become the new Adam and Eve, but she didn't seem to care for it.

The next week, Dr. Hodges, who was head of the directing program, came to rehearsal and told Fred to cut my song and tap dance. This was a relief to me, but I kept wondering if I couldn't have done better.

But Jody returned from school that day and told me Mr. Moller had given her the role of the witch in *Rashomon*, which he was directing on the main stage in late March. We celebrated by buying a bottle of champagne and going out to dinner. Then we returned to Elmwood Place and made love half the night.

"I'm so impressed," I told her. "What in the world did you say to him?"

"I just let him know I was unhappy," Jody said.

The three French farces were considered a disappointment, but I took most of the blame because of my inexperience.

Hoping to learn something about the theater, Jody and I went to see a touring production of Edward Albee's *Who's Afraid of Virginia*

Woolf? starring Uta Hagen and Arthur Hill as a couple who destroyed each other before our eyes. It is a stunning play and upset us so badly we couldn't talk to each other for days.

In late March, the week *Rashomon* opened, my parents called and told me they were coming down to Austin. They didn't want to see the show but asked me to find them a motel room. I was so busy that I forgot they were coming until Friday morning and could only find one in a Mexican-style motel on South Lamar with floodlit banana trees and a large green neon sign. Actually it wasn't such a bad place, and on Saturday evening, Jody and I took them to dinner at a restaurant called El Patio right across the street. My father was on his best behavior, and my mother complimented Jody on her clothes, asked what her parents did, and so forth.

As I drove Jody to the auditorium, she said, "I thought that went pretty well."

I asked her what she meant.

"I mean your mother liked me. She thinks we're going to get married."

"We're not, are we?"

"Maybe you should think about it," Jody said as she got out of the Oldsmobile.

This was a complete surprise to me. I decided it had been a sort of joke and hoped Jody wouldn't bring it up again.

Rashomon was based on the Kurosawa movie and the old Japanese folktale—four different versions of the story of the robbery of a merchant and the rape of his wife by a bandit. Jody was the witch who called up the spirit of the dead bandit at the trial. Cal played the bandit, and the wife was played by Kate, Professor Moller's favorite leading lady.

I went to the cast party, which was held at the home of an old grad student on a hill above North Lamar, and there I danced with a freshman girl to the Rolling Stones, mentioning to her that Jody and I were living together. For some reason she didn't know this, and I was strangely disappointed.

When Jody arrived, she went to the kitchen with Cal and Kate, where they drank scotch. She was having too much fun for me, throwing back her head and laughing, her throat exposed. Later we went out into the garden that was lit by Santa Fe candles in paper bags. All of Austin was moist and blooming that night, and I felt we were on Venus, the planet of love.

"If I didn't know you better," I said, "I'd think you were trying to make me jealous."

"Maybe I am," Jody said almost defiantly.

She was drunk, a slightly different person. So I took her home, but first we walked to Eastwoods Park and lay on the ground under our favorite oak. Lightning flashed in the distance. The first big thunderstorm of the spring was coming.

"What's going on with you tonight?" I asked her.

"There's this great empty space opening up ahead of me," Jody told me. "I didn't feel it a month ago, but now it's here. I'm graduating, and suddenly I don't know what to do with myself. I'd stay here in Austin if somebody asked me to." She looked at me. "Do you know what I mean?"

"I know what it sounds like."

"What?"

"It sounds like you're talking about getting married."

"Maybe you should start thinking about it."

"I didn't know we had to do that yet," I said.

Jody lit a cigarette. "Sometimes I think about going to California. Marry me, and I won't go to California."

"I'll be glad to marry you," I said, "but not for another year."

"Well, I call that pretty goddamned dull," she said and laughed humorlessly. "Here a girl throws herself at you, and you can't make up your mind."

To tell the truth, I was frightened. Of what? Making a decision, of course. There had been that first month, when we had made love every night without protection. If she had gotten pregnant, I would have married her. But then we had decided our freedom was the most important thing, hadn't we?

"We don't have to get married yet," I said. "I trust you."

"I'm not sure I trust myself. Time is getting a little short."

So we were facing time, the implacable enemy of lovers. Jody knew it was running out, but I didn't. Today, I can't understand why I wanted to wait that night. Was I incapable of making a Big Decision? Had I never grown up? Was I angry at Jody for forcing a decision on me as proof of her power? Or was I thinking, *Now that I have found Jody, there might be another, better girl out there, and I might meet her any day.*

All I could do was to repeat, "I trust you."

"Then you're a goddamned fool," Jody said. Suddenly she became bold, lustful. "Take me right now," she said. "I'm not wearing any panties." She meant she wanted me to make love to her without protection. I had found Jean Seberg, the disturbed girl of my dreams at last, and of course I did what she wanted.

It was pleasure, it was pain, I was out of control for one of the few times in my life, and we came at the same moment. Then there was thunder, lightning, rain, and hail. Soaked through, we ran back to the apartment.

"How did you like that?" she asked me when we were in the bedroom.

"It was just like *Lady Chatterley's Lover.*"

"Let's do it again."

So we made love without protection two more times that night. Jody was right; I was a goddamned fool.

The next morning was a Sunday. I drove out to my grandparents' home on old Highway 183 and met my parents there. My mother wanted to talk about Jody, but I felt a great sense of relief at being away from her. The cold front had moved through, and it was just another rainy day. After lunch, my grandparents and my little brother, Ray, watched *Lassie.* My mother looked at the *Saturday Evening Post,* and I sat at the dining room table, reading *The Collected Poems of William Butler Yeats.*

Then I had another mystical experience, the first one since the afternoon at the lake, five months ago. At first I thought the sun had come out. Some kind of light was shining on me, and I heard the crystalline music. *It's happening again,* I thought. But this time was a little different. I continued reading and found I could understand every poem in the book without effort. *A Reader's Guide to William Butler Yeats,* which I had long forgotten, came back to me. Meaning flowed through the poems like mercury, a dense mirror metal. Poetry was the real source of language. I understood that I could be a poet or a writer if I wanted, because it was my nature.

Finally I left the house and climbed the oak tree in the front yard to be alone with my thoughts. My father came out and asked me, "Sonny, what in the hell are you doing up there?"

I couldn't say. This mystical experience lasted, like the others, for about an hour, and as with the others, I have never mentioned it to anyone until now.

April came and, with it, the annual Shakespearian production, directed by old Dr. Payne. This year, it was *Measure for Measure*, and neither Jody nor I were cast, which was something of a relief.

I started sleeping a few nights a week in my room at Larry, Mike, and Shan's apartment, which I had been paying rent on all these months. Larry found a little book called *Leo Shull's Summer Theater Catalogue* in the library, and we took pictures of each other in Eastwoods Park and sent them off with our résumés. Both of us were accepted by outdoor dramas in North Carolina—me by *Unto These Hills* and him by *Horn in the West*.

Jody decided she would go out to California after graduation and stay at her uncle's house in Fresno. She also planned to go to Los Angeles and see Cal Hammer. A decision had been made, and marriage was no longer talked about. But one night I went back over to Jody's to get some of my things. She was so affectionate I spent the night there. Before we knew it, everything was as it had been before.

In May, Jody started leaving the bedroom door onto the screened-in front porch open so we could breathe the night air in our sleep. When we went to school in the morning, she sometimes took off her sandals and walked barefoot. The fast, low clouds of Austin rolled overhead, looking like stop-motion photography—the visible indication that time was growing short. By then, we had begun to make love almost every night without protection again. Jody was letting our bodies decide the future for us, as she had before. And I could not resist. She was right, I thought, to do this. Let life happen to us if it will.

One day, Larry called and proposed we all go out to Lake Travis. "I've been talking to my friends John and Julie," he said. "They go out there all the time, to this place called Windy Point, and they say it's really cool."

So on Saturday morning, everybody went out there, including Shan and his girl, Toni. It was the first time Jody and I had gone out with our friends in weeks. We bought a case of beer and rented a sailboat, a little fiberglass Sunfish, from the marina. John brought it around to Windy Point, and we took turns trying to sail it. Then we lay on the marble floor of Windy Point and watched the light change as thunderheads built up and the morning turned into afternoon.

"We should have done this a long time ago," Jody said as I rubbed Coppertone on her back. "This is so much better than going to the movies," she said, and I agreed, wondering why our lives couldn't go on this way forever. The sun finally set, and gradually night came on; but even when it was too dark to see their faces, I could still feel our friends all around us.

Finally, Jody and I drove back to Austin and made love, and afterward I thought, *Maybe it's time we left history and abandoned ourselves to a life without expectations.* For several days, it seemed to me that, in some alternate universe, we had already done this and would live in Austin for the rest of our lives.

Then, just three days before the end of school, Jody got her period.

Her mother came up from Houston to help her move out of our apartment—she was patient but clearly did not like me. I followed them down to Houston. Her family lived in the Heights, and her father was a bulldozer operator, his yellow D-9 Cat parked in on a flatbed in the driveway. He had been a SeaBee during World War II, but when I told him my father had also been in the war, he didn't seem to hear me. This was the sixties that would be remembered—parents were starting to distrust their children, and it would get worse as the decade went on. Her father did show me pictures of himself and his buddies on a Pacific island and said something I could not quite hear. When I asked him to repeat it, I was almost certain he said, "You couldn't have made it out there."

15

LARRY MET ME in Nortex, and we drove to North Carolina in three days, sitting shoulder-to-shoulder in his Volkswagen Bug. It was a dangerous journey. In Tennessee, we saw billboards printed in red ink—"Martin Luther Coon in Communist Training Camp"—and at every station the attendant asked us, "You boys sure you ain't got a nigger in the trunk?"

We drove on through the hillbilly foothills of the Smokies, past barns with "See Rock City" painted on the roofs. Then Larry dropped me off in the town of Cherokee, home of *Unto These Hills*, and went on to Boone, North Carolina, the home of *Horn in the West*.

Unto These Hills was staged in an immense outdoor theater on the Cherokee Reservation. The play depicted the history of the Cherokee Indians, and I was given the role of a Spanish conquistador who wore a steel helmet and a tin breastplate. Most of the other actors belonged to the drama department at Chapel Hill. History passed me by that summer—Martin Luther King spoke in Washington, but I don't remember hearing about this.

It was another time of intense boredom, like the A-Bar Hotel and the Victoria Shakespeare Festival. The director of the show was Harry

Davis, a former army master sergeant who ran rehearsals like basic training. Possession of alcohol, since we were living on the Cherokee Reservation, was punishable by immediate dismissal. Homosexuality was a crime. So, in a way, was heterosexuality. Males lived in an army barracks at the top of the hill, and females lived in one at the bottom, where we were forbidden to go at night.

Jody wrote me a letter from Fresno in her tight, little-girl handwriting.

> I'm staying here in Fresno with my uncle, and I'm not sure if I like it or not. Sometimes he gets a little too personal. The other night, he came into the bathroom and talked to me while I was in the bathtub. But I'm on my way to Los Angeles next week to see Cal and go to some auditions.
>
> Jody

This was the only letter I got, although I wrote her every day. It made me furious. Her uncle had talked to her while she was in the bathtub? What in the hell was going on in Fresno?

Gradually I made more friends in Cherokee. Lynwood was a carpenter with a full beard who looked like the Wolf Man and had a great sense of humor. Pete was an actor from Chicago who also wanted to be a writer. One weekend we hitchhiked to Asheville to visit Thomas Wolfe's childhood home, which was a boarding house. There Pete and I slipped into his bedroom, and I touched the keys of his old Underwood typewriter for luck. There was also a carpenter named Dick, who was from the same town as Carl Sandberg and took me high up in the Smokies one day to find a fallen tulip tree. He brought it back and gave it to a sculptor whose name I forget—who then carved it into a totem pole of his own design, which he left standing in the woods to be discovered. We did plays in the dining hall every Saturday night, and I had roles in *Beyond the Fringe*, *Becket*, and *The Fantastics*. I also read Tolkein's *The Lord of the Rings* and floated with Pete on inner tubes down the Oconaluftee River, where we spilled in a big rapids almost as bad as the one in the movie *Deliverance*.

One night toward the end of the summer, on a ride across the mountains to see Larry in Boone, the light shone on me again, and I heard music like the grinding of the stars overhead. This time the message took the form of an understanding that I needed the vertical world of the mountains for their heights, their depths, and their solitude—but I also needed the rivers flowing through them and would always be more interested in following them downhill than up. This was my nature and the conflict of my life—to seek summits but long for the mystery of the sea. It seems like a simple insight, but it was not. For thirty minutes, I knew the bliss of understanding and knew what I had to do.

In Boone, I stayed with Larry in the Gray House, where all the actors lived. He had a girl and was having much more fun than I was in Cherokee. After the show that night, there was a party at the Gray House. At four o'clock in the morning, I dropped several quarters into a pay phone, called Jody in Fresno, and asked her, "What the hell is going on with your uncle watching you in the bathtub?"

"Nothing's worked out for me here," Jody said. "I went to Vegas, and they told me I could be a showgirl, but I think they really wanted me to be a prostitute. I haven't been to Los Angeles yet."

"You have to come home," I said.

"I wish I could."

"I'll meet you in Houston at the end of the summer. Maybe then we can get married." I meant this. It was time to make the Big Decision.

"Oh, yes," Jody said. "I would like that very much."

"So it's decided."

"Yes. Then we'll be with each other forever."

Larry picked me up in Cherokee at the end of the summer, and we headed back to Texas. He took the southern route, through the bottom of the country and the radio dial, where Negro preachers in New Orleans prophesied the end of the world. We drove from Birmingham to Houston in one long day, finally reaching Houston after midnight.

I identified Jody's house by her father's bulldozer in the driveway. But there was another vehicle parked there, a little white Triumph sports car. All the lights were out as I knocked on the door of the garage apartment where Jody had told me she was living now and whispered, "It's Will."

Jody came out wearing a slip. But when we kissed, I remember it felt a little anticlimactic, as if her body was not quite the right temperature.

Larry joined us and we sat on the grass and smoked cigarettes. "It's wonderful to see you darling," Jody said. "And wonderful things have been happening to me too, ever since I got back from California."

Jody told me she had gone to an open call at the Alley Theater, where she had performed her audition monologue from Tennessee William's *Sweet Bird of Youth* and won a small role in the first production, *The Devil's Disciple*. Her father was so happy he had bought her the little white Triumph—she was a little embarrassed but loved it. Somehow marriage was not mentioned until the very end, when I asked Jody, "Do you remember our telephone conversation?"

"Of course, darling," she said. "But everything is different now."

"You mean you don't want to get married?"

"I want to marry you, darling. But now I have this job, so I've got to stay here in Houston for a while, and you've got to go back to school. Maybe we could get married next spring—and you could come to Houston."

I knew then that my Big Decision had meant nothing. I had made it just a little too late.

There was another painful month of lingering love. Jody drove her Triumph up to Austin one rainy day, wearing a putty-colored trench coat. She looked splendid—years older, even more beautiful, a professional actress. We made love, and I forced myself on her in a way that I knew she disliked—but I will omit the details. The week after that, I got a letter from her, which I found pinned to the callboard.

> I have to tell you I am marrying an old friend of mine, Darryl. He is a musician and has just gotten out of the army. If you knew him, I'm sure you would like him, but I am afraid our life together has come to an end. Sometimes I am afraid we are too much like each other and can never be happy. At other times, it seems like you have some idea of me I can never live up to. All I know is that I have tried as hard as I could. It may sound strange, but I am sure we will see each other again someday, and I hope we can stay friends because I will love you forever.
>
> Jody

It was almost the same letter I had gotten from Becky, right down to the statement "If you knew him, I'm sure you would like him."

Oh, sure, I thought again. *I'd like him. He's just like me—except he's better.* When I went outside, it was raining. Somewhat theatrically, I tore apart the letter from Jody, threw the pieces into Waller Creek, and walked home.

Larry and I had rented a furnished apartment, the second floor of a big Greek Revival house on Twenty-Sixth Street. I opened a bottle of scotch, Jody's favorite drink at parties, and poured myself a shot. Almost the whole time Jody and I had been together, I hadn't felt like drinking somehow. Now I sat in an old armchair in the front room and drank scotch until darkness fell.

I promised myself I would do anything to get her back, even cross the boundary of marriage, as Orpheus had crossed into the Underworld. I would make myself stronger, more heartless than ever before. Years would go by, and someday I would see her again. Then she would be sick of her husband, and I would have changed. She would beg me to marry her, and at first, I would refuse.

But it would be so much harder to make myself over a second time than it had been the first. Numbness was already settling over me, a complete absence of feeling, which was a kind of pain that I tried to think of as strength.

This was also the end of my mystical experiences for a while, although I'm not sure when or how this happened. Perhaps I thought they were part of my love for Jody and would go on forever, but they did not. One day, I found I could no longer remember how they had felt or what I had thought. I only knew that they had happened to me, and gradually I forgot even that. I was like a child who loves his favorite thing so much that he hides it away—hides it so well that one day he realizes he has forgotten where it is.

I CAN'T GET NO
(SATISFACTION)

16

Gabe returned from San Francisco on a Sunday morning in 1965, a couple of weeks before I received the letter from Jody. Larry and I had rented the second floor of the big old house on Twenty-Eighth Street. I was sleeping in my bedroom, which was off the living room, and my window was open because the nights were still warm. I woke when I heard a knock on the front door. Then the knob turned, and the door opened—we never locked it.

"Will?" someone called.

I had not seen Gabe for more than a year and a half, but I recognized his voice at once.

"In here," I said.

Gabe crossed the living room, opened the door of my bedroom, and entered without looking at me. He sat down at my desk, turned on the fluorescent lamp, and produced some Zig-Zag papers. Then he poured something onto them from a little black plastic film canister. His hair was cropped short. He wore plastic-framed glasses he must have gotten at the dime store, a black turtleneck, jeans, and big sandals with rubber tire-tread soles. Gabe had become a beatnik.

"How was it out there?" I asked him, still half-asleep.

"Groovy," he said.

It was just like Gabe to show up after more than a year with only one word to say—and a strange word at that.

"How long you going to be here?"

"I'm going to school here."

"Where you living?"

"With a guy named Pedro Fox. Met him in San Francisco. He's a merchant seaman, got a house out there and one here."

Gabe was rolling what had to be a marijuana cigarette with practiced, efficient movements that I couldn't quite follow, like a card trick. I watched as he licked and rolled it tightly.

"This is pretty good grass," he said. "Let's smoke it."

The apartment had a large screened-in front porch, and on it was an old sofa, swollen with rain. Gabe and I sat down, and I smoked my first joint. The streets were still, and there was nobody up yet. I must have gotten off, although I wasn't sure of it at the time, but I remember that I laughed a lot.

Gabe talked about San Francisco—the cable cars, the hills, the fog, the city that was like no other. He said I had to go out there as soon as possible. The best thing about it had been meeting Pedro Fox and some other beatniks from Texas who really had it together. But Gabe had decided to come back here, go to school, and get a degree in philosophy so he could teach for the rest of his life. "Sounds good," I said—thinking it sounded nothing like my own plan to go to New York City and become an actor. "What are you going to do for money?"

"Sell grass to people like you," Gabe said. "I'll give you a brick for a hundred dollars. Special introductory offer."

A brick sounded like a good amount of grass, and it had to be worth what Gabe was asking. I had some loose cash my parents had given me for the deposit on the apartment.

"I can go for that," I said.

So I bought a brick—I think it was half a kilo—in a rolled-up shopping bag for a hundred dollars, and Gabe threw in the little package of Zig-Zag rolling papers for free.

"You won't be sorry," Gabe said. "This is good grass, really groovy."

I must have given him a look because he added, "I know—it sounds funny to you. But in another week, you'll be talking just like me."

Then we went downstairs, and he got on a big black Triumph motorcycle that he said he'd bought in San Francisco and driven here. I envied him intensely for having the nerve to ride a motorcycle. Gabe said goodbye and drove off without giving me his address or phone number. He hadn't mentioned Jody either.

I went back upstairs, woke up Larry, and showed him the shopping bag. "I think I just got stoned," I told him, "and I bought us a brick of grass."

"No shit."

That night, Larry and I rolled a couple of joints and smoked them. This time I definitely got stoned—smoked so much my face turned into an Aztec mask of hammered gold. In another week, we were talking just like Gabe—everything was *far out, groovy, out of sight*.

Grass was just the thing for me. I figured that getting stoned might help me forget the events of last year. It was also illegal and seemed likely to make me what I longed to be—more *dangerous*.

Larry worked for the campus radio station, and they gave him a lot of British Invasion albums they didn't want. He brought them home, and we got stoned and played them every night. Eric Burdon was a joke, but we liked the Kinks, the Who, and the Yardbirds with Eric Clapton. The Beatles and the Stones were already famous.

The second week of school, Bob Dylan played Doris Miller Auditorium. I asked Leslie, the girl from the Victoria Shakespeare Festival who had just enrolled in the drama department. Before I picked her up, I rolled a joint. "You sure you want to do this?" Larry asked me. He was also going with his girl Karen, but we weren't sitting together.

"Absolutely," I said and smoked the joint.

By the time I picked up Leslie, I was completely stoned. She seemed to be wearing more pancake makeup than usual. Driving and finding a parking place near the auditorium was a problem—I was afraid I would never be able to find my car again—and Leslie wasn't sure she wanted to be there anyway. When we passed some beatniks in the lobby, she remarked, "These people are disgusting."

In the first half of the concert, Dylan appeared alone and played an acoustic set of every song on his album *Bringing It All Back Home*, which Jody and I had bought the spring before. When the curtain opened for the second half, he was joined by Mike Bloomfield and Al Kooper. Together they played everything on his new album *Highway 61 Revisited*, just as they had played it two weeks before at the Newport Folk Festival. The audience went insane. Old beatniks were shouting, "You scumbag." But the frat guys thought "Just like Tom Thumb's Blues," about a visit to a Juarez whorehouse, had been written just for them.

When the show was over, I found my car, no problem, but Leslie still wasn't sure what we had seen. "I don't like music if I can't understand the words," she told me.

The day after the concert, I went out and bought the new Bob Dylan album, which had a great cover. Then the Beatles came out with *Rubber Soul*, and the Rolling Stones came out with *Aftermath*. Larry and I got stoned and listened to them over and over.

That was the last date I had with Leslie. She later married a beatnik named Wesley and then complained to the cops when he smoked grass. He did some jail time, and I decided I had made a good move by dropping Leslie.

So I learned that grass made music better.

Grass was a secret too good to keep. Soon Larry got his girl, Karen, stoned, and she didn't mind at all—it made ice cream taste better, and what could be wrong with that? Grass was a mild and harmless psychedelic that enhanced all sensations and sent you on little *mind trips*.

We began getting stoned and driving around Austin in Larry's Volkswagen Bug. The brilliant emeralds and rubies of the traffic lights seemed miles away. Sometimes we went to art movies at the Texas Theater. On grass, Roman Polanski's *Repulsion* was the greatest horror movie ever made. Secretly, I preferred Richard Lester's *The Knack*, because Rita Tushingham reminded me of Jody—when she was depressed, her eyes got hard as nail heads.

One day, I ran into Fred, the grad student who had directed me in *Bobouroche*. "You smoke grass, don't you?" he asked me.

"I do," I admitted.

"I have an idea," he said. "I'm supposed to do a scene by one of the Greek playwrights for Demonstration Lab. It can be tragedy or comedy."

"Yeah?"

"The other students are doing tragedy, but I want to do the authentic Aristophanic comedy. I've found a script that was translated by William Arrowsmith—he's a professor here—and you're perfect for the lead."

That night I read the script. The translation was relentlessly obscene—there was no doubt this was the authentic Aristophanic comedy—and the next day I told Fred I would do it. So we began rehearsing the scene. There was one other actor in it, but he was a freshman and pretty much out of it. I want to say here that I never performed when I was stoned, but one day Fred and I did smoke a joint before rehearsal and decided that if this was going to be authentic Aristophanic comedy, I should wear nothing but a leather phallus.

In Demonstration Lab on that Friday afternoon, I bounded onstage wearing almost nothing and shouted, "Goddamn that whore of a city Athens and everyone in it." My mother and father would have been humiliated, but the scene created a sensation.

Later, Mr. Mott called me into his office and said, "Not only have you proven you have no polish; you have proven you are not a real actor at all."

But I thought I had proven I was capable of more *abandon* than any other actor in the drama department.

So I learned that grass made acting better.

It was now October, and I had lost Jody forever. There was no one to compare with her, of course, but I wasn't going to spend my last year at the university without a lover and was looking around for someone to replace her. To me, the choice was between two freshman girls. One was Dee, a girl from Dallas who seemed experienced; the other was Sandra, an innocent girl from Corpus Christi. I treated each according to what I thought were her needs. On Friday afternoon, I walked into the dance studio while Sandy was working out alone at the *barre*, wearing a black leotard.

Of course I took dance myself—it was a required course—so the studio wasn't a completely strange environment to me. I smiled approvingly and watched Sandy working out. Finally she became uncomfortable, stopped, and stared at me defiantly. So I introduced myself.

"I know who you are," she said. "What do you want?"

"I want to go out with you."

"O me."

"I just want to get to know you."

She asked me when I wanted to go out, and I said, "Why not tonight?"

Of course Sandra had nothing else to do that night, so I picked her up at eight o'clock, and we went to the bus station. There I suggested we get our pictures taken in the twenty-five-cent photo booth—something I had done with Jody and would do with all girls thereafter—tore apart the strip of photos, gave half to her, and kept the other half for myself.

When we said good night in front of her dorm, I gave her a polite kiss and told her we would see each other again. But I sensed she was not experienced enough for me, and didn't want to have to teach her everything, so I didn't call her back. In any event, Sandra had a crush on me for the rest of the year.

Dee was a little different. She also lived in a dorm but had already pledged a sorority and had a frat guy boyfriend. She was short with blonde hair and wore a miniskirt and smart black leather Beatle boots. When I took her out for a cup of coffee, she found a way to tell me she took birth control pills. Then I asked for a date, and she said, "I have a date Friday night, but why don't you come by for me after eleven?"

"Why?"

"Because the King will be bringing me back then, and it'll be easy enough for me to slip out later and see you." The King was her frat guy boyfriend.

But I didn't want to share Dee with the King and decided our first date needed an element of risk. So on Tuesday night, I got stoned and took her out to Ernie's Chicken Shack, a black club—we had started calling Negroes "black people" by then—on the east side of Austin, where you could sometimes hear Bo Diddley and other famous rhythm and blues performers. It was frequented by frat guys on weekends, but that night we were the only white couple there.

At one point, I went to the bathroom and was using the urinal when four young black guys entered and stood behind me. "What's happening?" I said.

"What the *fuck* you think you doin' here?" they asked me.

Things might have gotten out of hand, but turning away from the urinal, I improvised a series of what I thought were brilliant lies. "I can't believe this," I said sadly. "Here I just got back from Mississippi, where I was trying to help your people, and look at how you treat me now."

The black guys looked at one another and said, "Sorry, man."

When Dee and I got out of Ernie's, it was late and her dorm was already closed so I said, "Why don't you just spend the night at my apartment?"

That would be fine, she said—she could call her roommate, who would sign her in. When we got to my apartment, I asked Dee if she had ever smoked grass, and she said, "No, but I've always wanted to try it."

On that night, I learned what grass *really* did. It made sex better.

The week after that, I stopped smoking it completely. This was an experiment I performed to see if Larry and I were addicted. After seven days without grass, I went into the front room and told Larry, I had absolutely no withdrawal symptoms of any kind.

"Good," Larry said, lighting a joint and handing it to me.

Then he put on the Rolling Stones' *Aftermath* and turned on the television, but with the sound off. I took another hit off the joint and began free-associating.

Onscreen, Walter Cronkite was talking about protests against the war in Vietnam. Suddenly I saw we were all caught in some sort of time storm—time itself was speeding up, and successive waves of history were battering us. There were demonstrations all over the country— demonstrations for racial equality, demonstrations for sexual freedom, demonstrations both for and against the war. Cops were beating white demonstrators, National Guard soldiers with bayonets were threatening black protestors, and cars were being set on fire. In Vietnam, soldiers were jumping out of helicopters, napalm bombs were exploding, and somehow all of this was held together and *explained* by Mick Jagger singing, "I Can't Get No (Satisfaction)." Thousands of messages were being transmitted instantaneously by grass, music, and television, and understanding was everywhere.

Larry had just invented MTV.

LSD, or lysergic acid diethylamide, which everyone called acid, had been around Austin for a while now. There was a belief it was stronger than peyote, and it came in tablet form. Larry decided we had to take it, and that was fine with me, so I went over to Gabe's to ask him if he could get some for us. He was living in a converted garage under Pedro Fox's house, near Scottish Rite Dorm, and you knew he was home when you saw his Triumph chained to a cedar tree outside. I was a little nervous—lately I'd begun to think Gabe didn't take me seriously anymore because I was a drama major—so when I was around him, I tried to be the hippest person I could be.

"Come in," he said when I knocked on the door. His apartment had a concrete floor, no windows, and smelled strongly of jungle mold and Mexico. Gabe lay on the bed wearing his drugstore glasses, looking like a serious young Marxist, reading Sartre's *Nausea.*

Could he get us acid?

"Sure," he said. "But you've got to forget all that shit about *The Tibetan Book of the Dead.* You're not going to see your past incarnations."

"Good," I said. "I don't want to know anything about them. But we'd like you to take it with us."

He took off his glasses and polished them. "Why not?" he said. "I could always use another acid trip."

So one Saturday afternoon in November, Larry, Karen, Dee, and Gabe and I took the acid. Unfortunately, Karen got out of rehearsal late and didn't join us until almost five o'clock. Then Larry drove north on the Interregional Highway toward his father's farm, just outside of Waco, which we were supposed to have all to ourselves. If we could just get there before the hallucinations started, we would be all right.

But the acid began to come on as we approached Georgetown. I was sitting in the front seat beside Larry, reading the road map. Karen, Dee, and Gabe were crowded together in the backseat.

"It's illegal to carry this many people in a Bug," Karen said.

"Don't call my car a Bug," Larry said.

A long, uncomfortable silence came in as Larry drove on through Georgetown, past Rabbit Hill, and now the sun was going down. I felt a great urge to speak and finally said, "At least nobody's holding."

"I am," Gabe said. "I have got a bag of grass."

There was an electric moment. Then everybody in the backseat began talking about several things at once. Dee and Karen were obviously hallucinating, but I still thought I was all right until I glanced over at Larry, who smiled back at me—but seemed to be sitting on a sofa in a fifties living room, in front of a big Motorola television set.

The sun dropped below the western horizon as we passed through the small towns of Troy and Eddy, which I could not find on the map. When I looked back over my shoulder, Gabe's eyes met mine. "Make a wrong turn, and you end up in Dallas," he said.

Just then Larry found the gate to his father's ranch and turned in. We all piled out of the car like circus clowns and, for a while, wandered around in the dusk, along the limestone bank of a creek that crossed the property. The moon rose over the oak trees.

"I'm at the Grand Canyon," I shouted, and someone else shouted, "So am I."

Then we went into the house, which was empty of furniture. The walls were covered with knotty pine paneling and the floor with blue acrylic carpet. We were stuck here all night, and there was nothing to do. Gabe sat on the floor and rolled a joint.

Dee asked, "Should I take my clothes off?"

"Some girl always says that," Gabe said, already bored.

Acid was not as friendly to me as peyote had been.

"I'm having this electronic feeling," Larry said, "as if we were all on a television screen."

So was I, but it was not pleasant. I wandered from room to room and finally walked outside. The detailed ground at my feet was full of fossils, but there was no magic to this, as there had been on peyote.

When I walked around the house, the sky to the south glowed a radioactive red, like in the movie *Crack in the World*. For a moment, I thought I was going to fall on the ground and sob. Then I realized they were firing illumination rounds at Fort Hood. I also knew that this, like everything else that happened on our trip, was a sign—a sign of the Vietnam War. The army had just fought a big battle with the NVA in the Ia Drang Valley, and it was only a matter of time before we would all be called up for the draft.

Dee had followed me and stood beside me. She asked about the red glow, and I explained it.

"I love you," she said, "but I know what you're thinking about. You still love Jody."

"I guess I do." I said.

"You can't hide it."

Dee meant well, and I was glad she loved me. She was a good person with a good sense of humor. But she was a girl, not a woman like Jody. She was completely predictable, liked me more than I liked her—and I hated it when girls felt sorry for me. For the first time in my life, I was having a bad trip.

"Please leave me alone," I told her.

Dee went back inside the house, and I stayed there for a long time, staring at the glowing sky.

In December, Larry and I gave a cast party at our apartment, and a couple of frat guys tried to crash it. Cal Hammer, who was back in school for another year, beat them up in the front yard. I saw it coming, slipped away from Dee and went to my bedroom, where I watched the fight through the window. I was dreadfully ashamed of myself, but I wasn't going to go out there and get in a fight.

A week later, I went to the drama department Christmas party, which was held in the Laboratory Theater. The students whose dream it was to be in a Broadway musical did a song and dance number that was pretty funny. I had smoked a lot of grass before I came.

Cal Hammer was an old friend of Darryl, Jody's new husband, and suddenly I found him standing right in front of me, saying, "I just saw Jody and Darryl in Houston. I wouldn't think of it as a marriage of convenience if I were you."

I felt the blood leave my face and suddenly knew, with telepathic certainty, that Hammer knew I had hidden from the fight. "I'm not sure what you mean," I said, sorry I had smoked so much grass.

"I mean she didn't marry him because she was pregnant—if that's what you're thinking." He was standing so close to me I could feel his breath on my face. It was almost as if Hammer was trying to make me angry, so I would take a shot at him. "They're very much in love," he added softly.

Hammer had just played King Pentheus in *The Bacchae*, by Euripides, in which he had defied Dionysius and been punished by falling under the spell of the god. Then he had reappeared, wearing blue eye shadow and a transparent gown, and joined the other Bacchantes, who finally tore him to pieces. Somehow his effeminacy in the last scene had made him seem even more menacing.

"I have to go," I said.

I knew I had to get in a fight someday, but not with Hammer. If I lost, I'd have to see him every day for the rest of the year. As I left the building, I thought, *I should cut down on the grass, if it's going to make me this paranoid.*

But when I got to my car in the parking lot, I found myself thinking it wasn't really so strange for me to feel this way. Even Shakespeare plays were full of sword combat, and there was hardly a single American movie where the hero didn't get in a fistfight at some point. Of course he almost always won, and if he lost it was because he was outnumbered. The fight itself was brief and painless, and he almost immediately got over it. I doubted Hammer had ever lost a fight.

As I drove home, I wondered how I had ended up in a drama

department where the best actor was also the toughest, the best at beating people up. It was just like Zundy.

At Christmas, I did my duty and drove up to Nortex to see my family. The trees were bare and the grass yellow, but it had not yet snowed. My father was drinking hard and had lost his job as a consulting geologist for Red River Oil and Gas. But my brother, Ray, had started a rock band called Fast Eddie and the Electric Japs, which was becoming very successful. They rehearsed in the garage, and the neighborhood girls came over to watch.

When I got up on Christmas morning, my father said, "Come outside. I want to show you something."

My present was sitting in the driveway. It was an Austin-Healey 9000—a slightly old but beautiful British sports car painted racing green that my father had bought from an airman. At first I told him I couldn't accept it.

"But it's our gift to you," he said. "Why the hell can't you just take it?"

I had trouble explaining to him that Jody drove a Triumph, and if I started driving a sports car myself everyone would think I was copying her—and they would be right. It was just like my parents to give me a present I hadn't asked for and didn't really want. This had been a nightmare of mine since childhood.

I finally accepted the car but only drove it around the neighborhood and spent most of my remaining time in Nortex sleeping or wishing I had some grass to smoke. Once I spent an hour looking at the phonebook, curious to see who was still living here. Almost immediately I found "Cummins, Bobby Lee and Marilyn," who had an address on

Garfield Street, not far away. When it got dark, I drove past their house. There was a light on in the kitchen. I imagined ringing the doorbell and, when Bobby Lee answered, knocking him to the floor in front of his screaming wife.

Gradually I overcame my shame about the car—no young man can resist a sports car for long. On New Year's Day, I drove the Austin-Healey back down to Austin and found myself liking it more. The engine gave off a low hum of power as I went up and over the hills near Lampasas. Driving the Austin-Healey was like dancing with Julie Christie, a beautiful British actress in a green dress who wanted me to go faster.

When I arrived in Austin, I went over to show it to Dee at her sorority house. She thought it was really cool and rode with me out into the hills, where we made love on a blanket in the woods.

"Go ahead, take it out on me," she cried, her fingernails digging into my back.

Take out what? I wondered.

On a cold, gray afternoon in January, I went alone to a showing of *On the Waterfront*, starring Marlon Brando, at the Student Union. I'd never seen the movie before but had heard Brando got in a big fight at the end. Because I had never played a lead, I didn't bother following the plot, just concentrated on his scenes, one at a time.

But the best scene was not the fight. Toward the end, Brando sat on a rooftop, like Rodin's *Thinker*, pondering some important decision I couldn't understand. Then the music came in, and Brando made his decision—went down to the waterfront and got in the fight of his life, which he lost but somehow won.

I stayed and watched the movie again. The scene on the rooftop was still the best one, but this time I understood why. The most important thing for an actor to do was to show the moment of his Big Decision. It didn't have to be marriage—the decision could be a fight or anything that tied up all the loose ends of the story—the moment when the actor made the choice his character *had* to make. This was how you played a lead.

I went home and talked to Larry and Karen. "We're facing the same sort of choice right now," I told them. "Do we go to Hollywood or New York City? Try to make it in the movies or get into the Actor's Studio? Or do we just avoid the decision altogether?"

As I spoke, I realized this was also the decision Jody had faced last year. As it turned out, she had gotten a job at the Alley in Houston—a good job, a big role. But then she had married Darryl, and why? Was this the Big Decision she had been looking for? Was Hammer right, and did she love Darryl more than she loved me? Or did you sometimes make a Big Decision but make the wrong choice?

Larry and Karen were looking at each other.

"I don't know," Larry said. "I might want to go to Los Angeles and try to make it in the movies. Or I might want to go to San Francisco. There's a lot of theater out there."

Many Austin people had been going to San Francisco—Janis Joplin had headed out there not long ago—but they were music people, and there was no theater out there I had heard of. They did say drugs were almost legal.

"Like a friend of mine once said," I told them. "You have to do the things you're afraid of doing."

"I'd rather go anyplace than New York City," Larry said.

"You mean that?"

"Yeah, almost anyplace but there."

"I feel the same way," Karen said.

Secretly, I was also reluctant to go to New York. There might be no place to live better than Austin, which was becoming the coolest town in the world, unless it was San Francisco. Or was I just afraid of going anywhere?

In the drama school library, I found a one-act play by a new British playwright, Harold Pinter, called *The Dumb Waiter.* Two Cockney crooks are waiting in the basement of a restaurant for *someone* to show up so they can kill him. In the end, the victim turns out to be one of them. I liked this play and talked George, another actor in my class, into performing it with me for Demonstration Lab. I played the victim and found it was perfect material for me—a comedy of anxiety. The so-called mysterious pauses were moments of dread and could be played for laughs. Any good actor could see this. And when you got laughs in a Pinter play, it meant that the audience was following you and understood what you were doing and feeling. There was even a moment of decision when I found that I was the victim—I closed my eyes in resignation as George drew his gun, and the shot rang out in the blackout.

When Mr. Moller saw *The Dumb Waiter,* he said, "I couldn't tell if you were a good person or a bad. Look at the plays of Arthur Miller, who teaches us moral lessons."

But the other students liked the play, and I began to see that, in the Theater of the Absurd, there was no real distinction between comedy and tragedy and even a character actor could play a lead. This had been true in *Waiting for Godot,* and British actors like Tom Courtenay and Michael Crawford were proving it in the movies. To me, the secret of playing these roles was clear: Don't pretend to be other people; just play yourself in some way. Even if it's a character role, find a Big Decision of some sort and play it as your own.

In March, Dr. Hodges directed *Saint Joan*, and all the men had to get "pudding-basin" haircuts. Actually they looked like Beatles haircuts and turned out to be stylish. I played a French general in the first scene, and a British soldier in the last scene, for which I got good notices.

But sometime in the last year, when Jody and I had been in love, I had found myself and was no longer interested in playing somebody else. These were small character roles; the characters made no big choices, and it was hard to get excited about them. In the end I felt I had disappointed Dr. Hodges, who was the only one on the faculty who had ever encouraged me at all.

Everybody liked grass, even frat guys. By April, every student at the university was smoking it. That was the month Lutz appeared in Austin and took an apartment near Eastwoods Park. He arrived in secrecy, and I didn't learn he was there for more than a week. When I did, I went over to see him.

"I've dropped out of the University of Oklahoma," he said, "and I'm transferring here."

"Why'd you drop out?"

He looked around nervously and then confessed, "I got busted for smoking grass."

For the first time in years, I was impressed with Lutz. Getting busted was serious business. He showed me a copy of the *Daily Oklahoman* from a month before.

"Students Indicted for Smoking Marijuana," the headline said. "Fraternity House Burned Down. Fortunately No Loss of Life."

"I got off on the drug charges," Lutz told me, "but my frat brothers had a meeting in the basement of the frat house to decide what to do with me. I was already on probation for exposing myself. They voted to kick me out and told me to never come back. Then everybody went upstairs. Before I left, I threw my cigarette butt into the garbage can. I still don't know why I did this. There was a little fire burning when I left, but I thought it would go out. Then the next morning I read the article in the paper that said the frat house had burned down. So you can see why it's better for me to stay down here for a while."

I had to smile: he was still Lutz, the holy fool, and his foolishness had kept him out of jail. But when I mentioned this, he said he didn't want to be called Lutz anymore—just Danny—and he wanted to go to film school and make cinema verité movies like his favorite director, Jean-Luc Goddard (whose name he pronounced correctly, *Go Dar,* but with a frat-guy inflection). Then he told me I was stupid to go to drama school, even when I said I was learning about character and story and could learn about cameras and film later on.

"No, no, no," he said impatiently. "You're still trying to be somebody you're not. Cinema verité—the cinema of truth—is the only way to go."

I ignored the comment about "trying to be somebody you're not" and told him, "I can study cinema verité when I get to New York City, which is where I'm going to go when I graduate."

"I don't know how you can even *think* about leaving Austin," he said in horror. "It's the coolest place in the world."

"Then I'm sure you'll like it here."

By this time, I was wondering if my father could have been right. Did your old friends sometimes become your enemies and follow you around for the rest of your life? Before I left, Lutz asked me, "'Can you spare a dollar for a fellow American?'"—a line from the movie *The Treasure of the Sierra Madre*—and I gave him exactly one dollar.

Sometimes I stopped in to see Gabe when I saw his Triumph was chained to the cedar tree outside his door. He was always lying on his bed reading. When I mentioned I was reading this book or that, he had no response. Then one night, he showed me a paper he had written for Arrowsmith's course on classical civilization.

Arrowsmith was the brilliant professor who had done the obscene translation of *The Knights* that I had performed in Demonstration Lab. This assignment was on the Italian writer Caesar Pavese's *Dialogues With Leuco*, which he had recently translated—I have this book before me now.

Pavese is a forgotten poet and novelist of postwar Italian literature. His novels are set during the mysterious boredom of the German occupation, which has since spread around the world through art movies. In the last decades, most of his work has fallen silent. But *Dialogues With Leuco*—poetic dialogues between gods and men—still sings for me. Later Pavese committed suicide. He had fallen in love with the American actress Constance Dowling, who briefly returned his love and then married Ivan Tors, later the producer of *Sea Hunt*. ("Women," Gabe observed, "are the first to know and the first to forget.")

I was a little annoyed with Gabe, who I felt was moving in on my own interest, classical civilization—but then I read his paper on Pavese, which Arrowsmith had graded with an A+ and added, "Superb."

"How did you do this?" I asked him.

"I wrote it on the greatest drug of all," he said.

"What's that?"

"Methedrine."

Meth was around even then. There were several people in Austin who were supposed to be users, including Janis Joplin, who took it for the rush of energy just before she performed. But Gabe said it was a mind trip. I didn't know much about methedrine, but I knew that it had been invented by the Nazis, that it made you paranoid, and that users suffered from 'amphetamine psychosis,' as it was then called. The meth user's destiny seemed to inevitably be the insane asylum or suicide.

"What does it do for you?" I asked Gabe.

"You stay up all night."

"So what?"

"What's the first thing your parents told you not to do?"

I thought about this.

"Stay up all night," Gabe said. "Remember New Year's Eve? Your parents went to a party and left you alone. They told you not to stay up until midnight, but you did. For the first time in your life, you saw the hands of the clock go past twelve and heard the fireworks go off. And when you looked out the window, what did you see?"

I remembered that night well. Feeling a little sick, I had looked out my window at the backyard of my house, which was lit by floodlights, and what had I seen? The dead, yellow grass and the stars above, which had suddenly looked as strange to me as the surface of another planet.

"Loneliness," I said.

"I began to see things the first night I took meth," Gabe said. "When I stayed up working on that paper, I could see things right through that wall—and I don't mean the kind of things you see on peyote."

"What *do* you mean?"

"Strange things. There were people out there. Things that had happened and things that may happen yet. I think I was seeing what Heraclitus called the River of Time—I mean the world as seen from more than one point in time and space."

This was impressive.

"But you've got to shoot it up to get the full effect," Gabe finished.

Then he took out his works—a needle fixed to an eyedropper and his stash of meth. "You want me to give you a hit?"

I had sworn to myself that I would never inject drugs and said, "It's not for me."

Then I left, got in the Austin-Healey and drove away.

My last year at the University of Texas was coming to a close. As in my senior year of high school, every moment seemed to be happening for both the first and last time. Dee and I went dancing at the New Orleans Club where a group called the Thirteenth Floor Elevators played almost every night. Afterward we made love, but I will admit the woman I was thinking about was Jody.

In another month, school would be over forever, and the great emptiness Jody had felt was now opening before me. To think ahead drained me of all energy. The year had come and gone, and I had not become as dangerous as I had hoped. I could get (no) satisfaction.

In the end, it always came back to Jody. With her I had been better than myself and thought I had won her forever. But I had never really touched her at all. *You always had some idea of me I could never live up to*, she had said in her last letter. Why had she married this guy Darryl anyway? If he was a friend of Hammer's, he must be a tough guy who got in a lot of fights, who was dangerous and sexy. Maybe I should just give her up.

No, I thought with sudden anger. *Forget that. Jody is still your destiny, and if you give her up it will be the end for you. You need to find something stronger than she is, something that will make you even more dangerous than you are now.*

Finally I went back to see Gabe. When I told him what I wanted, he removed a section of his bathroom wall and took out a large amber glass bottle full of white crystalline powder, with a cork on top.

"This is a one-hundred-gram bottle of laboratory pure," he told me. "Pedro Fox got me a doctor's letterhead, and I ordered it straight from Burroughs Wellcome. It should last me five years."

He spilled some powder into a spoon and held a burning match under it until the meth bubbled and cooked up. Then he sucked it up through a little ball of cotton into a #19 needle, which he had fixed to the end of an eyedropper with some twine and a little coil of toilet paper. I sat on the toilet and let Gabe drive the needle into the large vein in my elbow.

It was sordid, it was erotic, it was the worst thing I had ever done, but it filled my brain with hot light. Then I found Dee, and we went to the New Orleans Club and danced to the Thirteenth Floor Elevators until long after midnight.

17

I WOKE AT DUSK in Larry's old room on the top of the Gray House in Boone, North Carolina. This summer, we were both working for *Horn in the West*. I had followed him here in my Austin-Healey, driving for two days and nights on meth, pouring it into Cokes and drinking it down— it was too dangerous to shoot it up while you were on the road—finally arriving at dawn, falling into bed, and sleeping for another day.

Larry was standing at the end of my bed. "I don't feel so good," he said.

"Neither do I."

For the past two months of school in Austin, we had taken meth almost every day and night—to write papers, to take finals, to go dancing. I had even written a play for my playwriting class based on an article in *Life* called "The Panic in Needle Park," but my characters had taken meth, not heroin. Finally, we had graduated and driven here, and now the meth was finally gone. Rehearsals for *Horn in the West* would start tomorrow morning.

"Meth scares me," he said.

"It scares me too."

"I have to tell you," he said, "I'm going back to Texas. I have to be with Karen again. She's the only one who can help me."

"You're coming down. You're depressed. What about your job here?"

"You can have it."

I couldn't believe it. For more than two years, Larry and I had been close. We had lived together, discovered drugs together, told each other everything. Now he was going to turn around and go home, just as Joe Hollis had gone home when we had reached Colorado because he couldn't live without Jayne's love. He was weaker than I'd thought.

But I couldn't convince him to stay. He talked to the director, left Boone that evening, and drove back to Houston in his Volkswagen.

Meth was not physically addicting, like heroin; there was just a slight psychological dependency, and this would be a good time to stop taking it. Maybe by the end of the summer, I could find somebody here who was willing to go to New York City with me.

The director of *Horn in the West* decided not to give me Larry's role of Judge Henderson, although I was supposed to be his understudy. Instead, he gave the role to Bruce, a new actor who had played leads at the University of Oklahoma. I was to understudy Major McKenzie, the British officer who terrorized the American colonists (probably because I could do an English accent), and the director promised me I would play it at least once. Meanwhile, I took the small role of a settler who had no lines.

I began dating one of Larry's former girlfriends, Dottie. She was a big blonde girl from Florida who looked a little like Monica Vitti. In a week or so, we became lovers, which made me feel considerably better. Some members of the company stayed up all night after the show at the Gray House—playing cards, drinking moonshine, and telling ghost stories—and Dottie and I soon joined them. The stories that particularly frightened me were stories of the ghosts who inhabited mirrors. One night we all drove out to the Blue Ridge Parkway to see the Brown Mountain Lights, pale fireballs that shot up from the woods below. At the Gray House, I also heard the greatest UFO story I have ever heard. A girl in the company told me she had seen an unidentified flying object—a triangle of lights that hovered over the Blue Ridge Parkway for an hour. Her story was so detailed I had to believe it and still do.

At the first light of morning, I drove Dottie back to her house, which was on the side of a hill near the edge of the deep woods. It was lovely to make love to Dottie in the morning, when the honeybees droned in the garden and her long, naked body smelled like baking bread. Then we slept until the afternoon.

In July, it rained every day, and the rhododendrons gave off an almost sickening sexual reek. Dottie and I became friends with Bruce and his wife, Lisa. I told him about *The Dumb Waiter*, my favorite Pinter play, and we started working on it, with Lisa directing.

That month, I was short of money and went to work at the Tweetsie Railroad, a theme park where I played Daniel Boone and walked around in the rain carrying a rifle and wearing a coonskin cap. Kids followed me, yelling out, "You're not the real Daniel Boone." Only one kid believed I was the real thing, and he was mentally handicapped, so I took him to the General Store and bought him a soda. But a depression about the whole acting profession began to overtake me.

I had bought a paperback book before I left Austin—*The Moviegoer* by Walker Percy, whose hero, Binx Bolling, drove a sports car. For some reason, I couldn't finish it, but Dottie did and said Binx was just like me. At first I was flattered and then asked her, "Because he drives a sports car?"

"No," she said. "Because he thinks he's smarter than everybody else."

This didn't sound good at all, and I asked her what she meant.

"He dates girls who are dumber than he is so he can feel superior to them."

"I don't think you're dumb."

"No, but you treat me as if I was," she said.

This led to an ongoing discussion between Dottie and me about my nature and hers. It was all right for me to be a better actor than the others, but I definitely didn't want them thinking I felt superior to them. Finally I decided they thought I was standing off somewhere watching them—that I was *uninvolved* again.

In Texas I had taken drugs to become more involved and more dangerous. I was not taking drugs now, or even drinking that much, so perhaps this was what people sensed. But I was not a bad person like my roommate.

My roommate, Matt, the local guy who played Major McKenzie, had been cast as the bad guy because he *was* a bad guy—he was my roommate, and I know. Matt carried a gun, stole my change, cheated at cards, and once I heard him hit his girlfriend. But he was no Cal Hammer, and I was not afraid of him. In fact, I felt contempt for him, because he couldn't be trusted.

In August, Bruce's wife, Lisa, talked a closed movie theater in Boone into giving her the stage on a Monday night, and Bruce and I performed *The Dumb Waiter* for the company. By this time, I had my performance nailed, and almost everyone liked it. I had made people laugh and was forgiven for sometimes being uninvolved. Instead of having a cast party, we went to a local restaurant and ate fried chicken, and later I followed Dottie back to her house, where we made love. I had successfully pretended to be an ordinary guy, which most actors thought was the hardest role to play.

Later I would finish reading *The Moviegoer* and be astonished by how closely the author, Walker Percy, had described my thoughts at that time.

Today I regret that I ever left North Carolina. The people there were smart, as smart as Texans. They loved the mountains, moonshine, Thomas Wolfe, and Appalachian music. I wish Dottie and I could have stayed there in her little house on the side of the hill by the edge of the deep woods forever.

But one afternoon toward the end of the summer, Dottie and I were with Bruce and Lisa when we heard on the radio that a sniper named Charles Whitman was shooting up the campus of the University of Texas from the top of the Tower. He killed fourteen people before the cops finally got him, and I decided I wanted to go home.

So I wrote Gabe and asked him to send me some meth. He sent me an envelope with an eighth of an inch of white crystalline powder on the bottom. On the night the show closed, I got in the Austin-Healey and started back for Larry's apartment in Houston.

And on that drive, I lost my mind. I am not sure what happened, but it took me three days and nights to cross Alabama and Mississippi and reach Houston. On the first night, I saw a huge meteor shooting overhead through the Appalachian mountain fog. On the second day, I thought something was wrong with the Healy and spent the second night in a motel. I took the meth the third day, licking it off my fingers. That night, I somehow got off the map and found myself driving on an elevated blacktop road across the swamps of Louisiana, the full moon shining in my face. It was a nightmare that ended only when the sun came up and I could finally tell which direction I was going. Gas flares burned above a refinery to the south. At Port Sulphur, I pumped gas into my car, standing beneath the floodlights, feeling like a fly trapped under a crystal paperweight.

Finally I reached Houston, where I woke up Larry. When he answered the door, he seemed to be able to *see right through me*, and there was nothing left inside of me but fear.

It was another warning, but I ignored it.

18

It had been the strongest paranoia I had ever felt, but after I slept for a few hours, the fear faded away. Then I did an unbelievable thing— auditioned for the Alley Theater and got a job. Of course this was the same job Jody had gotten a year before. I performed a monologue from the play *Dylan*, and Nina Vance, the artistic director, accepted me and said I could be an apprentice—play small roles, work in the shop, eventually join the company and get my Equity Card. Mr. Moller sent me his congratulations.

It sounded good until I reported to the shop on the first day. There I met Jerry, another apprentice, and told him I was here to get my Equity Card.

"Yeah, that's what Nina promised me," he said, "five years ago."

I worked for the Alley for three months. At first I was afraid Jody would show up in her Triumph and see I was also driving a sports car. Then Jerry told me she had left the company when she'd married Darryl and not come back. Soon I understood why—apprentices were seldom given even a small role. Most of our time was spent building and moving scenery, although Nina did ask me to follow her around the day the National Endowment came and light her cigarettes for her.

I lived with Larry and Karen in Montrose, an old bohemian neighborhood, which was very much like New Orleans, full of gays and prostitutes. Larry worked as a disc jockey for a local country and western station that wouldn't let him play Bob Dylan because they said it was "'nigger music."

People had now taken to calling this decade the sixties. The Beatles had come out with the *Revolver* album, the Stones with *Big Hits*, and Bob Dylan had put out *Blonde on Blonde*. Our arguments about which was better grew more serious. When I came back from work in the evening, Larry was usually stoned, and we talked about the alien abduction case of Betty and Barney Hill, which had just been written about an article for *Look*. The aliens had somehow erased all memory of the abduction from the minds of the Hills until it was uncovered by hypnosis, an idea that fascinated and frightened us both. My fear of mirrors returned, and one night, flying saucers were reported over Houston.

It was clear the country was becoming increasingly polarized and that we lived in one of its most conservative parts. The Houston cops had noticed my sports car, and sometimes I found a ticket on the windshield for illegal parking. Police surveillance seemed like a real possibility. And all that fall, we heard constantly about Timothy Leary, acid, and San Francisco.

One night, I came home, and Larry told me, "I've decided to quit that redneck radio station. Karen and I are going to San Francisco. I think we can be free out there."

I was dubious, but two weeks later, Larry and Karen threw

everything they had into the back of his Volkswagen and headed out for San Francisco. I watched them drive away, impressed that they had actually *done something*, and wished I could also change my life.

The week after that, I resigned from the Alley, which was difficult because I had to tell the director of *The World of Sholem Aleichem*, on which I was working backstage.

"But I was just about to give you a couple of lines," he said.

If I had known this, I might not have quit, but it was too late to back out now.

So on a rainy day in late October, I dropped my rent check in the mailbox and drove up to Austin. There I found a one-room apartment behind an antique store on Red River Street. The walls were white stucco, the floor was covered with blue acrylic shag carpet, and the yard was full of old tombstones, scattered around like so many marble pages. Behind it was an empty garage in which I parked the Austin-Healey.

The next day I took a part-time job at a textbook store on Duval Street, and went to the Green and White Grocery Store, where I bought tortillas, beans, and some Mexican comic books. I decided not to tell Dee or anybody else from the drama department I was here. After a few days of resisting the idea, I went over to Gabe's apartment, because I had come back to Austin to take meth.

There will be no apologies here for taking meth. Recently there has been a popular cable television series called *Breaking Bad*, about a college chemistry professor who is dying of cancer and becomes a meth chemist to provide money for his wife and children. I can't watch it.

I didn't sell meth, I just took it—but not because I was dying of cancer and wanted to help my wife and children. I took it because I was willfully destroying my past as an ordinary guy, and I liked the rush. There had been that spell of intense paranoia on the drive back from North Carolina, and it was clear that meth was dangerous—but I wanted to do something *dangerous* again, so that when Jody came back, I would be ready for her.

Gabe was living a few blocks away; he had a large split-level apartment in a new complex made of gray barn wood. His new girl, Kitty, who had been a Tri Delt cheerleader when he met her, answered the door.

"How did you get her?" I asked Gabe when we went upstairs, where he kept his meth.

"Gave her a hit," he said. "Now she's my sex slave forever." This was a joke, if not completely funny, and also the truth—some girls were turned on by meth.

I sat on the toilet and let Gabe shoot me up. Then I hung around for the rest of the night while Kitty, who was an art major, made charcoal drawings of Gabe and read the *I Ching*. I wanted to talk to Gabe about Pavese, but he was now reading Ouspensky, Gurjieff, and a novel called *The Recognitions*, by William Gaddis, a writer he recommended.

Toward morning, some people showed up who had something to do with the Thirteenth Floor Elevators. Gabe was now a meth dealer to the stars.

At dawn, a pale fisheye moon hung in the greenish sky. "Stick around and have another hit," Gabe said. "It doesn't mean anything until you've stayed up two or three nights."

I had another hit and bought a gram of meth and a fresh needle from Gabe so I could shoot myself up. Then, because his motorcycle was almost out of gas, he asked me to take him to the 7-Eleven to buy a carton of milk for Kitty. As we started into the store, a frat guy came out and said, "Get out of my way, you fucking beatnik."

"You fucking asshole," Gabe said.

"What'd you call me?"

"Asshole, asshole," Gabe said, hit him with three or four punches, and knocked him to the ground.

"All right, enough," the frat guy said, covering his head.

I decided that Gabe was the toughest guy in the world, tougher than a Nortex hood—the more meth he took, the more *dangerous* he got.

When I reached my apartment, I assembled my works, fastening the #22 needle to an eyedropper with thread and toilet paper. First, I cooked up a hit of meth and went through the sordid but necessary injection ritual. Then I sat down at my typewriter, which I had placed on a card table in the center of the room and began to type out the story of Jody and me and our love for each other.

I spent the next six months in Austin, living on Red River Street and working at the textbook store. In the middle of the winter, I played the role of Davies, the tramp in a production of Harold Pinter's *The Caretaker* at a local theater. It was a character role, but I was onstage almost every minute, and when the show was over, I had learned how to play a lead. When I was rehearsing and performing, I took no meth— but for the rest of my time there, I did.

I should have known from the first that meth was going to be the most addictive drug for me, because the rush produced a feeling not of excitement but of infinite calm and concentration—alert vigilance, as the behaviorists put it. There were no withdrawal symptoms, I just slept it off. The cops and the doctors had lied about grass, and they must be lying about meth—if Gabe could take it, so could I.

On weekends, I went on "runs," staying up as long as forty-eight hours, from Friday night to Sunday morning. Almost all I did was set down my memories and this went on for six months. I took my first hit of meth on Friday afternoon when I got off work and sat down at my typewriter. After midnight on Friday, I began to come down.

Soon I learned there were withdrawal symptoms after all. The pain was mental, but far worse than any physical pain I have ever felt. In the end, there was a wall of pain between me and the world, and I lost my belief in everything. This was when I first tried to read William James's *The Varieties of Religious Experience,* but not the chapter on mysticism. Instead, I read the chapter on the divided self and the account of a fall into despair by a French philosopher, Jouffroy:

> I shall never forget that night in December, long after the hour of sleep had come. Anxiously I followed my thoughts, as from layer to layer, they descended toward the foundation of my consciousness, scattering one by one my illusions ... Vainly I clung to these last beliefs, as a shipwrecked sailor clings to the fragments of his vessel. But the inflexible current of my thought was too strong—parents, family, memory, beliefs, it forced me to let go of everything ...

I allowed myself another hit of meth on Saturday morning and two more on Saturday night. Each time I had to take more, because I quickly built up a resistance to it. Soon I began to need meth to think at all.

When I took meth, I ran out of clock time. The sun seemed to rise and set at random intervals. Sometimes, when I went out, the sun was rising; sometimes it was setting; and sometimes I couldn't tell the difference. At night I went out for long walks, afraid to drive my car. Austin was changing. At two and three in the morning, the streets were blocked by old houses being towed to new lots on huge flatbeds. They moved with incredible slowness, in almost complete silence.

Finally, I began to have what Gabe had first told me about—the strange, toxic hallucinations of meth that Gabe had called the River of Time, things that had happened and things that might happen yet. In reality, they were the hallucinations of delirium, the beginnings of amphetamine psychosis, and could seldom be remembered the next day.

On Sunday, I slept through the afternoon and night, and on Monday morning, when I went back to work at the textbook store, it seemed that years had passed.

In November, I got a notice from the Nortex draft board saying I had to report for my induction physical. It was easy enough to get out of the draft—all you had to do was say you took drugs—but I was worried enough to get a letter from a Nortex doctor saying I had allergies and would probably develop asthma in the presence of jungle foliage.

In December, I flew up to Nortex on a Trans-Texas turboprop. When my father picked me up at the airport, I could tell he was worried—didn't want me to die in Vietnam but didn't want me to be a coward either.

On the way home, I told him, "Look, I can't make up my mind. When I get there, I just might enlist."

I could tell this made him feel better. "Just do whatever your conscience tells you to do, Sonny," he said, staring straight ahead.

That night, I couldn't sleep. The next morning, my father took me down to the bus station before daybreak, and I climbed aboard and took my seat. It was like a grim high school reunion. Half my senior class was on that bus, but they were all people I didn't really know. And I couldn't remember their names—except for Wayne Follet, who had helped Bobby Lee Cummins beat me up that night in high school and who now sat right across the aisle from me.

I touched the doctor's letter in my pocket, making sure it was still there, but had already decided it was best not to mention it to anyone. The bus pulled out of the station and headed for Dallas. It was a cold, gray day, and the sun refused to rise. I turned to Wayne Follet and nodded, but I could tell from the way he nodded back that he had forgotten me.

"Where's Bobby Lee?" I asked him.

He gave me a blank stare.

"You know," I said. "Your friend Bobby Lee Cummins—he married Marilyn Donahue."

"She died of cancer," he said. "And Bobby Lee's in prison for armed robbery."

"Oh God," I said.

"No," Wayne said. "It's a good deal for Bobby Lee. He's white middleweight champ of the Texas Prison System—and he don't have to go to Vietnam, that's for sure."

A couple of hours later, the bus reached Dallas. The induction center was on Dealey Plaza, just across from where Kennedy had been killed. The contempt of the military for us all was plain to see. Naked, we stood in line to give a urine sample. "Alla you who can't piss," a sergeant said, "stand aside." I was unable to produce a single drop—it was like my old gym class at Zundy.

I showed my letter to a doctor, who glanced at it and said, "Why don't you just get the hell out of here?" I finally got a marine at the desk to tell me I had been rejected and demanded that he stamp my papers, which he did angrily. Then we all got back on the bus.

Wayne Follet was walking the aisle of the bus asking everyone, "Did you get induction?"

I lied and said I had.

On the way out of Dallas, Wayne forced the driver to stop and bought two cases of beer at a convenience store. Just as we got back to Nortex, a fight broke out. The last I saw of Wayne, he was punching some guy in the face who had not gotten induction. I jumped out of the emergency door, ran three blocks, called my father, and asked him to pick me up. When he did, he asked me if I had been drafted, and I said I didn't know yet.

All this left me with a feeling of deep shame. But Wayne Follet survived Vietnam, returned to Nortex, and became a cop. A few years later, he beat a suspect to death, and when they searched his apartment, they found several Vietcong ears, strung on a wire like dried fruit.

That spring, Danny, who was majoring in film, asked me to play a role in the 16-millimeter movie he was making, and I agreed. The film was about a student who was late for class, and Danny wanted to shoot it in Eastwoods Park—I think because it looked a little like the London park where David Hemmings had seen the murder in *Blow-Up*, which had opened the week before.

On the morning of the shoot, I took so much meth that when I glanced at my watch, the numbers were swimming in and out of focus. So I threw the script away and told Danny I was going to improvise. We shot a few scenes at his apartment and then went to Eastwoods Park. While I was doing a scene, Dee showed up. I had never told her I was back in Austin, and taken care not to run into her. She was angry at first, so I told her that she could stick around, and I'd talk to her when we were finished shooting.

But when I finished a scene, I looked up and saw she was crying. "Why are you doing that?" I asked her.

All she said was, "You're not yourself anymore." Then she left.

When the shoot was finally over, we went over to Danny's apartment, and I smoked some grass to try to cool out. But of course the grass on top of the meth made me paranoid, and things got a little confused. Danny said maybe it was time to head for San Francisco. I kept saying I was only interested in going to New York. Suddenly he was frowning at me and asking, "What are you, an anti-Semite?"

"Not at all," I said.

At that moment, I heard a police car radio crackle outside, and when I looked out the window, I saw a black-and-white gliding soundlessly to a stop in front of Danny's apartment.

Instantly, I was full of profound fear and, without another word, turned and ran out the back door, leaving Danny sitting there alone. I ran through his backyard and climbed the fence, not really knowing why, except I was sure there was going to be a bust of some sort. Then I ran across a wooden bridge over Waller Creek into Eastwoods Park.

It was a warm day, and now the park was covered with dozens of couples sunbathing on blankets, who stared curiously at me as I walked rapidly toward the trees at the north end of the park. I was already telling myself I had been foolish when I heard the rumble of police motorcycles behind me, driving up each side of the park and surrounding me. Now the sunbathers were staring at me with pity. A police cruiser reached the top of the park at the same time I did, and a cop wearing big mirrored sunglasses got out and motioned me over.

I said, "What's the trouble?"

"You stole that motorcycle, didn't you?"

I almost fainted with relief—it wasn't a bust! Somebody had stolen a motorcycle, and the cops had taken me for the perp. "You got the wrong guy," I said, shaking my head.

But the cop told me to turn around, put my hands behind my back, and handcuffed me.

Then other cops took me to the garage where the stolen motorcycle had been left—behind the house whose backyard I had crossed, of course—and kept me there while they fingerprinted it. They slapped me around a little and told me, "You might as well confess, 'cause when we get your prints, you're gon' be charged."

"With what?" I asked.

"Stealing that motorcycle, resisting arrest, vagrancy, and we'll think up a few more things later on."

Then they took me down to headquarters and threw me in a cell. I lay down on the metal sheet of my bunk—there was no mattress—and after a while, my cellmate woke up and asked me what I was in for. I told him I didn't know yet.

I slept for a couple of hours, and the cops finally let me out late that night without ever charging me. Gabe (who knew the owner of the motorcycle of course) told me the guy had stolen his own bike to get the insurance settlement and was really relieved that I had gotten caught, not him. My paranoia was so bad I was getting busted for things I hadn't even done.

When I looked at the rushes several days later, I saw Dee had been right; I looked dreadful, my eyes dead, my face closed like a fist, just like it had in my Zundy yearbook photo.

Not that I didn't have some good times that spring. I started hanging out with John and Julia. One day, there was a big thunderstorm, and it rained for hours. That night, we got stoned and went to Barton Springs, climbed the fence, and went skinny-dipping. The full moon broke out of the clouds, and the water was warm with rain. The guard knew we were there, and so were several other people, and he didn't do a thing about it.

On a rainy day not long after that, I walked past the little hobbit house where Jody and I had lived and then wandered into Eastwoods Park. A crowd of longhairs were there, celebrating Eeyore's birthday. Some wore big papier-mâché heads, and others were blowing bubbles and passing out Kool-Aid and joints to everyone. They looked and acted just like the "hippies" of Haight-Ashbury who had recently appeared on the cover of *Ramparts*. Then, as I watched from a safe distance, some frat guys appeared and joined the party. They were drinking beer and soon got rowdy, knocking down Eeyore and Pooh and rolling them and their papier-mâché heads through the mud. When the cops arrived, they arrested the hippies and let the frat guys go.

It was time to get out of town, as Gabe had said once, when we'd been staying with Lutz in Norman.

I walked back to my apartment on Red River Street and looked through the huge pile of typed-up pages that were lying on the blue acrylic carpet. I had begun by writing down the simple facts about Jody and the past, but the closer I got to the present, the more unintelligible the pages became. And there were some sentences I could not remember writing at all.

The rush of meth got shorter and shorter, and only a few minutes after a hit, I started coming down. Then I slept without dreaming. I was subjecting myself to terrible pain, and I was not getting more dangerous. Suddenly, I realized I was learning nothing from all this. I was punishing myself for losing Jody by destroying my mind, and I had to stop taking meth. But I was no longer sure that I could.

One by one, I picked up the pages and threw them into the wastebasket. Then I went into the bathroom and forced myself to stare at my reflection in the mirror, looking for signs of neurological damage.

The dry spell came. Gabe's one hundred-gram bottle had, unbelievably, run out. But we had enough left for one more run, and he had a plan. Tommy, who worked for the Thirteenth Floor Elevators, had gotten busted, pleaded insanity, and was now at the Austin State Hospital. There was a rumor that, just before this, he had stashed several grams of meth and some money in a safe-deposit box.

Gabe and I went to see him at the state hospital, which was in the middle of a north Austin suburb called Hyde Park. My grandfather's used car lot, where I had spent much of my early childhood, had been only a couple of blocks away. I remembered how he had told me that sometimes lunatics came running down the street, trying to escape. Somehow Tommy had gotten us on the list of relatives who were allowed to visit him, and we were let in through the gate. It was a cloudy spring day, and thunderstorms were predicted.

Tommy met us by the gate and said, "Let's go to lunch."

Then he took us to "the Sub," which was short for "the Submarine," a big modern dining hall with steel shutters. There we ate Salisbury steak and mashed potatoes, the same institutional food I had eaten at Seaton Hospital when I had worked there. Some of the diners were throwing their food and crying out. There also was a strange fecal smell that I decided to ignore.

"I won't be here much longer," Tommy said. "Just a couple of months, and then they'll let me go home."

Later, we walked outside and stood by the chain-link fence. Gabe went into his pitch: Tommy would give him the contents of the safe-deposit box, and Gabe would give him a percentage of the profits.

I knew from the beginning it wasn't going to work. I had also identified the smell here. It *was* fecal matter mingled with stale fish, dead brain cells, electricity, and crystal meth—the smell of insanity. I could smell it on myself and was afraid they would never let me out.

Standing by the chain-link fence while Gabe and Tommy talked, I watched the traffic going by on North Lamar. Big yellowish cumulous clouds drifted overhead, showing no concern at all for our sufferings down here on earth.

That night I finished the last of my meth at the end of a three-day run. But when Gabe came over, he had a little left, so we shot it up, got the rush, and smoked some hash, and everything changed. Once again, we were safe for a few hours. A green crumb of hash fell off the table, and I saw it as a tiny frog that stared back at me with emerald eyes. No matter where I went, that frog was looking at me, and when I tried to pick it up, it jumped away. I knew the frog was a toxic hallucination of meth and that, most likely, I would not remember it tomorrow.

Gabe said, "I know some people who've still got meth. But they've moved out to the Serpentarium."

The Serpentarium was a snake house on the other side of Lake Travis, which had closed down—and then been rented by some meth freaks who wanted to get away from the Austin cops. It was more than sixty miles out there and back, and Gabe said his motorcycle didn't have enough gas to make it.

"You think we've got to go there?"

"I think so," he said.

"Then we have to take my car."

"That's what I'm saying."

When we walked outside, the night was full of hallucinations. Pachucos were sitting in every parked car, their switchblade knives pointed directly at my heart. I was higher than I had ever been in my life, but I felt no fear, not even when a pickup truck—driven by narcotics detective Harvey Gann, Gabe told me—pulled in behind the Austin-Healey and started following us. But he turned back just as we passed the bright green neon sombrero of El Mat on Guadalupe Street, big as a flying saucer.

Relief flooded through me, and I drove faster. As we left town on Bull Creek, I began to see more hallucinations, and the faster I drove, the more convincing they became. The limestone beds of the road cuts turned into layers of Egyptian hieroglyphics and statuary. Crossing a low-water bridge, I drove up onto a plain where cactus and insect life predominated, going faster and faster. Now the pavement rolled like a grindstone beneath my car, and microscopic cockroaches were jumping through the headlights and disappearing into the night.

I slept for an endless time without dreaming, and when I woke, I was back in my apartment; the sheets were soaked. Looking out the window, I saw dry, heatless sunlight flooding the street.

I had a dim memory of reaching the Serpentarium. The walls of the concrete rooms had still been covered with faded murals of snakes. One of the meth freaks had told me I could have a hit if I let him shoot me up. His face had been white and smooth, and he told me he had just shed his skin. That was all I could remember.

But my mind was still working at incredible speed. As I looked around the room, there were shadows everywhere. But when I looked closer, they filled in with thoughts and faces. Gabe would know how to get over this. I dressed slowly and carefully, trying to avoid the concentric shells of reflections that surrounded my body. Then I drove over to Gabe's and knocked on the door.

After a long time, Kitty opened it.

"Gabe's been busted," she said.

"When?" I asked her.

"This morning."

"Can you tell me about it?"

"This guy we knew came over to buy some grass. When Gabe gave it to him, he showed his badge and said, 'Can I pay you in gold?' Then he put handcuffs on Gabe and told him he was under arrest."

She started to close the door.

"Where's Gabe now?" I asked her.

"In the city jail," Kitty said.

On the way home, I stopped at a 7-Eleven for cigarettes. I felt that the counterman could *see right through me* and also knew what he was thinking about me: *This guy is a meth freak.*

My mouth filled with saliva, and the corner began to jerk uncontrollably.

Back at my apartment, I lay down on my mattress but was unable to sleep or think clearly. Finally I wandered out into the garage.

There was an old Mason jar of clear green glass full of kerosene, which had sat on the shelf for so long it had settled into two layers. The top layer was clear, and the one beneath was a dense, red fluid. Between them was a thin, reflective surface, like a floating mirror. *This is my mind*, I thought. The reflective layer was a one-way mirror of pain and failure, floating between me and the outside world. I could not see out, but anyone could see right into my soul. My mind was split away from my body again, and this time the split would last forever.

Amphetamine psychosis—I had finally taken the trip from which there was no coming down.

JOURNEY TO THE WEST

19

I N J UNE 1967, Danny Abrams and I finally took the Journey to the
West, as we had long promised ourselves we would. The hippies were
supposed to be creating a utopia out there in San Francisco. I didn't
really believe it was going to work, but thought I might be able to find
a girl there. They said it was going to be the Summer of Love.

After Gabe was busted, I was no longer able to get meth and had
finally quit. As before, the cure was sleep—I slept for a week, until my
tic and my tremor disappeared. When I couldn't sleep, I exercised until
I was exhausted. I saw nobody, seldom left my apartment, and when
hunger finally drove me out, I drank milkshakes.

My sufferings had not made me stronger or more dangerous—they
had almost destroyed my mind. I could never take meth again. For that
matter, I could never again take drugs of any kind. The last few days
of taking meth I had gotten too close to the edge and been unable to
stop seeing what was waiting for me down there—insanity.

Sometimes I still felt the hint of a split between mind and body,
and terrifying paranoia. Sometimes I still thought I smelled of
schizophrenia. Mirrors were still dangerous to me, and I had to be

careful to look normal at all times. But as long as I got enough sleep, I thought I was going to be all right.

On the other hand, Austin was getting too dangerous for me. The cops followed me everywhere, and this was not just paranoia, but the result of the fact that I drove a conspicuous car. Sooner or later I would get busted; evidence would be planted on me; and after that, there were only two possibilities.

One was prison—Joe was now doing two years in Huntsville— which I knew I couldn't handle. The other was an insanity plea, which meant I would be sent to the state hospital and given shock treatments until my mind was destroyed.

But Larry had written and said things were a lot cooler in San Francisco, so Danny and I had decided to head out there in the Austin-Healey. He had gone back to Dallas for a few days, and I was driving home to Nortex. Danny would come there on a bus, and we would leave for San Francisco.

That morning, I put a suitcase full of clothes, my sleeping bag, my typewriter, and two books I had long promised myself I would read— Hesse's *Journey to the East* and Kierkegaard's *The Sickness Unto Death*—in the trunk of my car. I also took several of my favorite comic books, including the first "Fantastic Four," the first "Zap Comix," by R. Crumb, and "Jepe Basura" or Hippy Garbage, a Mexican comic by Jose G. Cruz. Then I dropped the key in the mailbox and drove out of Austin on North Lamar.

Of course a police car fell in behind the Austin-Healey and followed me all the way out of town.

When it finally turned around at the city limits, I decided I would say goodbye to John and Julie, who were now living out at Lake Travis. So I turned off on the Comanche Pass road; drove out to Lake Travis; and then headed down a side road, past Hippy Hole, to their cabin.

John was repairing cars now, and the yard was full of Volkswagens in various stages of disrepair. Their cabin was empty, and I was looking in the refrigerator for a beer when Julie came in, wearing a black nylon bathing suit. She looked good—tall, blonde-haired, and sleepy-eyed. I had always liked her.

"John's not here," she told me. "You want to go for a swim?"

I got my bathing suit out of my car and followed her down past their garden, through the cedars to the shore of the lake. There I swam for fifteen minutes and lay on the rocks in the sun to dry. Julie offered me a joint, which I refused and then told her I was on my way to San Francisco.

She and John had just been out there the month before. "Be sure to go to the Muir Woods," she said. "Those big old redwoods were the best part for me."

Julie asked me why I was going, and I said I hoped to find a girl out there.

"You haven't been the same since you lost that girl," she said. "What was her name?"

"Jody," I said. "She was the girl for me."

"Yeah, I thought so too."

"Trouble was, she didn't think I was the guy for her. Now it seems like I can't get it together until I find the right girl—and I can't find the right girl until I get it together."

This was something I often told people then. Some laughed, but Julie nodded seriously, and I felt she was on my side.

"If you can't find the right girl out there," she said, "just come back to the lake. Problems don't last long out here."

I looked around at the lake—the limestone cliffs, the cedars, the ink-blue water. Here, John and Julie had found happiness. They knew I had a problem with meth but were too polite to mention it. They were perfect hippies, and I wanted to be just like them.

I drove away, feeling healthy, normal, and slightly sunburned.

At the top of Comanche Pass there were two ways to go. To the east was the highway home. To the south were the road to the dam and the Serpentarium.

I was looking for a road map when I found the last of my crystal meth, which I had hidden and forgotten under the dashboard. Unfolding the square of tinfoil, I licked off the meth, smelling its mineral stink, and told myself one more taste wouldn't hurt me.

Then I drove on to Nortex. As I went through Lampasas, the meth came on, and a line of thunderheads rose in the west. At Mingus, a highway patrol car fell in behind me and followed me almost all the way to Graham. Dusk fell as I drove through Archer City and up onto the high plains, where the ground turned to red clay. I was filled with dreams of power, but the moment I saw the red lights of the broadcast towers in Nortex, I began to come down. Passing the Speedrome and the state hospital, I finally turned into the driveway of my home as lightning flashed to the west.

My father was playing the piano and had of course been drinking. "Hello, Sonny," he said. "I've been waiting for you."

Danny woke me the next morning when he called and told me he would be in Nortex on the afternoon bus. My brother had gone to school, my mother had gone to work, and my father was playing the piano in the front room.

Nortex seemed even more hopeless than it had the year before. There was an article in the paper about a local man who had found a joint in his son's shirt pocket when he took it to the cleaners, so he had shot his son in his head while he was sleeping. "Better he die by my own hand than live forever as a drug addict," the man had told the judge, who had given him a suspended sentence.

My father went on playing the piano, the air conditioner roared all day long, and the grass was already dead. When my mother came home, I talked to her for a while. She was now working as a secretary at the state hospital and had started reading Freud.

"I never knew toilet training was so important," she said. "Now I'm sorry I made you and your brother learn how to do your business so early. Maybe that's why you've both had so many problems."

"Don't blame yourself, Mom," I said, smiling. "It's not your fault."

"You're not taking drugs, are you?"

"Not anymore."

"Just promise me you'll tell your brother he shouldn't take drugs."

I promised her that I would.

My brother, Ray, came home, his blond hair now as long as a girl's. He had come in last night while I pretended to sleep, and we hadn't spoken. Now he told me his rock group was the most popular in town—he played the saxophone and the flute and sang lead vocals, and they covered a lot of songs by the group Chicago.

Danny called me from the bus station at five o'clock and said he had gotten in, so my brother and I drove down and picked him up. He had brought an expensive 35 mm Bolex camera—he pronounced it as *Bo Lex*—and several cans of film he had stolen from the film department. He had also grown a thick black Zapata moustache. I wasn't sure either of these were good choices.

"Who cares if I stole the film?" Danny said. "We're never going back to Austin anyway."

We ate supper at my house, watching Walter Cronkite on television. Then Danny and my brother and I went to the old Bar-L Drive-In, where we sat in the car and drank Red Draws, beer mixed with tomato juice. My brother produced a joint and asked us if we wanted to get high.

"I'll take some of that action," Danny said.

"I don't take drugs anymore," I said. "And you shouldn't either— not even grass, and especially not methedrine. They'll destroy your mind."

"Man," Ray said, "I can't believe you're telling me that. I've been smoking grass for a year now. It helps me play better, and every girl in town is following me around. Thing I want to do now is get some acid."

"Don't take acid."

"Isn't that what you're going to San Francisco for?"

"No," I said. "I'm going to San Francisco to get my shit together."

They laughed and it sounded dubious, even to me.

Danny and I left the next morning at sunrise. My brother and my mother were still asleep. My father, who had stayed up all night practicing Schumann's *Kinderszenen*, embraced me before we left. I felt the bristles of his beard and smelled the yeasty smell of alcohol on his breath.

"I'm afraid you'll never come back," he whispered to me.

"Please try to stop drinking, Dad," I said.

"Just be careful of Lutz," my father told me, repeating something he had first said years ago. "He's a Hebrew, and they'll always try to ruin a Gentile if they can."

But once Danny and I were driving across the Panhandle, we started having the greatest conversations we'd ever had. We talked of Gabe, who had taken the Journey years before we had and wondered how he was doing in Huntsville.

"If he was with us he would wish us well," Danny said. "Just keep driving, and we'll absorb the lessons of the road."

Then he read me passages from Hermann Hesse's *Journey to the East*, his favorite book. Hesse had belonged to something called the League for Spiritual Discovery, which had traveled around Europe seeking enlightenment in the twenties. The initials of this group, as Danny pointed out, were LSD, which Sandoz was making back then—therefore, Hesse must have been taking acid.

"But we're not headed for the East," I said. "We're headed west."

"In America, we take the Journey to the West."

He told me the Journey had begun in childhood. Our best games then had been cowboy games, which we had played in the summer—games that were so good they went on long after dinner and into the night. When our parents finally called us in, we always promised ourselves we would continue them tomorrow but never did. Now we were being given a chance to play them forever.

We were also headed for the old frontier, the land of endless possibility, where our cowboy games had come from in the form of movies starring Gene Autry and John Wayne—some of them directed by the great John Ford. In San Francisco, we would find what we had always been looking for, the secret of life. Maybe I would fall in love and again learn how to play roles for fun, as I had when I'd first entered the drama department. This had become impossible for me since I had freaked out on meth and gotten paranoid. The only role I could play now was that of a normal guy, so I wouldn't get busted. Maybe in San Francisco I could stop worrying about this.

Danny and I drove beyond Albuquerque that day. When the sun was going down, we bought steaks and cooked them under a bridge, as Kerouac had done when he had hitchhiked back from California in *The Dharma Bums*. Then we lay down in our sleeping bags on the sand of the dry riverbed. I found it difficult to sleep and could hardly wait until tomorrow, when the Journey would begin again.

At first light, we got up and drove on though the Malpais, the lava beds. Beyond the town of Grants, the landscape turned to pink and gray rock, and now we began to see others who were on the Journey. Near Gallup, we passed a bearded hippy with his thumb stuck out. Danny wanted to pick him up. "He seems to know what he's looking for," Danny said. "Maybe he could give us some guidance."

"There's no room," I told him. The Austin-Healey had a small backseat, and I needed no guidance.

We drove on that day through the Painted Desert of Arizona, where I had come with my father in the fifties when he was looking for oil. In the afternoon, we passed the Navajo Motel, where my father and I had stayed, and ahead we saw the volcanic cone of Humphrey's Peak, near Flagstaff. Here Danny shot footage of old billboards and abandoned gas stations, which he said would someday be part of his great cinema verité film about the journey of our generation. (Maybe he was right; parts of the movie *Easy Rider* were later shot here.)

I wanted to spend the night at the Little Colorado Canyon overlook. Just before the turnoff at Flagstaff, we saw another hitchhiker wearing a combat jacket. "You have to pick this guy up," Danny said, and this time I did.

He was a Vietnam vet. "Thanks," he said when he got in the backseat. "Just got back from 'Nam. Got my discharge at the Oakland Army Terminal. Spent three days in the Haight trying to get fucked.

Started hitchhiking back to Pennsylvania. Spent last night in a ditch. Dreamed some fucking zip was trying to crawl down my neck. Now I'm headed back to the Haight, and this time I'm going to get properly fucked."

"We'll take you all the way," Danny said.

We reached the Little Colorado Canyon overlook at dusk. There were some German tourists there in a microbus. Danny shot footage of the vet talking to the Germans, who were worried about the future of our country. "Yeah, I killed people in Vietnam," I heard him say, "maybe even babies. I don't know."

The Germans seemed impressed—maybe they were just frightened.

I sat on the edge of the canyon, staring down into an abyss of black rock. I had always enjoyed heights. Crows hovered above the infinite depths.

The vet sat down next to me. "Long way down," he said.

"Yeah."

"I know; you want to jump. I had the same thought every time I was in a helicopter in 'Nam. It wouldn't be a bad way to go. You'd have a hard-on all the way down."

I wondered why I was destined to meet these people. "Leave me alone," I said.

He got up and walked away. I slept on the rocks in my sleeping bag that night. In the morning, the Germans were gone, and the vet had gone with them, taking the Bolex.

"No blame," Danny said. "Maybe we'll meet in him San Francisco. He is the first prophet of our destiny."

"I never want to see that guy again."

The last day of the Journey was the best. We drove on across the Mojave and up through the central valley of California, past Bakersfield and Fresno. The hills were covered with yellow grass, and on the radio, we heard "A Day In the Life," a great new song by the Beatles, which proved that these were historic times.

We passed through Oakland as night fell and crossed the Bay Bridge. I found the house on Turk Street where Larry and Karen lived and rang the bell. Larry threw open the door with theatrical suddenness, wearing a green air force parka and love beads, his red hair as long as Prince Valiant's. His and Karen's faces were smooth, and their eyes were dilated, big and black as buttons, and they seemed to *look right through me*. I was paranoid again.

20

ALL NIGHT WE argued. They had dropped acid before we came, and Larry kept insisting, "If you just take enough acid, you see the clear white light. Then you lose your paranoia forever, and you'll never get busted."

Paranoia—it was just a word to them, but to me it was a horrible reality, the endless fear I would face if I ever took drugs again.

"I think they're right," Danny said. "Let's trip."

Still I refused, and when Larry offered me a chance to go in on this big mescaline deal he was setting up, I told him I wasn't interested. Larry and Karen were terribly disappointed in me. Finally, Danny and I slept on the futons on the floor by the bay window, and they slept in their bed, which was separated by a low partition from the rest of the room.

The next morning, we drove across the Golden Gate Bridge and out to Marin County, so Larry could show us the mescaline laboratory. He and Karen rode in his Volkswagen, and Danny and I followed in the Austin-Healey.

The lab was in a rented suburban house. There we met Angel, a dude from Galveston who claimed to be a chemist. His wife Nova was eight months pregnant. In the bathtub, fifty pounds of peyote buttons were cooking down to green soup, and the kitchen was full of laboratory glassware. All this could be seen through the windows, and the landlady had a key. "Yeah, she was snooping around here the other day," Angel told me. When I asked him what he had done, he laughed a big laugh—haw, haw, haw—and said, "Tol' her to get fucked."

Then Angel handed me a joint, the remedy for all paranoia. By now, mine was coming in waves. Pretending to take a toke, I looked out the window. Parked just down the block was a Pacific Bell panel truck—the favorite vehicle of narcs on stakeout.

"I've got to get out of here," I whispered to Danny.

So we drove back across the Golden Gate to the house on Turk Street, and almost the moment we stepped into the apartment the phone rang.

"We got busted," Larry said. "Right after you left. This is my phone call. Clean out the apartment and be at the Marin County courthouse at noon tomorrow."

I had never played the role of the guy who cleaned out the apartment but found I could perform it easily. Danny and I then drove to the bus station, stashed the dope in a locker, and slept that night on Farallon Beach.

The next morning, we drove to the Marin County courthouse for the arraignment. But to my surprise, the judge turned them all loose and didn't even confiscate their cars or have the apartment searched.

"I was right, wasn't I?" Larry said. "Drop enough acid, you lose your paranoia, and nothing bad can ever happen to you again."

I had lost my paranoia, but for another reason: I had learned I was no fool—the bust had finally come, but I had seen it coming and gotten the hell out of there just before the cops arrived. I was feeling better about myself than I had for a year.

At first I liked the house on Turk Street—a big old white wooden preearthquake Victorian house, ten blocks from the Haight and one block up from Fillmore Street, which ran through the heart of the black ghetto. It had bay windows and corner turrets, and all sorts of people lived here—old beatniks, merchant seamen, and a married couple who were dancers for the San Francisco ballet. On the top floor lived beautiful Dolores, who was an artist for the Rip Off Press. In the side yard was a mossy garden with oak trees and a green glass reflecting globe on a pedestal. Just down the hill was the First African Baptist church. It seemed to me that I could fit in here.

Karen decided the bust had been a good thing, and it was time we all got healthy. So we went on the macrobiotic diet, which was based on the Taoist principles of the great polarities of the universe, yin and yang. Yin was the female principle of darkness, brown rice, and the Beatles. Yang was the male principle of light, red meat, and the Rolling Stones. The aim was to get as yin as possible. We ate only brown rice and a few dried vegetables. Most Americans were yang from eating too many hamburgers. This was the basic cause of the Vietnam War.

She made an altar in the kitchen with a little gold Buddha, and we ate with chopsticks from a common bowl. Every bite had to be chewed twenty times to get the full food energy—if you didn't do this, there was some danger of starving. Karen closed her eyes while she chewed and wore a headband with a green stone in the center of her forehead—chrysacolla, which was recommended by Edgar Cayce to increase your psychic powers.

For the first time, I felt the righteous power of natural food, which some woman would always be discovering for the rest of my life. Danny was unhappy with this diet, but as I pointed out, it had one great advantage—it cost almost nothing.

Larry took us to an army-navy store in the Tenderloin, where I bought a green wool Pendleton shirt and a gray army combat jacket, the uniform of many hippies. I also bought a canvas army map case with a shoulder strap and put my notebook into it. My hair was still too short, but it would grow.

I felt so good about myself that I even let Larry talk me into taking acid. "You were the first guy in Austin who was into peyote and *The Hobbit*," he said. "We need your ideas." He proposed we all go up to Mount Tam, drop acid together, and get some answers.

After all, I told myself, acid wasn't like meth—I was spiritually advanced and could handle it.

So on a Sunday morning, we all got into Larry's Volkswagen, and he drove across the Golden Gate to Mount Tam. Under a sky the color of ice, we hiked up a trail through the Muir Woods. As Julie had told me, the redwoods were impressive. At the top of the trail, we crossed a meadow, entered a high forest, and lay down in the center of a crater that a redwood had torn out of the earth when it fell. There we dropped the acid, closed our eyes, and waited for it to take effect.

After a while, I thought I could hear something like electronic music. Then I got up and told Larry I was going for a walk.

"Go ahead," he said, his eyes still closed.

I left the others, walked back down the path for a while, and sat on a redwood stump. The radians of cracks and the circles of growth rings began spreading out until they were the only things I could see. Suddenly, a sort of electric shock went through me and knocked me off the stump.

Holy shit, I thought. *That was the clear white light*. It had been green instead of white, but no matter.

I walked on to the meadow, where the fog was clearing. A score of deer ran out across the meadow and into the trees. I thought of *Bambi* and cried a little. The ghostly shapes of redwoods covered the slope below, fading into the fog like the Zen painting *Rivers and Mountains Without End*. Snot ran from my nose, and I was full of acid joy.

Soon my friends appeared out of the woods and joined me. But Danny seemed to feel ill. His eyes were rolling, and saliva ran down his chin. "Look down there, into the fog," I said. "Can't you see those big redwood trees in the valley below us?"

"No, I'm seeing swords and stars," he said, "big De *Mo* lays."

There was something odd about the way he said this, but I tried to ignore it.

"I feel a little strange myself," Larry said. "I think this acid's got a lot of meth in it."

Meth! The moment he said this, I began to think we had been poisoned. Then Danny told us his stomach was upset.

"I'm sick," he complained in a childish voice, his face pale. I decided he was in for a bad trip. Larry and Karen walked away, while I tried to talk him out of it. But Danny kept insisting, "*You're* the one who's having a bad trip."

"I am *not* having a bad trip," I said firmly.

"You're playing a role, like your drama friends here," he continued. "You've been doing it ever since you were master councilor of the order of De *Mo* Lay."

"That was a long time ago," I told him. "And stop talking like that."

"You're always looking for love. And who but an actor would accept the love of total strangers?"

"They're not total strangers," I insisted. "They are my friends."

Larry and Karen were standing a few feet away. "What are they talking about?" she asked him.

"I think he's saying Will is a ho *mo* sexual," Larry said.

Concentric shells of paranoia were closing in around me—memories of every lie I had ever told, every role I had ever played, every time I had been false or dishonest, even every article of clothing I had ever worn that was faintly wrong for me. I tried to get Danny to look at the redwoods appearing and disappearing in the fog below us, but he would not.

We stayed up there on the top of Mount Tam for a couple of hours and finally walked back down through the Muir Woods as night fell. Then I drove Larry's Volkswagen back to San Francisco. Danny had another bad moment after we had crossed the Golden Gate Bridge and called out from the depths of his bad trip, "Stop the car—I need to be sick ... for a few things." I pulled over to the curb. He opened the door of the Volkswagen and vomited onto the street.

Finally we reached the house on Turk Street. There we fell into an uneasy sleep, Danny and I lying on our futons, Larry and Karen on their bed behind the partition. Once during the night, I woke up and thought I saw Danny standing over me naked, his penis almost hidden in the curls of his black pubic hair.

When I got up the next morning, Danny was gone. But when Larry appeared, he told me, "Your friend Lutz tried to show Karen his prick last night."

"Don't call him Lutz," I said. "He doesn't want to be called that anymore. What's the big problem? I've always known Danny was a flasher, and I thought you did too. He's harmless."

But Larry said, "I refuse to let him stay in this apartment anymore."

When Danny returned, I told him that Larry and Karen wanted him to leave.

"Fine," he said proudly. "I have my own friends here in San Francisco—I'm sorry you won't get to meet them. They work for the Rip Off Press and are *real* artists."

So Danny packed his bag and left. He was a flasher—and instead of talking about it, he always hinted that I was the one who had sexual problems. I had problems, but they weren't sexual, and I was tired of his hints. Also, this was the second time in a month I had broken my promise to myself and taken drugs, and somehow Danny was responsible. Anyway, he had a place to go, and I didn't.

Larry and Karen and I ate a bowl of rice for dinner and went to bed early. But that night I woke on my futon and heard Larry and Karen making love on the bed behind the partition. The next day, I moved into the big walk-in closet across the hall.

At first the closet was not so bad; it was six feet by four, with a naked electric bulb hanging from the ceiling. I put my sleeping bag on the floor, along with my books and my typewriter. In the morning, I ate a bowl of brown rice with Larry and Karen and then set out to explore the Haight. The Austin-Healey wouldn't start—it often had electrical problems—so I left it parked in front of the house on Turk Street and took public transportation, bus and cable car.

I had hoped to meet up with Sandra, the innocent Austin girl who had come out here a month or so earlier, but Larry told me she was now making fuck movies for the Sexual Freedom League. In Golden Gate Park, I met some hippy girls, but they distrusted me—my hair was still short, and they seemed to think I was a narc. Most of them were barefoot anyway, and their feet were dirty.

I soon learned that the Haight was a fabulous temporary society, ruled by behavioral codes based on the bipolar ethics of drugs and music. Jefferson Airplane (who took acid) were good. Quicksilver Messenger Service (who were said to take meth) were bad. Nobody had a last name or a past, and everyone communicated by code phrases—*being yourself, doing your own thing, getting your head together,* and *going through changes.*

In the beginning, these codes were easy for me to understand. But I could never quite understand *going through changes,* and the longer I stayed, the more mysterious these *changes* became. Finally they began to mean something I could not comprehend.

Spirituality was a constant concern. Karen was always telling me about Edgar Cayce, and there was perpetual talk about reincarnation, flying saucers, and the lost continent of Atlantis, or Mu. All of this, of course, I had heard from my father years before. The old spiritual legends were coming back, and several people told me that the hippies were the next step in human evolution, as predicted in *Childhood's End.* Everyone was interested in everything—the *I Ching, Stranger in a Strange Land,* and *The Lord of the Rings*—but nobody could *do* anything except *talk* about things, and decisions were bad form. These people had lost touch with reality.

Feeling that I needed to see more of the country, I decided to go to Monterey for the Pop Festival. My friend Shan was the technical director of a summer theater near there and told me I could stay at his apartment.

Larry gave me a ride to South San Francisco, and I hitchhiked the rest of the way, wearing my old cowboy boots and carrying in my map case a can of chili, my Zap Comix, my loafers, and a spare pair of jockey shorts. The coastal range was emerald green, like an expensive golf course. Pelicans soared like pterodactyls through the fog over the prehistoric beaches of Big Sur. I was finally doing the Dharma Bums thing, and it felt great.

Shan had once dated Jody at the University of Texas, but I didn't think he had slept with her. He had also bossed my set-building crew and taught me carpentry. Shan could *do* many things—could build and paint scenery, knew about plumbing, and could even install a toilet. We went to a restaurant for a hamburger, which made me a little sick but filled me with energy. Then he took me to the theater, where I met the carpenters, who were all good guys. Before I went to sleep on the couch that night, Shan hinted that I might be able to come down there and work as a stage carpenter myself.

We went out for breakfast the next morning, and then Shan had to go to the theater for the matinee. I spent a pleasant day in his apartment, writing in my notebook. The kitchen had a red tile floor and casement windows that looked out on yellow hills. I managed to set down a few good paragraphs about the Haight before I lay down on the couch and slept.

I woke when Juan entered. Juan was a big blond guy with a full Mr. Natural beard. Shan had said to leave the door unlocked, and I was sure that Juan was a friend because he was so easy. After we introduced ourselves to each other, Juan took a shower and changed his clothes. Then he picked up the phone and said, "I'm going to make a couple of calls—Shan won't mind."

I changed into my loafers because my feet hurt, left my cowboy boots under the bed, and headed for the theater. As I left, I thought I heard Juan talking to an international operator in Paris, which seemed a little strange. But it had to be all right because this was the Summer of Love, and everyone in utopian California took everyone else at his or her word.

When the show was over, I met Shan in the parking lot and told him that Juan had stopped by.

Shan's face went expressionless. "Juan?" he asked me. "What did he do?"

"Nothing," I said. "He just made a few calls."

"We'd better go home," Shan said.

On our way there, he told me that Juan was a notorious local character with powerful friends, and I shouldn't have let him in. When we got to Shan's place, the door was open, the lights were on, and Juan was gone. So were Shan's guitar, most of his power tools, a roll of duct tape, and my cowboy boots. Shan called the cops.

The cops explained that Juan had been on acid and had stolen goods from several local people before he had started over the hill to the house of his old friends, the sisters Joan and Mimi Baez. On the way, he had lost control of his Land Rover, gone off the road, and rolled hundreds of feet down to the floor of the canyon, landing in the organic garden of someone who lived at the bottom. But by a miracle, Juan had survived. Now he was recovering at the Baez house and was contrite—called and offered to give everything back if charges were not pressed.

Shan told me it was time for me to return to San Francisco, and I realized I had lost my carpentry job.

"Not until I get my boots," I insisted.

The next morning, before I hitchhiked back to San Francisco, Shan took me over to the beautiful glass and redwood house, which was on a cliff overlooking the sea, surrounded by impressive trees. The sisters Baez were reluctant to let us through the gate but finally did. Shan was told to stop in the driveway. They stared down contemptuously from the deck, and everybody was nervous—it felt like a drug deal.

Finally their go-between brought my cowboy boots, which Juan for some reason had wrapped in gray duct tape. This depressed me so much I almost started crying. I'd had those boots forever—since before I'd met Jody. For the first time since I had been in California, I realized who I really was here—just another hippy, not an artist, just one of those people who had no money and could do nothing. It didn't feel good.

21

THE SUMMER OF Love wore on. Fog hid the sun for days at a time. Karen made God's Eyes, crosses of sticks woven with colored yarn. I was still looking for love, and there was one girl in the house who was perfect for me—Dolores, who wore velvet dresses and high-topped black boots and rolled her own macrobiotic tortillas.

One night we all went to see Janis Joplin at the Matrix. She had come a long way since the night I had met her, six years before, at Scottish Rite Dormitory in Austin. Of course I had heard about her after that, singing folksongs at Threadgills, becoming popular, finally coming out here to San Francisco and starting a group called Big Brother and the Holding Company. Now she had become a great blues artist, and she sang a song, written by her friend Powell St. John, that I had been hearing on the radio ever since I'd gotten to San Francisco:

> A man and a woman
> Need each other now, baby,
> To find their way in this world
> I need you, baby,
> Like a fish needs the sea.

Don't take your sweet, sweet love from me.

Janis had transformed herself into the greatest performer I had ever seen. This was the kind of love I needed—not flower power love or hobbit love, but the love of a real woman who had to go on loving or die.

We walked back from the Matrix to the house on Turk Street, and that night, Dolores asked me if I would like to stop at her room for ginseng tea.

Everything was perfectly arranged in the corner turret, her drawing table, fans of coral, and prisms hanging on threads in the window. On her bedside table was *The Love Book*, by Lenore Kandel.

Dolores had high hopes for the Haight. It was a beautiful place, where we were going to generate enough love energy to change the world.

I admitted that I had some problems with it. "Nobody here can *do* anything," I said, "except for the musicians. I mean, nothing practical."

"The Diggers give food to the poor," she said. "We're building a new society here, and everybody has to come up with his own way of contributing. I should think that would be easy for you."

So I told her a little about my troubles, and something about the way she listened made me think she understood. But the more I tried to explain them, the more complicated the subject became. In the end, all I could say was, "I have to make a move of some sort"—not sure if I was talking about my life or some move that I had to make right now, in this room.

"Then why not consult the *I Ching*?" Dolores asked me.

The *I Ching* was the bible of the acid gospel—the ancient Chinese *Classic of Changes* that foretold the future. It was a book I both believed and disbelieved in; like astrology, it always seemed to tell the truth, or at least part of it. I didn't want Dolores to see my paranoia, so I decided to go ahead and try it. She had the real Chinese coins, the yarrow stalks. As I threw the coins, the candle, for some reason, began to sputter very fast, like a strobe light.

I got the po hexagram—*falling apart.* The commentary said, "It will not be advantageous to make a move in any direction whatsoever."

At the end of July, Karen decided we weren't yin enough and put us on diet number seven—brown rice alone. For two months, I had eaten almost no protein and had lost so much weight my clothes no longer fit. When I was around people, I felt I had to control myself like a robot, consciously moving my face and body. This took an effort "like thousands of tons" as the Zen masters said and left me exhausted. But Larry told me the diet was good for us. The Vietcong ate only one bowl of rice a day, and soon we would be able to lose our egos and trip without drugs.

Down Fillmore Street was Do City, where the brothers got their hair conked, and next to it was a joint called the Pig Stand. My hunger drove me to slip down there sometimes. The floor was tacky with grease, there was a Huey Newton poster on the wall, and the brothers called me a hippy motherfucker—but a pork sausage cost only fifty cents, and I couldn't resist them.

"Try this," I said to Larry one day, giving him one.

He bit into it, his eyes closed. "Pure poison," he said, pork juice running down his chin. "Don't tell Karen I did this."

The black people of San Francisco were getting angrier every day. This was, after all, the city where the Black Panthers Party had been formed. Already there had been riots in Harlem and Oakland. Detroit was in flames. "This city's going to burn," people said almost gleefully. "It's going to burn right to the ground."

But Larry and Karen's case was going well, and Larry decided to give a party for the whole building to celebrate. As I walked up Fillmore Street that evening, I saw a crowd on the sidewalk and heard a burglar alarm ringing. Suddenly, a bottle full of gasoline flew through the air and exploded on a parked car. The riot was definitely on.

I ran back to the house on Turk Street and up the stairs to the apartment. Everyone in the house was there for the party, including Dolores. Through the bay window, we watched as the rioters set fire to a building on Fillmore, which sent up great clouds of smoke shot through with comets of burning tar.

"I told you this would happen," Larry said. "I wish I had a gun. I'd be down there with them."

Dolores, who was looking at him with admiration, asked, "What if they come up here?"

"I'll just give them the television set," Larry said. "They don't hate us—all they want is material goods."

"I'm not sure that's all they want," I said.

"Oh, you're so *heavy*, Will," Karen said. "You're the heaviest guy in San Francisco."

"I know," I said humbly. I was the only guy in the Haight who didn't smoke grass or take acid, the only guy who hadn't found spiritual perfection—plodding around as if I was on the planet Jupiter, crushed by the weight of my own self-importance.

Finally I left the party and went across the hall to the closet. I had already finished *Journey to the East* by Herman Hesse but didn't like it much. There was only one good scene: The League for Spiritual Discovery conducted a trial of Hesse and charged him with trying to reveal their secrets. But the final verdict of the jury was that Hesse could never reveal the secrets of the league because he had forgotten what they were looking for.

Now I lay on my sleeping bag and began reading Kierkegaard's *The Sickness Unto Death*. I was expecting some humorous remarks about love, boredom, and repetition, but it turned out to be the only philosophy book I had ever read that told me what the real problem of life was.

The real problem of life was despair, and I had only read a few pages when I realized I was reading about myself. Despair was the shame of being hit in the face at Zundy, the pain of losing Jody and knowing it was my fault, the paranoia of meth, and the feeling that people could *see right through me*. They were all forms of what Kierkegaard called despair, mind split from body, self from soul.

But Kierkegaard was a Christian, and to him despair was a sin. Like any sin, it was shameful, and the shame of being split in two led to indecision, which he called reflection.

I had lost Jody because I hadn't asked her to marry me until it was too late. But with every decision I failed to make, the harder they got, until finally I began to postpone all decisions, chose reflection instead of immediacy, and gradually drifted from grass to acid to meth to amphetamine psychosis.

There was more, and it got worse. The hippies weren't the only people who had lost touch with reality and couldn't *do* anything.

Gabe was confined to a cell in Huntsville. He had chosen to break the law, and it was, therefore, necessary that he lose his freedom for two years. When everything was necessary, nothing was possible, so he was suffering from the despair of necessity.

And I was confined to a closet in San Francisco, which was about the same size as Gabe's cell. But because I was an actor, I had fallen for the idea that I had not one self but many and might play any number of roles, do any number of great things. When everything was possible, nothing was necessary, and now I was suffering from the despair of possibility, worst of all forms of the Sickness Unto Death, because now I could not even will myself to die.

The night wore on and the sirens outside rose and fell, and I found I could read faster than ever before and finally understood *everything*. In the morning, the fires were out, the air was full of smoke, and my mind was still burning with the knowledge I could never forget.

But I was still in despair, for which Kierkegaard said there was only one cure—to make the leap of faith, to be transparently grounded in God and believe he had the power to heal anyone. And how could I do this when I had no faith in anyone or anything and didn't even believe there *was* a God?

By August, I knew I was in deep trouble.

For another week, I lay on the floor of the closet every night, reading Zap Comix and *The Sickness Unto Death*. One morning I was eating breakfast—another bowl of brown rice—when I heard a song on the radio by Donovan called "Celeste." He was singing about wandering through "crystal halls" and "the changes I'm going through."

Suddenly I knew as clearly as if someone had spoken in my ear that when Donovan said "crystal halls," he meant *crystal meth*, and that by taking meth, I had put myself through irreversible *changes*.

When I stood up, the blood ran from my head, and I almost fainted. I had kept my promise to myself and not taken a drug of any kind for almost two months. But I was slowly starving to death, and this had apparently brought on a psychotic episode. Half of my mind knew I was just hearing a popular song; but the other half was hearing messages in the lyrics—a common affliction of the stoned and the insane.

I left the apartment and took the bus to the Haight, looking for Danny. Things were going from bad to worse. When people on the bus glanced at me, I thought they could *see through me* and knew I was contemptible—that I had lost Jody, taken meth, postponed every decision. When I got off the bus I saw myself reflected in the blue mirror of a storefront—a skinny meth freak with what looked like dyed blond hair—and knew they were right.

I finally found Danny sitting on a bench in Golden Gate Park, and somehow this did not surprise me—another bad sign. He was wearing sandals, and his hair was now down to his shoulders. I sat down next to him, and after a while he said, "I think I know you."

"Oh, stop this horse shit," I said. "You're pretending to be Leo in *Journey to the East.*"

"So you have finally read it?"

"Yes," I said, "and it didn't do much for me. The important thing is that the Journey isn't working out for me. I'm hearing messages in the lyrics of songs, for God's sake—you've got to give me some help."

Danny just stood up and said, "Follow me."

I followed him to the Strand Theater in the Tenderloin, a neighborhood for bums, where we watched the movie *Shock Corridor,* directed by Samuel Fuller. It was about a detective who went to an insane asylum to save a girl who had lost her mind. Of course he ended up losing his own. What was Danny trying to tell me? I thought I detected the fecal smell of schizophrenia on myself, and when I went to the men's room, there were two sailors having sex in a toilet stall.

When we came out, it was dark. I followed Danny to the sandwich shop across the street, and he told me to buy a hero, which I did with my last dollar.

"The Strand Theater is my cinematheque," he said, "I come to the matinee every day to learn its lessons." He looked at me sadly. "I see you are on the edge of a great discovery. But you are still playing a role."

"Yes, I'm still playing a role," I said. "I'm playing the role of a normal guy so I won't get thrown into an insane asylum."

"Is it so important to be normal?"

"If you haven't got any answers for me," I told him, "then take me to your friends."

"I'm not sure I want you to meet my friends. They are serious people."

A black derelict stepped between us and said, "Gimme a bite."

Danny held out the sandwich, and the derelict dove in like a shark, his hands in his pockets, bit off most of it, and disappeared.

"He needed it more than we did," Danny observed.

"Just take me to your friends."

Danny sighed. "All right, then," he said. "Let's go. As it happens, there's a party tonight."

Danny lived near Golden Gate Park, in a large apartment on the ground floor. It was owned by a former nun who had given up the Church. There were some young hippy girls there and an older guy who had a somewhat clown-like appearance—he wore a wig, had a red rubber bulb for a nose, and boasted that he was a member of Ken Kesey's gang, one of the Merry Pranksters. "I've been to his ranch at La Honda," he told us. "Ken has painted the woods behind it Day-Glo orange to duplicate the acid experience. He gave a party and invited the Hell's Angels—it was the first Acid Test."

There was some acid Kool-Aid going around. "You should drink it," Danny said, tossing off a paper cupful.

He told me he was taking acid several times a week. Then he introduced me to someone who had just come from the Tassahara Zen Center, who proved he was completely spontaneous by picking up a cockroach and eating it.

The vet who had taken the Bolex was also there, making movies, but Danny said that didn't matter anymore.

"Come on," he said. "I'll show you the Next Great Guy."

The Next Great Guy was sitting in a chair in the next room, surrounded by hippy girls. He was small, his face was almost hidden by a black beard, and his burning black eyes reminded me of a daguerreotype of a Civil War soldier. I couldn't stay in the same room with him for more than a few seconds.

"He's like Preacher Harry Powell in *The Night of the Hunter*," Danny said as we left the room. "But I think maybe he's a prophet and a teacher."

"I don't trust prophets," I said. "My father trusted a prophet named Dr. Truman, who told him he would have something called a cosmic illumination, and he was never the same. That's when the trouble starts—when prophets get a corner on enlightenment."

"There are those who try to lead," Danny said quietly, "and those who are not born to lead. The ones who think they are born to lead—as you do—mostly end up in insane asylums."

"I don't want to lead, and I definitely don't want to end up in the asylum," I told Danny. "I just want to *go home*."

There was a large pantry in the kitchen, and someone who had been listening asked if he could show it to me. So I stepped inside and saw the walls were lined with shelves of canned goods. Then the guy closed the door behind me and locked it. I heard people laughing outside as he did. It was completely dark in there, and I couldn't find the light switch. Finally it came to me that nothing had really changed—I was just in another closet. So I sat on the floor and waited to be let out.

But Danny and the rest of the people there had forgotten all about me, and nobody let me out until morning.

A couple of days later, I started walking across the Golden Gate Bridge. When I reached the middle, I looked both ways. Behind me was San Francisco. Ahead was the rest of the country. The strong wind blew right through me. Big cumulous clouds were rolling in over Mount Tam and blowing out over the Pacific. The summer was almost over, and the weather was warm and dry.

I was working on a Kierkegaardian proposition. If one could summon up the will, then one might do something irrevocable— might throw oneself over the edge and let gravity take over. And in doing so, might one not lose his or her despair completely? In the fall, there would be a moment of freedom in which one became his or her *true* self. If one survived it—and there was a chance one would—then he or she would have found the way to cure despair, and would never suffer from it again.

Since then, I have seen a television documentary about people who walk the Golden Gate Bridge and finally jump, their suicidal leaps recorded by automatic cameras. Almost every one has a history of drug addiction, mental illness, or both. I was surprised by how closely I fit the profile. But there was a strong feeling of freedom out here, and I told myself I wasn't really thinking about jumping—just playing with the idea.

For three hours, I walked back and forth across the bridge, stopping at the overlooks to stare down at the water. There, a Park Ranger approached me. Could I be thinking about jumping?

"Absolutely not," I said. "I just came out here to clear my head. It's a great view."

He walked away, and I resumed leaning on the low stone wall, staring down at the water far below. Suddenly, I realized that I really *was* thinking about jumping.

Another hour passed. When it got dark, I left the bridge and rode the bus back to the house on Turk Street. But the feeling of freedom I'd had out there was gone. With every step, I dragged along my body, which weighed thousands of tons. I had come to San Francisco to find a girl and make the Big Decision, which Kierkegaard called the leap of faith—now all I could think of was leaping off the Golden Gate Bridge.

At the top of the Turk Street hill, I got off the bus and met the Japanese lady who was always there giving out handbills. "You want to go to the Buddhism Society?" she asked me. I told her I did not, but when she wanted to know if I was troubled, I admitted that I was.

"Pray to Buddha for an answer," she said. "Ask him to show himself. I promise that if you put your soul in his hands, he will answer your prayers."

I went back to the closet and sat under the naked bulb, praying for the first time in years. I was now willing to accept any faith, any solution, and so I prayed to Buddha. Prayer meant you had faith, didn't it? But you had to pray out loud or it wouldn't work, and as hard as I tried, I couldn't. It was like the fairy tales of my childhood, in which the hero was confined to a prison and could only escape it in one way—by somehow learning the words of the spell that would make his wishes come true.

Larry and Karen told me they were getting married and wanted me to be their best man. I had often put them down in my thoughts for not having any real belief in what they were doing. But in the end, I admired them for taking an action and was absurdly happy to have been chosen to play this role—it proved I was a good hippy.

Larry sent me to the African Baptist church next door to ask the black minister if he would perform the ceremony. So I went to the little red granite church and rang the bell. The minster's wife was clearing the dinner plates, and his children sat in front of a black-and-white television, across which a plastic screen had been pasted. Almost nobody had color TV then, and this was a substitute. The screen had three bands—the top band was blue for the sky, the middle band was pink for faces, and the bottom band was brown for the earth.

The minister and I then went into his study, and there I told him that two young people who lived next door sincerely loved each other and wanted to be married. He said he would be happy to do it for them.

The ceremony was performed in the garden that afternoon. For some reason, almost no one in the house came. But I played the role of best man perfectly. Larry and Karen were married next to the green reflecting globe, and he placed his mother's wedding ring on her finger. Then I gave the minister twenty-five dollars. I was happy for Larry and Karen, who were in love and had done what I had not been able to do—they made the Big Decision. We went to their apartment and opened a bottle of champagne. No honeymoon was planned. They had each passed a civil service exam and were both going to work the next day for the post office.

Then I went upstairs to see Dolores. I was wearing a suit and tie, and this left me feeling strange and able to do carefree things. So I asked her if she wouldn't like to come downstairs and see Larry and Karen.

"I don't know," she said. "It's getting so I hate to leave this room. Have you noticed how many freaked-out people there are on the streets? Sometimes I just sit here and throw the *I Ching* twenty or thirty times a day."

"Nothing very bad could happen to you downstairs," I said.

She sighed, sat down at the table, and threw the *I Ching*. I held my breath. The coins clicked together like stones underwater.

"I got 'the perilous pit,'" she said. "That's K'an above and below, water, a pit, danger. There will be evil for three years."

I left her staring out the windows at the distant green hills of Marin County.

RETURN TO TEXAS

22

I WAS LYING IN the closet that night when Larry knocked on the door and said, "You've got a phone call." He and Karen were both looking at me strangely as I picked up the phone.

"Hello?" I said.

"Hello, darling," Jody Brown said to me.

It was like what I had imagined electroshock therapy to be—the blood drained from my head and my eyes went dark. When I came back to myself, Jody was telling me she had left Darryl.

"Oh," I finally managed to say. "I love you."

"And I love you. I want to come out there and see you."

"Don't do that," I said. I told Jody I was just leaving San Francisco, and that I would meet her in Austin, seven days from now.

When I hung up, tears were running down my face. My life had become such a desert I was surprised there was any moisture left in my body. "She's left her husband," I told Larry and Karen. "And I think everything's going to be all right."

But by the time I returned to the closet, I was in despair again. The miracle had happened—but it could not have come at a worse time. I had promised myself that when Jody returned, I would be a stronger person, but it would be harder for me to win her back now than ever before. I had lost more than thirty pounds, I was living in a walk-in closet, and now I had to cure myself of the Sickness Unto Death in one week. But I told myself that life had always been harder for me than other people. And now I had something to live for.

Necessity worked wonders on me. I stopped walking the Golden Gate Bridge, phoned my parents, and got them to wire me some money. I found a sports car repair shop, bought a new battery for the Austin-Healey, put up a note at the Haight-Ashbury Free Clinic—"Riders needed for trip to Austin"—and got two takers, a hippy couple. Then I went to a cafeteria and ate a huge protein meal of roast beef and mashed potatoes. Finally, I went to say goodbye to Danny.

"The outward appearance of the Haight may be bullshit," he said. "But there is a real spiritual energy here, and that girl is not going to bring you happiness."

"How would you know?" I asked him. "You've never had a girl."

Larry and Karen wished me the best, but I could tell they were worried about me. On the morning of the fourth day after Jody had called, I picked up my riders and left on a journey of over seventeen hundred miles, which I had to make without chemical help.

On the first day, I drove down through the yellow hills of the central valley. When I got out of the Healy to fill the tank with gasoline, the blood ran from my head and I fainted. My riders helped me back in the car, but I still refused to let them drive. That afternoon, I drove over Cajon Pass and down into the Mohave Desert on the other side. Night fell; the moon rose; and, at a roadside park near Needles, I lay on the ground in my sleeping bag with my eyes closed, while my riders slept in the car.

At sunrise of the second day, I got back behind the wheel. That day, I drove on across the Painted Desert and past the Navajo Motel. When there was no traffic, I pushed the Austin-Healey up to ninety miles per hour—singing and eating sunflower seeds and dried apricots. My riders were worried about me because I wouldn't stop and I wouldn't let them drive the car. Night fell beyond Gallup, and the moon, growing fuller, rose before me a second time. I felt I had to get back to Texas before it was completely full. Just before I reached Albuquerque, I turned south and drove down through the gray lava beds and then across the Trinity Site, where the first atomic bomb had been set off. There I pulled off the road and slept behind the wheel for a while.

At daybreak, I crossed the Texas border. Near Lamesa, I came to a crossroads where a pickup had just turned over. Two cowboys were climbing out, but I didn't stop to help. I drove on through Coleman, Brady, and Rising Star, arriving in Austin around two o'clock on a very hot afternoon. It was the end of the greatest drive I had ever made, more than seventeen hundred miles in less than fifty-two hours.

I dropped off my riders and their bags at the bus station—still had no idea where they were headed and didn't care. John and Julie had moved out to the lake but kept an apartment in town. It was the same apartment where Jody had lived with her gay roommates, a coincidence that could be good or bad, but could not be ignored. From there, I called Jody in Houston, gave her the address, and told her I would meet her in Austin tomorrow. Then I fell on their bed and slept forever.

When I woke, a light rain was falling. It was early evening. I walked to Eastwoods Park, where I had seen the cops bust the hippies on Eeyore's birthday and then past Jody's house on Elmwood Place, where we had lived together for the most glorious months of my life. Complete darkness fell as I walked across the campus to Guadalupe Street, where there were now hippies begging for money. It began to rain harder. I had not drunk alcohol for a long time, but before I turned back, I stopped at a liquor store on Guadalupe and bought a half pint of vodka, clear as rainwater, which I drank as I walked across the campus. When I reached John and Julie's apartment, I had finished the bottle and felt numb all over.

My paranoia was coming in waves, so I lit a Diamond Strike Anywhere match from the little box I had been given at the liquor store. *You will be yourself,* I thought, *as long as you can hold your thumb in this flame.*

When my thumb was blackened and burnt, I fell into bed again and lay there trying to sleep. Even pain was better than the pain of feeling nothing, the pain of despair.

At noon, the skies cleared and Jody drove up in her white Triumph, wearing a stylish yellow vinyl miniskirt with horizontal black stripes, like a bee's. I put on my sunglasses to conceal my eyes and stepped out on the porch. "Hello, my love," she said as she walked up to me.

When we kissed I felt only a slight electric charge. I carried her suitcase into the apartment, where I gave her a glass of iced tea and asked her how long she could stay.

"I don't know," she said. "I'm not sure what I'm doing here."

"I like your miniskirt."

"Thanks. I wore it for you. You've lost a lot of weight."

I told her I had eaten nothing but brown rice for three months.

"Are you on drugs?"

"I don't do drugs anymore," I said.

"I thought you'd be having a great time out in California, doing drugs," Jody said. "That's why I wanted to meet you out there."

"It's horrible out there," I told her. "I'm never going back."

"But we had such a good time when we took peyote, didn't we? I loved you so much then."

A silence came in that got longer and longer. Finally I asked her, "What did you expect from this?"

"That you'd throw me down on the bed, make love to me, and tell me I had to divorce Darryl."

This had been my hope as well. But I could already see it wasn't going to happen.

"Could I ask you to do something?" she said.

"Yes."

"Take off those sunglasses."

When I did, her eyes met mine, and she *saw through me*. At the same instant, the corner of my mouth jerked. It was like smashing through mirrors, the concentric shells of reflection that cut me off from the world. My face felt torn and bleeding, and I couldn't look at her.

"You're in a bad way, darling," she said after a while. "I'm afraid it's too late for us."

I knew I had lost her forever and wanted to die.

"Give me a couple of days to get myself together," I said.

Jody stood. "No, I should go back to Houston."

"Just let me … touch you."

She did, and again I felt that faint electric charge.

"Spend the rest of the day with me," I said. "Let's go out to the lake."

"By the time we get there, it'll be dark."

"Not quite. We can watch the sun go down."

"All right," she said finally. "I'll get my bathing suit."

So we got in the Austin-Healey and drove out to the lake. Jody was surprised that I also drove a sports car, but it wasn't as shameful as I had expected. I think by now we had both given up and knew this meeting was not going to renew our love. But in a way, this set me free. I even asked her about Darryl, shouting over the roar of the wind, "Why did you marry that guy?"

"Because I slept with him."

"What does that mean?"

"He seemed to know what he wanted, and you didn't," she said. "Now all he wants to do is fuck me in the ass."

"He's been seeing too many foreign movies."

"He says he still loves me."

"So do I, but I've never wanted to fuck you in the ass."

We reached Comanche Pass and drove on down to John and Julie's cabin. They weren't home, but we put on our bathing suits and walked along the shore to Windy Point. There we found the grove where I had first read to her the description of the golden age. I stepped out to the end of the marble slab and dove in. The water was warm with the heat of summer.

Jody didn't go swimming. But she came down with the blanket and sat beside me when I got out, wrapping it around us both. The sun was just setting and the full moon, which I had seen before me on the way back, was just rising over the hills on the opposite side of the world, a faintly transparent gold coin. I had reached here just in time—at least I had done that much. Everything was the same as it had been on our first night here, almost three years ago.

Then I heard the music.

Sometimes, when I went swimming, a drop of water got caught in my ear, so it sounded like pebbles rolling back and forth. Then my hearing cleared, and I was able to hear the sounds of the world around me. Something like this happened to me now. Gradually I began to hear everything—the sound of Jody's bare feet on the limestone, a dove calling in the distance, even the beating of our hearts. The continuous static of my thoughts had died out. All around us, the crystalline clockwork ground on, giving off its eternal music, and I knew *who I was* and *where I was in time.*

It had all happened before. I was having a mystical experience, and now I could remember all the others—at my grandfather's cabin, here at the lake, in the mountains of North Carolina—every one that had ever happened to me, going back to my childhood. I could remember it all, my whole life, and what I was here on earth for—to know this moment.

When I kissed Jody, the power of our lives flowed between us again, and for the first time in almost a year, I had a hard-on.

"You're like Jesus," Jody said as she touched me. "You're so thin I can feel every one of your ribs. But your hands are warm."

"So are yours."

"What's happening to us, darling?"

"Maybe it's the moon," I said.

An endless time passed. The sun was gone, and the moon rose higher, and then it was night. The stars came out, and the moon was so bright it cast faint shadows.

"Let's go back to Austin and make love," I said.

"I wasn't going to do that."

"Bullshit," I said, laughing.

So we went back to Austin and did what I had for so long wanted to do—made love without protection. The moon was so bright that night that a mockingbird in the tree behind the apartment sang to it, and we heard its music all night long.

For the next three days, I was in the same blissful state I had known before. This time, because I had been reading Kierkegaard, I thought I had made the leap of faith. I was cured of amphetamine psychosis, had cast reflection out, and was now transparently grounded in God. My face was clear, my eyes were opened, and all sensations had returned. I could complete a sentence, and I could make love to Jody. I had been healed by some higher power—had a mystical experience so powerful that I would never completely forget it.

Not long ago, I read a new explanation of amphetamine psychosis on a *Wikipedia* page of the Internet:

> As a result of methamphetamine-induced neurotoxicity to dopamine neurons, chronic abuse may also lead to a dopamine shortage. The symptoms, which persist beyond the withdrawal period, may last for months, even a year. But when they are relieved, normal consciousness returns.

This could mean that my amphetamine psychosis was partly a dopamine shortage, a loss of the brain chemical that gives one freedom of movement. This could explain my paralysis, the jerking of my mouth, my withdrawal into the closet, my complete inability to take action.

At the time, I thought my problem was the despair of possibility as defined in Kierkegaard's *Sickness Unto Death*, and I still think this book is the best description of my thoughts then. But when Jody came back, my body began to produce dopamine again, and my symptoms suddenly disappeared. I was like one of those patients with Parkinson's disease who were given dopamine by Dr. Oliver Sacks—as described in his book *Awakenings*—and returned to a normal state in little more than an hour.

But this does not explain the mystical experiences I have had from childhood or why I forgot them or why they happened when they did. So I have settled on another explanation. There was another kind of force at work here that was neither completely chemical nor completely natural.

I believe it was eros that had brought me back from despair. It was love, the healing force, which has existed for all of human time, although its existence can never be proven. Love may be an evolutionary strategy for ensuring that the human race survives—and the music may be the music we hear when time chooses a new path. Whatever it may be, eros is the force that, as the Greeks said, brings all things to pass, and it was powerful enough to bring me back from Hades. I have never felt anything quite like it again.

Jody and I stayed together for three more days. She took my recovery for granted—she had barely seen me when I was sick—and we never talked about it.

On the morning of the fifth day, she went back to Darryl, promising me that she would see a lawyer and set about divorcing him. Then we would get married.

23

THERE WAS A little wooden shed on John and Julie's property, which they used for storage, and they told me I could stay there as long as I liked. I cleaned the windows, hammered down the old nails protruding from the floor, and put in a mattress. Then I bought groceries and a kerosene lamp. It was very much like my Grandpa Thorn's fishing cabin and a big improvement over the closet in San Francisco. Every morning, I put on my bathing suit and walked down to the shore. I felt a few traces of the sickness lingered in my mind, and the cure I had chosen was water.

First I swam far out into the lake. There I practiced drownproofing, which I had read about in the *Reader's Digest*. The human body floated if you were completely relaxed. Sailors who fell overboard had practiced this method and remained alive for several days. First, I emptied my lungs and loosened my muscles. Then I sank until my feet touched the cold layer, ten feet down.

I kicked once, and my body rose until it broke the surface. Taking another breath, I exhaled, and sank again. Once the slow, hypnotic rhythm established itself, I took only one breath every forty or fifty seconds. It was a form of meditation. First I saw the hills and the sky and felt the sun on my shoulders. Then I sank down into the cold, green water and my dreams. Finally I rose in silver bubbles to the surface and saw the clouds and the sky again.

After an hour of this, a deep calm settled over me. I swam back to the shore and lay on a limestone slab in the sun, feeling empty and strong.

At night, I walked to John and Julie's for supper but never smoked grass with them. I was gaining weight, and my brain no longer felt like compacted dust. Everything flowed. The moon was waning now, and every night, it appeared later and later. The night was a beach of black sand, the moon a white shell, and the stars glittered like precious stones.

Sometimes I still heard the music of the other universe where I had been with Jody, although it was growing fainter. This universe was not made of matter, but of time, which enclosed but did not imprison me. Sometimes I stayed awake until the tide of light rose in the east. This was the perfect life I had always dreamed of.

One day I went into Austin to buy some groceries and met Dee at the Tower Drug. It seemed to me this was not completely accidental. I felt fortunate in those days, when I had won Jody back—thought I was destined to meet everyone I had ever known. And Somehow Dee knew everything that had happened.

"I know I've lost you," she said, "but I'm not angry about it."

When I told her that Jody and I were going to get married, she wished us the best. Dee was so happy for us that I forgave her for being someone I could not really love. At least she had tried to be that girl as hard as she knew how.

Then my mother called me at John and Julie's, and told me that I had to come home. My brother had tried to commit suicide with my father's rifle.

I drove up to Nortex on a long September day. The intense solar radiation of the summer had turned everything brown. As I approached my hometown, I had a premonition of loss. *I don't want to lose my strength here*, I thought. *But I have a duty to my brother.*

That night I talked to Ray and was shocked by his appearance. Like me, he had lost a lot of weight. His face was thinner, and there were dark blue circles under his eyes. But in a strange way, his suffering had made him stronger-looking. My little brother had finally grown up.

"Nothing makes a shit," he told me, lighting a cigarette. "Dad drinks, and he and Mom fight every night since you went to California. I cover my head with a pillow, but I still can't sleep. When they started in the other night, I went to the kitchen and told them, 'If you don't stop I just might kill myself.'"

"Jesus," I said.

"They didn't pay any attention to me. So I went to the garage and got Dad's rifle. Found some bullets and loaded it, went back to the kitchen and said, 'Watch this.' Then I pulled the trigger, but nothing happened. I must have loaded it wrong."

"Jesus."

"They started crying and saying they were sorry. But the next night, they were fighting again. Now Mom wants me to go see the psychiatrist she works for. Nothing makes a shit."

"What do you want to do now?" I asked him.

"I want our father to take us on a camping trip up to Lost Lake," Ray said, "like he used to do, when we were kids. And when we get there, I want him to promise us he'll stop drinking."

"That sounds like a good idea," I said, turning away so he couldn't see the tears rolling down my face.

I was still feeling the glow of what would be my greatest mystical experience—I would hold onto it for some time—and saw everything in its light. My feelings were strong, but I was quiet. I felt I had endless time to set things straight.

Lost Lake was in a park in the Wichita Mountains, a series of granite hills on the Comanche reservation near Lawton, Oklahoma, forty miles to the north. My father agreed to go, and on Friday afternoon we drove up there and pitched camp. My brother, who was an Eagle Scout, cooked hot dogs and baked beans as the sun went down. Then we started talking to my father about his drinking.

"I'll stop drinking," he finally said, "if you boys will stop taking dope."

"We're not taking dope," I told him.

"Don't give me that shit."

"Look, we've taken dope, but not tonight. And we'll never take it again—if you'll stop drinking."

My father thought about this and then offered his hand and said, "All right—it's a promise."

Ray and I shook hands with him, and for a while it seemed that we had accomplished what we had set out to do.

But after supper, my father wandered off into the woods. We found him staring at the yellow stars dropping slowly over Fort Sill, where they were firing illumination rounds. "I've seen the same thing in Europe," he said sadly.

My brother and I looked at each other. From the quality of his sadness, we knew our father had a bottle hidden somewhere and was still drinking.

Nobody could sleep, so we drove to the top of Mount Scott, the highest point in the Wichita Mountains. The parking lot was full of Lawton teenagers—when we got out of the car we saw glowing cigarettes and heard snatches of music on their car radios. "Look out there," my father said, staring across the moonlit prairie. "I can see almost all the way back to your mother."

My brother shook his head and walked away.

"Please don't do this to my brother," I said.

"Oh, fuck you," my father said angrily. "You don't feel sorry for anybody but yourself. The great actor!"

"You the one who told me I should major in drama."

"You're a draft dodger too—told them you were a queer to get out of serving your country, didn't you? Christ, I was so ashamed of you when I saw you up there on that stage, wearing tights and lipstick. And your brother's no better."

I had gotten out of the draft with a doctor's letter, but my father had never known for certain and had assumed the worst. I also recognized the moment he was talking about—it had been in *Julius Caesar*, in my senior year, and I had been on meth. I looked away, thinking about this.

When I turned back, he had disappeared, and I had lost both him and my brother.

I waited there for a while, staring at the moon. Then my brother returned, and we got in the car and started looking for our father.

Finally we found him walking along the side of the road. "I thought you'd forgotten me," he said tiredly, "so I was headed home."

My brother and I talked him into getting back in the car, and then I drove down to Lost Lake, where we lay in our sleeping bags for hours, pretending to sleep. But the moon was so bright sleep was impossible.

On that night, it seemed to me that the great time storm of the sixties had finally destroyed my family. Event after catastrophic event had crashed down on us, and the Vietnam War had been the worst of them all. In many ways, it was a replay of the Civil War. You tried to stay out of it, but you had to take sides. Our parents hated us, and we hated them, and nobody knew why—just that it had to be.

Finally my brother fell asleep, and my father began talking to me—or to himself; I wasn't sure which.

"I don't know," he said. "But I felt all my life there was some kind of secret nobody would tell me, not even my real father. I learned to play the piano, I went to college, I married your mother, and I went to war. That was quite an experience, and I thought it might be the secret, but it wasn't. Then I got out of the army, and we had you. But—I don't want to hurt your feelings, Sonny—you weren't the secret either. Nothing was. I had a great life, but I always thought I deserved more."

"You only feel that way because you drink, Dad," I said, but my father didn't seem to hear.

"I only found the secret once, at Aum-Sat-Tat," he went on. "I saw the real colors, the real light that shines on us all; saw the way everything is always moving and changing and trying to become something else. And I heard the perfect music I'd been trying to play forever." He was silent for moment and then said, "I lost it for good not long after that. But trying to find it again is all that keeps me going."

At this moment, I suddenly knew with absolute certainty that my father was not talking about a natural mystical experience, like the ones I had known. *Dad thinks he had a cosmic illumination, but Dr. Truman gave him mescaline or acid at Aum-Sat-Tat.*

The experience had been too difficult, too hard for him. And he talked about it too much. It was not natural, not *his.*

In the years to come, this idea would grow even stronger. Even on that first night, it somehow made me feel better. The memory of my last mystical experience was still fresh, and I understood everything without effort—even mysteries that had bothered me since childhood.

But when we returned from the Wichita Mountains the next day, I learned that Jody had called and told my mother I had to get down to Houston right away. There was a problem.

24

JODY LIVED IN Montrose, the same neighborhood where I had lived with Larry and Karen. The night was foggy and smelled of petrochemicals. Her apartment was on the top floor of an old 1920s Greek Revival house. I rang the bell. She let me in, and I climbed the stairs and knocked on her door.

The change in her was immediately apparent. Her beautiful red hair was dull; she wore no lipstick or makeup. Her eyes, which had been green, were now colorless, and the pupils contracted to hard little pinpoints.

"Hello, my love," she said tonelessly, standing aside to let me enter. "How do you like my apartment?"

I didn't like it at all. The wallpaper was brown, the color of endless disappointment, the ceiling stained with leaks. Dim light fell from a globe overhead. Jody gave me a glass of scotch and put on our Rachmaninoff record, *Rhapsody on a Theme of Paganini.*

I sat on a sofa covered with some sort of hard plastic material, and Jody sat on another. She crossed her legs beneath her, lit a Pall Mall, and closed her eyes as the music played on. Every move said, *Don't touch me.*

What was going on here? What had happened to her, and why

had she changed so much? When the important part of the music had played, she opened her eyes and I asked her, "What's the problem?"

"The problem," she said, "is that this isn't going to be as easy as we thought it was."

"How do you mean?"

"When I got back here, I told Darryl we were going to get married. He told me I was insane to think about such a thing, and for a while, I was inclined to think he was right."

"I see."

"That was the low point. But then I did a good thing."

"What was that?"

"Went to see Dr. Harris. He's a psychiatrist and a good person, and he told me not to do anything until I was absolutely certain that it was what I wanted to do."

The record was over. She lifted the needle from it and lit another cigarette.

"Let's go back to Austin," I said. "Let's go back to the lake. You don't need to see a psychiatrist. We can solve this problem ourselves. We're in love, aren't we?"

She shook her head, staring off, and said, "I've got to stop pretending."

"How long have you been pretending?"

"All my life."

This sounded bad.

"You see, I've always tried to be a good little girl—first for my father and then for you and then for Darryl."

"I didn't think you were pretending in Austin."

"Dr. Harris says I was—and so were you. It was all a lie. Now I know the truth. I've been dreaming my whole life, and this apartment is the nightmare where it all ends."

This sounded very bad indeed.

"Everything will be all right if we just go back to Austin," I said and told her about the cabin I had prepared for us out at the lake.

"That's so sad."

"Why?"

"Because I can't leave here until I find myself. See, you and Darryl are fighting over me. Both of you want to control me. The only person who really understands me is Dr. Harris. Here's what I want you to do. Stay here in Houston and see Dr. Harris."

Jody gave me his card, which I put in my shirt pocket.

"I'll see him," I said, "if Darryl will see him too."

"Don't worry about that. Darryl's already seeing him. Maybe Dr. Harris will give you pills so you can sleep, like he gives me."

"I don't need pills to sleep," I said, standing up. "I can sleep right now."

"You can't sleep here."

"I thought we might make love."

"No, I can't let you make love to me now. Give me a call when you've seen Dr. Harris."

She held the door open for me, and I left.

The change in her was incredible. As I went down the stairs, I thought about her talk about "pretending." She suddenly felt she had been false, playing a role. This must be the reason why she had left Darryl. I had been so concerned with myself that I hadn't even noticed she was also in trouble. I would have to explain to Dr. Harris that she didn't need his help. Then I had to make Jody understand that psychiatry wasn't the only way to understand what was happening to her. We were in love, and that was the way out of this. We had to get back to where we had been back in Austin, at the lake.

But when I got outside, I stopped and looked up at her lighted windows. *Now I have to do the impossible again,* I thought. *Stay here in Houston, get a job, see Dr. Harris, and somehow convince Jody to come back to Austin with me. How many times will I have to prove myself to her before this is over and she's mine forever?*

I found a motel room and the next morning went to see Larry's father, who ran the Montgomery Ward Department Store at Sharpstown Center. He gave me a job with the display department. "We had one of these drama boys here before," he told the display director, "and he worked out real well." The display director was clearly gay and kept giving me approving looks, but this didn't bother me, since I'd known so many gays in drama school. *I'll only have to do this job for a little while,* I thought.

Then I drove around Montrose until I found a small apartment for rent not far from Jody. I had the phone turned on, called Dr. Harris's office, and was told I could have an appointment in about a week. Then I tried to call Jody, but a recorded voice told me her listing was unpublished, and she had not given me her number.

Fine, I thought, *I'll wait for her to call me.*

I waited through the weekend, but she never called. On Monday morning I got up at six o'clock and drove to work at Montgomery Ward, which was on the other side of town.

For five days I worked, and finally, I went to my first meeting with Dr. Harris on Friday evening.

His office was near Rice University. I was early and waited for half an hour in a comfortable outer office, with a tank full of tropical fish and the latest magazines.

He was about thirty years old; wore a brown corduroy suit; and had prematurely white hair and a medical degree from Tulane. I had expected someone older, and found his youth slightly disturbing. When I asked if I was supposed to lie on the new leather couch across from his desk, he said, "No, you can sit in the chair if you wish."

This can't be so different from an acting scene, I thought. *All I have to do is tell the truth, or most of it.*

So I spent most of the first hour giving him an honest version of my life—how I had met Jody and so forth. But when I finished, there was a silence that was a little too long—like the silence following a performance that had not quite come off—while he made notes.

"There are a few things I don't understand," he said finally. "Could you clarify your state of mind in San Francisco for me?"

"It doesn't matter, does it?" I said, determined not to get into methedrine or Kierkegaard. "I was depressed and I wasn't eating right, but I had stopped taking drugs before I ever got to the Haight. Then Jody called and said she was leaving her husband, and I drove back to Austin and met her."

"Go on," he said.

Why not just tell the whole truth? I thought.

"It sounds a little strange. I was nervous around her for the first fifteen minutes or so. Then we went out to the lake, and then it was like a strong light was shining on me. All my doubts just went away, we made love, and we knew what we had to do."

He wrote all this down and then said, "So now you're here to talk Jody into marrying you."

"That's pretty much it."

"I'm not sure I can let you do that."

"Why not?"

I didn't even know he was angry with me until he said, "Because Jody doesn't agree with you, that's why."

"She agreed with me in Austin."

Dr. Harris went on, carefully choosing his words. "You're telling me you're fine, but what you just told me sounds to me like a psychotic episode. You come in here and tell me a story like that and expect me to believe you're not on drugs?"

"But I'm *not.*"

"I think you are a much more disturbed person than you are willing to admit, and you are a danger to both her and yourself."

I realized I had to be careful here. "All right," I said. "I was a little sick, but I'm not anymore."

"Then why are you here?"

That was a hard one.

"Because Jody wants me to be here."

He stared at me until I had to look away.

"Fine," he said, taking out his notebook and pencil again. "I'll try to treat you. You obviously need help. But you have to do everything I ask, and you can't see Jody unless you have her permission to do so."

"That's easy. Jody hasn't given me her phone number, and I haven't seen her at all."

"What drugs are you taking now?"

"None."

"Jody also tells me you are a homosexual."

"She couldn't have said that."

We stared at each other again, and this time he looked away.

"Well, she said something like that."

"And I'm telling you that I'm not."

But I was thinking, *Did she really say that?*

Dr. Harris put down his notebook and pencil. "You'll have to go to one of my groups."

"Why, if there's nothing wrong with me?"

"My belief is that nobody can solve these problems themselves," he said. "But if you're doing as well as you say you are, what could be the harm in it?"

I had to agree there could be none.

Four nights later, I went to my first group. There were three of them. Jody was in one, Darryl was in another, and I was in the third. They met in the living room of Dr. Harris's comfortable house in River Oaks, a wealthy neighborhood of Houston.

Group was not as easy as I had thought it would be. First there was coffee and classical music. Everyone seemed a little strange, and I felt that I was stronger than they were. But it was like trying to join an improvisation that had already begun.

The subject of this one was suicide. An attractive young woman gave us a long monologue about the time she had recently tried to kill herself. "It was the most wonderful moment of my life," she said. "I took all my pills. Then I filled the bathtub with warm water, got in, and slit my wrists with a kitchen knife. For the first time, I was *doing something for myself.* And when I woke up in the hospital and was still here—it was a big disappointment."

After group, we all went to a bar where we sat in a booth together and drank beer. The young woman who had talked about suicide sat right next to me. She seemed to feel just fine now, completely normal, even happy.

I noticed everyone was being careful to keep at a distance from me. Their eyes never met mine. But was that my problem or theirs? The young woman's hip was touching mine, and I thought about the story she had told us, which I doubted somehow. Sure, I had *thought* about suicide when I was walking the Golden Gate Bridge—but it had not been the most wonderful moment of my life. Maybe if I had really jumped, it would have been.

Suddenly I couldn't stand this room, these people, and put my hands over my eyes. At that moment, the girl who had tried to commit suicide leaned over and whispered in my ear, "Do you feel threatened? Do you feel left out?"

Every day I worked in the windows with the display director, dressing mannequins in bras and panties. Since childhood, I had been fascinated by the smooth pink plaster bodies of mannequins and admitted this to the display director.

"Sometimes I take their panties home and try them on," he said. "It gives you a big hard-on. But I'm sure you already know that."

"Not me."

He laughed and asked me if I'd like to go out for a drink sometime. I accepted because I was hungry for someone to talk to.

That night I met him at what turned out to be a gay bar in Montrose. It had white wrought iron patio furniture, and the jukebox played Cole Porter.

"You're queer, aren't you?" the display director asked me casually.

"I don't think so."

"Maybe you are, but you don't know it."

"I've heard that before."

I began to feel a little guilty. Probably the display director thought I was leading him on. But nobody believed you were straight if you wanted to be an actor. For a fact, men in the theater were often gay, and women were hard to get—I knew all about that.

I gave him the most honest look I could, and said, "I've got a girl here in Houston."

"So what?" he said. "I've got a wife and two kids."

I nodded and took another drink, as if I knew what he was talking about. Suddenly, the depth of our loneliness struck me. But the display director seemed to have adjusted to it.

I went home feeling a faint anxiety, which took the form of graphic fantasies of Jody and Dr. Harris having sex.

The next time I saw Dr. Harris, I told him about going out with the display director, which he seemed to find interesting. I wanted to talk about Jody, but he refused to tell me anything about her. Instead, he kept coming back to the gay bar.

"How did you feel about being there?" he asked me.

"A little embarrassed."

"Is that all?"

"Look," I said. "I know it's hard for you to believe. But I've never had sex with another guy."

"Never?"

"Not since I was in the Cub Scouts."

He gave me a look of serious concern. "That must have been traumatic."

Dr. Harris had no sense of humor; that was for sure. Or was it me who was to blame?

"Not at all," I told him. "We were friends."

"How would you describe it then?"

"Innocent fun."

He laughed. "You are hard to pin down, aren't you? I thought maybe we were going to have a *real* discussion for a change."

For a moment, I almost liked him. But it was Jody I wanted to see, not Dr. Harris, and I couldn't contact her and was afraid to drop by for fear she wouldn't let me in.

A couple of days after that, I called my old companion, Joe Hollis, who was now a teaching assistant at Rice and working on his master's degree in logic. When I asked if we could talk, he said, "Not on the phone. It might be tapped."

I was a little surprised at this—it was what all the hippies were saying in Austin now.

"I'll meet you," Joe told me, "but it has to be a public place."

I suggested the place where I ate supper—Cokin's Restaurant, which had a red neon sign on the roof and pine tables. It was always dim and deserted, but it was public.

Joe's hair was thinning, but he still looked like Marlon Brando, the greatest hood of them all. As he sat down, he glanced at his watch and said he had exactly thirty minutes to talk to me. After that, he had to go home and study—he was learning Vietnamese. Then he told me, "You look to me like you're on drugs."

I admitted that I had taken them but not recently.

"I hope not," Joe said. "The reason I don't take drugs is that I'm afraid they'll destroy my mind."

"They can," I agreed. "But I didn't come here to talk about drugs—I came here to talk about Jody."

"Your girlfriend? Remember my old high school girlfriend, Jayne? She turned out to be a lesbian."

"I heard about that."

"But I'm still in love with her."

"Of course you're still in love her," I said. "You're right to love her."

Then Joe changed the subject to logic, talking so fast I could hardly follow him. He mentioned that he spoke fluent Russian and was an expert in Russian logic, which was top secret.

"Russian *logic* is top secret?"

"Their mathematical logic is. The theorems are used in computers. They're called algorithms."

He had just come back from Russia, where he had met some of their greatest thinkers. The FBI had been following him for a year because he refused to get a security clearance. Then he switched to talking about this country.

"There's a war going on in this country between men and women," he said. "Of course women are entirely in the right, and for a while, I turned my house into a home for battered women. Don't interrupt me—I haven't got much time left. My first wife is trying to steal our children, and the FBI is trying to steal my logic. So you can see I have my share of problems."

"So do I," I said, and managed to get in a few words about Jody—told him how our problems were being negotiated through Dr. Harris.

"Do you think women will ever forgive you?" he asked me.

"I have my hopes."

"Why, you're as naive as a child," he said, laughing. "Look, I don't know why you are in this situation with this girl Jody, but I'll tell you this—you have to be careful. If you have a child by her, I can promise you that she will try to destroy you. I could tell you about some things that have been done to me … but I haven't got time," he finished, looking at his watch and finishing his coffee. "Anyway, it's all classified, and you have no need to know."

Joe stood up suddenly.

"Wait," I said. "Tell me more."

But he walked out the door and was gone.

Joe was still the smartest guy I had ever known—a math genius, a Dharma Bum. I did not doubt he had done important work for the government. But he had no time to talk to me, and as he put it, I had no need to know.

My days grew longer and my nights shorter.

After work, I began sleeping from 6:00 until 10:00 p.m.; woke and went to eat at Cokin's, where I always ordered the same thing, a hamburger steak; went back to my apartment and fell asleep until 6:00 a.m. Then I got up, showered, and drove back to work at the Montgomery Ward store in Sharpstown Center.

Once a week I went to see Dr. Harris, and once a week I went to group, but I contributed almost nothing. To me, it was like the Society of Friends; I wasn't going to speak until I had something to say.

On Saturdays and Sundays, there was nothing to do. I sat in a chair outside the door of my apartment, pretending to read *The Moviegoer,* waiting for Jody to give me a call. Sometimes I got in the Austin-Healey and drove past her apartment, and sometimes I drove around to escape the depression that followed.

Once I drove all the way out to Buffalo Bayou to see the San Jacinto monument and the old battleship *Texas.* But it turned out that seeing old battleships was also depressing. On the way home, I saw a sign advertising a Sunday morning tour of the Astrodome, and it came to me that I could put on a coat and tie and show up for the tour. This would be so depressing that I could then go back to my apartment and commit suicide in some way. Maybe it would be the best day of my life.

I was losing ground, and I knew it.

Jody finally called and gave me her phone number. I wrote it down and said, "I want to come over right now."

She told me I could, so I drove over to her apartment.

"I hope you're learning something about yourself in group," she said, inviting me to sit beside her on the plastic-covered sofa.

"Not really."

"Then I feel sorry for you."

"Why did you tell Dr. Harris I was a homosexual?" I demanded.

"I didn't."

"He said you did."

"No, I told him that I thought Darryl might be a homosexual."

"Why?"

I was learning to ask "why?" It was very important in therapy.

"Darryl always wanted to fuck me in the ass," she said, "if it's any of your business. Sometimes I think every man I've ever known is a homosexual."

"I am not a homosexual."

"No, but you once said you wanted me to be your mother."

"I never did. Can we just stop all this psychiatric talk? Can't we just talk to each other like we did back in school? Could we go swimming together and then make love? And do you think you could you turn on that lamp?"

"Why?" she said.

"I can't even see your face. If you would just let me hold you …"

Instantly she was on her feet. "Stay away from me."

"For God's sake," I cried, standing up and taking a step toward her. "Won't you even let me *touch* you?"

She took a step back. I was doing the unthinkable thing—losing my temper. But even as I was trying to control my anger, I thought, *Good—she's afraid of me.* Then Jody closed her eyes, and her head dropped submissively.

I touched her, felt electricity flowing back into my body, and when I took her in my arms, the difference was immediate; I could see everything clearly, smell her hair, even hear a television set playing downstairs in the silence.

"Thank God you let me do that," I said a little later.

We were sitting on the sofa. My arm was around her, and her head was on my shoulder.

"I'm sorry, darling, but—"

"I know. You're afraid of everything."

Jody looked up at me. Her pupils had expanded again, and her eyes were bottomless. "I feel like I'm falling all the time," she admitted. "I was always a dirty little girl, and I liked it when my uncle came in and watched me taking a bath. That time we took peyote in Austin, I kept thinking I'd like to take your friends into the bedroom and fuck them while you watched. Did you know that?"

This hurt, but I knew she thought she had to tell me. "Everybody thinks things like that sometimes," I said.

"None of it's our fault anyway, is it? It's just the way we were treated when we were children, isn't it?"

"I'm not sure about that."

"Dr. Harris says we're not responsible for our actions."

"Maybe he's not right about everything."

"You sound so sure of yourself."

JOURNEY TO THE WEST

"I am when you're listening to me. I love you."

"It does sound good when you talk like that."

"Let's go back to the lake. Just for the weekend. It will save us both."

"You're always saying that. What happened to you there?"

"I don't know. I think I gave up my unhappiness."

"No, it's better when you hold me and we don't talk," she said. So I did, but then she asked, "What's *wrong* with us anyway?"

"It's a sickness. But it gets better."

"What makes it better?"

"Water. Air. Light. If we could just go back to Lake Travis—"

"What if it follows us?"

"It will. But you have to give me a chance. Let me be strong for you. I can be strong, but sometimes being with you is like—fighting air."

When I kissed her, she closed her eyes and said, "Do that again."

I did and then said, "You should listen to me sometimes. I know a little about these things."

"What else do you know?"

"We have to live this life—and go back to work."

"Oh, I can't think about work again," she said. "You have to pretend to be somebody you're not."

"Yeah, but they pay you for it. And there's a way you can play a role but stay yourself—"

"No," she said, suddenly getting up. "Dr. Harris knows what's best for us."

"Can't we make love?"

"Too much is happening to me tonight," she said, staring down at me. "Please go home now."

"All right."

But at the door I stopped and said, "Can't we just do something meaningless, like going to a movie together?"

To my surprise, she agreed. "There's a movie called *Point Blank* I'd like to see," she said, "starring Lee Marvin and Angie Dickenson—I think they look like us."

I didn't, but it sounded like a completely normal thing to do. So I made a date for Saturday night and told her I would pick her up at seven. Then I drove back to my apartment, singing along with a song on the radio.

Two nights later, I picked her up, wearing my slacks and dress shirt from work. I noticed she was wearing makeup and new shoes and thought that was a good sign. The movie was playing at a neighborhood theater in a shopping mall, and she had to give me directions there. As I stopped for a light, Jody said, "I've been thinking about our conversation the other night."

"Good."

"Can you talk again about what happened to you out at the lake?"

"I think I finally gave up my unhappiness," I said, concentrating on the light. It was easy to talk about these things while you were driving.

"But how did you do that?"

The light changed. I drove another block, pulled into the theater parking lot, and found a place.

"I don't know," I said. "You have to want it. Then you have to wait for it to come."

"For what to come?"

"I don't know what to call it."

"Are you telling me you have to pray?"

"No, but you have to wait forever. Finally it just happens."

She got out herself, on her side of the car, and we walked toward the theater. I couldn't tell what she was thinking.

The theater was fairly crowded, but I found us two seats at the back. It was a little warm, and Jody began to shift uncomfortably.

Finally there was a scene where the stars made love—Lee Marvin was lying on top of Angie Dickenson, his face pressed to hers—and they *did* look exactly like us.

Jody stood up abruptly and said, "Take me home."

Everyone was staring at us, and I was filled with shame, wondering what I had done wrong.

In October, it turned cold. I began to have nightmares where mannequins came into my room and turned me into one of them. My brain felt like compacted dust again, and I sometimes thought I gave off the mineral stink of insanity and crystal meth. It was clear that Jody had contracted a serious case of the sickness, and I couldn't handle it. I was losing my strength, and this was sad but somehow inevitable. One Sunday, I spent an hour staring at my reflection in the bathroom mirror. I felt I was approaching some dangerous point when I might see something I did not want to see.

That weekend, I drove up to Austin, where I stayed with John and Julie out at Lake Travis and went swimming one last time. "When are coming back again?" Julie asked me.

"Not right away."

"Just don't forget about the lake," she said. "You can always stay here as long as you want."

Then I drove back, through Austin. But there I stopped for a cup of coffee at the Tower Drug. Dee came in, just as I had somehow known she would, and sat down with me.

"How are things going with Jody?" she asked me.

"I don't really know."

Then Dee told me she was going to graduate at midterm and was thinking about going to New York City, where she had some relatives.

"I'm impressed," I told her. "That's a big step. But you might have the right idea—stop playing it safe and just *go*."

"I'm ready if you are," Dee said suddenly, putting her hand on mine. "I think we could make it up there, Will."

Just for a moment, it seemed possible. Then she added, "But of course we'd have to get married. My mother couldn't stand it if we didn't get married."

"Yeah, well, of course we'd have to get married."

But I knew I could never do this, so I said goodbye and drove back down to Houston.

I worked the rest of the week at Montgomery Ward and, on Friday evening, saw Dr. Harris. "How are things going with you?" he asked me abstractly.

I told him about taking Jody to the movie and how she had walked out.

He was a little surprised we had gone out together and asked me, "Why do you think she was angry at you?"

"I don't know."

"You must have a theory."

"I think she's getting worse," I said.

Dr. Harris looked out the window and thought for a while. There was something going on here—he knew something I didn't, and I waited for him to speak.

Then he turned around in his chair and said, "I think you are also getting worse."

I thought of my growing fear of mirrors, of my feeling that I had to control my every movement. Dr. Harris was saying he would like to give me medication but couldn't because of my history as a drug addict, and I thought, *I'm losing ground, and it shows.*

"You, of course, are a good patient," he finished. "But I think you are deeply disturbed. You had a psychotic episode."

"Go on."

"Here's my proposition. This might be a good time to put you in a private clinic. Not for long, just a few days. I know of such a clinic, and I can write you a letter that will help you with the expense."

"For how long?"

"Three days of electroshock therapy, about a week altogether. Now I know there are a lot of bad stories about it, but the procedure has been much improved. You'll be thoroughly sedated and well taken care of."

In fact, I had heard all this before in group and thought Dr. Harris might be right. The procedure had been much improved and probably wouldn't harm me. It would also be an admission that I was helpless, but in a way, this was appealing to me. Wasn't this what I had needed? Someone like Dr. Harris, someone who cared, someone who could help bring me to my senses?

When I was walking the Golden Gate Bridge, I might have gone for it. But suddenly I thought of the time, two months ago, out at Lake Travis with Jody, when I had heard the music more clearly than I had ever heard it in my life. Dr. Harris thought that was a psychotic episode. But I had remembered who I was and what I had to do, and what if I lost my gift, my strength, my firmness of mind, and never heard the music again?

I stood up and said, "I'll have to think about it."

"I hope you're going to take me up on my offer," he said, a little surprised.

"I'll have to think about it," I repeated.

Dr. Harris stood himself and offered his hand, which I shook. It was warm and dry.

"Then do," he said. "I hope you decide to go through with this. I've come to think of you as a friend—and I sincerely think this is the best thing for you and Jody both."

From that moment, I think my mind was made up. Perhaps, like the girl in my group, I felt I was doing something for myself for the first time in my life.

I went back to my apartment and packed up my things. Then I dropped my rent check and the key in the mailbox, drove to Jody's, and rang her bell. Finally she let me in.

I had grown to hate her apartment, and tonight it seemed to me that it held that faint, stale chemical or fecal smell that I had smelled at the Austin State Hospital and on myself.

"Dr. Harris wants me to have shock treatments," I told her.

"Yes, he suggested the same thing to Darryl."

"I'm not surprised."

"Darryl won't go for it."

"Neither will I. I'm leaving town tonight, and I'd like to take you with me."

"I can't go," she told me. "I'm pregnant."

It was like being hit. My face went numb, and we stared at each other for an endless moment. I was completely lost, struggling to make sense of what she had said, doing sums in my head and trying to figure out the timing.

"Yes, the poor little rabbit died," she was saying. "Maybe that's why I've been so impossible."

"Is it mine or Darryl's?"

"It's so like a man to ask that. I don't know," Jody said. "I did make love to Darryl one more time after I met you in Austin. But it might have been you, on one of those nights we spent in Austin."

The pain of her telling me she had made love with Darryl after seeing me in Austin was incredible.

"It's strange, isn't it?" she said. "All that time when we lived together and made love night after night, I wanted to have your baby, but I couldn't get pregnant. Now that I am—either one of you could be the father."

"Yeah," I said. "It's strange."

"Dr. Harris wants me to have an abortion and says he can arrange it for me. Darryl says he doesn't care. So I guess you'll have to make up your mind about it."

This is why Dr. Harris wanted me to have shock treatments, I thought.

"Why do I have to make up my mind about it?" I asked her.

She frowned. "Because ... I don't know; it might be yours."

"Look," I said. "All I know is, I have to get out of here, and I want to take you with me. If we stay here, we'll both be lost in the questions, the doubts."

"I'm not leaving Dr. Harris. He's the only one who can help me. But you have to stay too."

"I can't stay."

"If you love me, you'll take care of the child, even if it's not yours."

Here it was, the great choice of the decade. That I had to face it now was strange beyond belief. Strangest of all was the fact that I had a hard-on. Knowing that I might have gotten Jody pregnant on one of those nights in Austin made her incredibly attractive to me.

Everything for years had led to this moment, and tonight I could make her mine forever.

"Darryl doesn't give a goddamn," Jody said, coming closer. "Touch me." She took my hand and put it on her belly. "I know you're strong enough to help me raise this child."

"No," I said. "I'm afraid I'm not." I hadn't known I was going to say these words until I did.

"You told me you were strong."

"Not that strong."

"But what about the baby?"

"It's up to you, not me."

"Don't you care about it?"

"You shouldn't have slept with Darryl."

"Dr. Harris says I'm not responsible for my actions."

"Dr. Harris is wrong. We are responsible for who we are."

Already, something had changed. The light seemed dimmer, the room looked far away, and so did she. "Dr. Harris said if I wanted to have the baby, then I should do it for myself."

"That's always the best way, isn't it? But I have to go."

"Right now?"

I nodded and took her in my arms. "Look, I'll call you in a couple of days," I said. "Things will look better tomorrow. I'll probably change my mind."

Jody followed me downstairs to the Austin-Healey.

When I got in my car, I said, on a sudden impulse, "I'm going to write about this someday."

"I know," Jody said. "I know you want to be a writer; that's another reason I love you."

But I couldn't stay in Jody's presence for another minute. So I drove away and left her there in Houston.

In the country between Houston and Austin—at a grove called the Lost Pines, some very tall pine trees that had somehow grown up here a hundred miles from East Texas—I pulled over to the side of the road and stopped. For twenty minutes, I could go neither back nor ahead.

It seemed to me that I could faintly hear the music, but it was very far away. Finally, I started the Austin-Healey again and drove on.

When I reached Austin, I called Dee and asked her to meet me in Eastwoods Park.

After twenty minutes, I saw her coming toward me. We sat together at an old picnic table, whose linoleum surface was covered with years of carved initials.

"Let's get married," I said, "and go to New York together."

Dee gave a sharp intake of breath and started to tremble. "Oh yes," she said.

It was like jumping off the Golden Gate Bridge. I had finally done it—made a Big Decision that was irrevocable, that there was no going back on. In doing so I had saved myself, and I think I even felt relief. But I had not been able to save Jody. This time, I had lost her forever.

FINAL JOURNEY

25

JANUARY 1968: ON the morning I saw the gray-gold towers of New York rising ahead of us, I felt such anxiety that I could no longer drive. So she took over the driving, and we roared through the Lincoln Tunnel, emerging into the shadowed canyon of Times Square. I remember there were theater posters everywhere, with solarized photos of hippies, advertising *Hair: The American Tribal Love-Rock Musical.*

Dee and I had gotten married the month before, in Dallas at the First Methodist Church of Highland Park. My parents were very happy that I had finally done it. Dee's mother was appalled. The sickness had begun to return, and in photographs of the wedding, my eyes are completely empty. After New Year's, Dee and I headed for New York in her Volkswagen Bug. It seemed the only way to defeat the Sickness was to keep throwing myself into new situations—so I had chosen to play the role of a young husband in the worst city in the world.

Dee and I spent that night in a motel near LaGuardia Airport and, the next morning, met her cousin at her home in Queens. Her cousin told us the best place to live was LeFrak City, but there were no vacancies. So we went to a real estate agent and, by the end of that day, found a studio apartment in a brick building just off Queens Boulevard with a sign on the wall that said, "Now Renting—One, Two, Three Bedroom Apartments." The next day, I signed a five-year lease, telling myself I would live here for the rest of my life. Walker Percy, who was becoming my favorite author, said that some people come to New York to be remembered and others come to be forgotten. I had come to be forgotten.

New York probably was the worst city in the world back then, but at least you could find an apartment, and jobs were easy to come by. Dee and I became office temporaries, riding the subway into Manhattan every morning and reporting to a temp agency. If there were no typing jobs, I went to the public library, where I spent hours reading old magazines, and ate lunch at the Automat. At dusk, Dee and I rode the F Train back to the last stop in Queens and walked to our apartment. There she made dinner, and we watched the news on television. On Sunday mornings, I put on my coat and tie and went to a small Episcopal church a few blocks away.

During the four months we lived in Queens, Martin Luther King was shot and killed in Memphis, Columbia students took over the campus, and Dee and I kissed in the lobby of a residence hotel on West End Avenue when we heard Lyndon Johnson say on the radio, "I will not seek or accept the office of president of the United States." To my great surprise it was possible to get non-Equity acting jobs. I found two—one was in Pinter's *The Room* at a girls' college near Milbrook, New York, and the other was in Clifford Odets's *Waiting for Lefty* at the old Roundabout Theater, then in the basement of a Chelsea supermarket.

At night, Dee and I lay in our bed in the dark telling each other stories of our childhoods. We had no friends here, but in this way, we discovered the happiness of early marriage, when it is just the two of you against the world. In the end, we did fall in love, and it seemed these nights would go on forever.

In May we were suddenly homesick for Texas. So on a Friday evening, we abandoned our apartment, threw everything in the back of her Volkswagen, and drove until midnight, when we stopped in Pennsylvania at the Mallard Motel. For years I was afraid the real estate agency in Queens would come looking for me, for breaking our lease.

Two days later, we reached Austin, where we found an apartment north of the campus and enrolled in the drama department. Both of us took a set design class, which would count toward our master's degrees, and I worked part-time as a delivery boy.

Larry and Karen had returned to Austin when the charges against them had been dropped. Larry worked as a disc jockey for a local radio station, and Karen was pregnant with their first child.

Danny had also returned. He had hung out in San Francisco with Mr. Natural and the Next Great Guy for another month. Then the "family" had bought a bus and driven to Los Angeles, where they ended up living at a house in Topanga Canyon. As the years went by, I realized the clown-like prankster we had met in the Haight might have been Hugh Romney, also known as Wavy Gravy, and the Next Great Guy might have been Charles Manson.

But Danny was more than ever a prankster, a holy fool, and I began to think of him as Lutz again. He was always getting in trouble and slipping out of it at the last minute. One night, he was at a party when the cops arrived, and he jumped out the bathroom window. Unfortunately, the house was on a hillside, and he fell twenty feet to the ground, breaking his leg. The doctors put a cast on it and gave him Nembutol. Sometimes I brought him a Frisco Burger and we talked—Lutz so stoned that food was falling out of his mouth—about the theories of R. D. Laing; that the insane were really the sanest of all, and so forth.

When Lutz was able to get around on crutches, he hitchhiked to the Drag and begged for spare change with the Vietnam vets. He also tried to enlighten me in the prankster way, by putting me in dangerous situations. One day, we drove to San Antonio to see Sam Peckinah's *The Wild Bunch* in an old movie theater with a diorama of the Alamo above the screen. We were the only gringos there, and during the final shoot-out, Lutz cheered for the Wild Bunch and the Pachucos cheered for the Mexicans. Later, they surrounded us in the lobby and called us *Jepe Basura*, but somehow Lutz talked them out of killing us by making them laugh. He was invulnerable in those days.

That summer, we watched the continuing disintegration of the United States on Larry's television or mine. We saw Bobby Kennedy assassinated in Los Angeles by Sirhan Sirhan, Hubert Humphrey nominated at the Democratic convention in Chicago while the cops beat up hippy protesters outside, Richard Nixon nominated at the Republican convention in Miami and being hugged by Sammy Davis Jr. On rainy nights we went skinny-dipping in the flood pools along Bull Creek Road. On hot days, we went to John and Julie's cabin on Lake Travis, sometimes renting a sailboat and sometimes just lying around on the shore.

I remember one such afternoon. Larry was talking to John about getting into Volkswagen repair, Julie was smiling like a cat in the sun, and Lutz was sleeping on the rocks with his leg in a dirty cast. Austin was still the coolest place in the world, but when Dee and I looked at each other, we knew it was our last summer here and, in the end, were glad to return to New York.

Just before we left, I talked on the phone to Jerry, the apprentice I had worked with at the Alley. He told me that Jody had gotten a divorce from Darryl and married someone she had met in one of Dr. Harris's therapy groups. She must have had an abortion, but he knew nothing about that. I told myself I would see her again, on the Journey.

On our way back to New York we stopped in Tulsa to see Gabe, who had just gotten out of Huntsville. He had married Kitty, moved here, and was now working as a janitor and on welfare. But he looked good—a lot healthier than he had looked the last time I'd seen him.

Later that day, we went swimming at a lake near Broken Arrow, and I saw his arms were huge; Gabe had spent much of his time in prison lifting weights so nobody would fuck with him. At first I was afraid he was angry with me because I had never been busted, but Gabe was easy to talk to. In prison he had played baseball, taught himself Classical Greek, translated the Book of Revelation, and never gotten in a single fight.

"Getting busted probably saved my life," he told me. "There's no way I could have survived another year on meth."

It seemed to me that, in prison, Gabe might have experienced Kierkegaard's despair of necessity. In your cell, where everything was necessary and nothing was possible, you were forced to find faith in yourself and in God, if not Jesus Christ. But Gabe didn't talk much about his religious beliefs. When the time came to break his silence, he might tell me something—but not now.

This time, Dee and I went straight to Manhattan, where we rented an apartment on the top floor of a building on West End Avenue. The windows opened onto the airshaft, but from the roof, you could see the Hudson River and the industrial coast of New Jersey. We sold Dee's Volkswagen; she got a job teaching at a private school; and I went to work, first as an office temporary again and later as a theater carpenter.

We stayed in New York for almost two years and made many friends. I never told them anything about my past in Texas—I was trying to forget my past then—although Dee and I often went to the Thalia Theater, near our apartment, to see the art movies we had first seen in Austin for a second time. Nixon was elected president and promised to end the war in Vietnam.

At Christmas, we watched the astronauts make the first orbit of the moon on television and read to us from the Book of Genesis. And we went to plays. Broadway was a slum then—there were more porno movie houses than stages in the theater district—but we saw *The Great White Hope*, *Rosencrantz and Guildenstern Are Dead*, and *Hair*. Gradually, we began to understand how to make our way in the theater. I found a good acting class and began working as a stage carpenter. Ice floated down the Hudson River all that first winter, but spring finally came.

Then flew back to Dallas, feeling like a great deal of time had passed. Earlier, my brother, Ray, had called and told me that our father Harmon had stopped drinking and joined Alcoholics Anonymous. He had even taken a trip to Dayton, Ohio, to see his real father, who was now retired and living on a farm again, to make amends. When I went back to Nortex, he was working as a janitor at a dance hall on the Amarillo highway, and my brother and I went over to see him. He had completely lost his anger, seemed years younger, and was the father I remembered from my childhood.

"You boys thirsty?" he asked at one point, and when Ray and I said we were, he told us, "I can take care of that."

Then he opened the soft drink machine with his key and gave us two Dr. Peppers. I have never been so proud of my father as I was that day.

That summer, I worked as a carpenter for Joe Papp at the Delacorte Theater in Central Park. On a hot night, Dee and I watched Neil Armstrong land on the moon, on our little black-and-white television. Later an old actor friend of mine from *Unto These Hills* dropped by and told me that Pete Peters, who wanted to be a writer, had gone to Vietnam but had stepped on a mine and lost both legs. Pete had written an angry letter from a hospital in the States, before he'd died of an infection the army doctors could not cure:

> Those Commie motherfuckers have blown my legs off.
> If you ever get to Vietnam, kill a Commie for me.

I watched the moon, a tarnished coin, sink into New Jersey. The fact that Pete had died left me in a state of depression that lasted for months.

I decided to get serious about the theater and finally got my Equity Card by stage-managing a children's show. Then I began going to auditions. But professional acting jobs were hard to get. It was a very frustrating time for me, because I was obviously one of the best actors in my class. I had it all figured out, including how to find the choices in a scene, how to take the big moment, dress right for an audition, and play myself. But I still couldn't get cast—and unless you got cast, you couldn't get an agent and couldn't go anywhere. The winter was long and snowy, and I walked around Manhattan in my cowboy boots, wearing a black funeral coat I had bought at a thrift shop and a blue button on my lapel that said, "End the War Now."

Finally I started writing a series of audition scenes for myself. These became a play, which I sent to the Yale School of Drama with an application. Dee also applied in theater administration.

A month later, we received a letter saying we had both been admitted.

The Yale School of Drama was a good place to hide out in the last years of the sixties and the early seventies. The Vietnam War was still going on, and Nixon was still president, but somehow we no longer had to worry about it. Dee and I were there for three years, and I read every play in the drama school library. When I wasn't reading plays, I was swimming in the pool at the Yale Gym or taking long, solitary hikes in the Connecticut woods.

At first I went to church but found prayer increasingly difficult now that I had lost the feeling that something dreadful was about to happen to me. Exertion was still the best way to overcome the lingering traces of the sickness.

In my first year at Yale, the play I had submitted—about an office temporary who was almost driven insane by the meaningless routines of the job—was produced as a freshman acting class project. But I was disappointed in my work.

By that time, I had rediscovered Chekhov, whom I had not paid much attention to in Texas—but he is the greatest playwright since Shakespeare and not a realistic writer at all. I had also read the fiction of Larry McMurtry, who was from Archer City, a small town near Nortex, and particularly liked his early novel *Leaving Cheyenne*. From it, I learned that the Texas plains were not so different from provincial Russia and that my hometown could be a place to set plays after all.

That summer, I wrote two plays, one after the other. The first, *Lifeguards,* was set at a swimming pool after it had closed for the night. Two lifeguards and two girls had a long conversation, lit by the green glow of the pool, which held real water.

The second play, *Cactus Courts,* was longer and took place a year later. It was senior night. The boy and girl in *Lifeguards* had gotten married and were spending their honeymoon at a motel called the Cactus Courts, in a room lit by fluorescent light. Four of their friends dropped in to see them, but when the play ended, the couple was left in the bed at center stage, where they had been discovered at the beginning.

The conversations in both plays always came back to the emptiness of the plains, and the subtext of both was silence. While I was writing them, I achieved a state of concentration where I played every character; but I also felt the play had already been written, and all I had to do was get it down.

The plays were performed as a project by my acting class and were very successful, and I decided I had a talent for playwriting.

One of the new characters I introduced in *Cactus Courts* was a hood, who was short, bowlegged, and wore motorcycle boots. Anger came off him like heat off a hot stove, and at one point, he talked about beating up his girlfriend. This character I called Bobby Lee, after Bobby Lee Cummins, and I remember that I thought, *Now that I have put him in a play, I don't have to fight him, and he will never bother me again.*

During this time, Lutz was writing me short but interesting letters about his exploits, in the voices of his many alternate personalities, like Dr. Strange and Mr. Hebrew.

> I am in Cuernavaca, following the trail of Malcolm Lowry in *Under the Volcano*. Have just been to the Farolito, the little lighthouse where the counsel was shot. Mescal forever!
>
> Stanley Cortez

Stanley Cortez was another one of these personalities, as well as the cinematographer who had shot *Night of the Hunter*. When Dee and I read these letters, we shook our heads in admiration and dismay.

Then, in the fall of 1971, I received another letter from Lutz:

> Something unbelievable has happened. A few weeks ago, I began receiving messages that a spaceship was landing in New Mexico. I started heading there, but my car broke down, and I hitchhiked back to Dallas. I got a ride from a trucker who wanted me to give him a blow job. When I got home, my parents wouldn't believe me, so I butted my head against the wall until they saw the blood and sent me to the loony bin. There I heard voices telling me that I am the secret husband of Evonne Goolagong—but that's another story. Some of the people here are insane, but I'll be out in a few weeks. Keep watching the skies!
>
> Chief Broom

The return address on the letter was Rusk State Hospital.

Fall 1971 was also the time of my ten-year high school reunion—suddenly it had been that long—and Dee and I flew back to Nortex. The movie version of Larry McMurtry's novel, *The Last Picture Show,* had just come out. Filmed in nearby Archer City, it was set in the fifties, at the time of the Korean War, and almost every scene featured a period article of clothing or song. But there was no great difference between then and now, and seeing the local terrain onscreen seemed to give our lives a new importance.

Everyone was at the reunion, including most of the beauties, favorites, and hoods. Some had done their military service, and a few had died in Vietnam. But most people, like me, had gotten out of the draft and were now devoted to making and losing money.

Toward the end of the evening, Bones, Pud, and Pigs Garland all came up to me and asked, "Where's Lutz?"

I told them I didn't know, but later I found out Lutz had tried to come to the reunion. He had broken out of Rusk, stolen his mother's car, and started for Nortex. But when he'd arrived, he had gone to the airport for some reason, where he was seen wandering around the terminal, saying, "I'm just trying to get home. Can you loan me some money?"

Finally somebody called the cops, and he was taken to the state hospital, where he tried to make an escape—ran for the fence and was caught by a guard, who threw him to the ground and broke his arm.

On the same Saturday night I was dancing the Dirty Bop to "Peanuts," "Sherry," "Only the Lonely," and "Will You Still Love Me Tomorrow," Lutz was out there at the state hospital—the very place where we'd had our first important conversation—but locked in one of those little brick buildings with wire screens on the windows, his arm in a cast.

So ended the sixties. But life, unlike entertainment, cannot be divided neatly into decades—and our lives would go on.

26

Joe Papp decided he wanted to do my play *Cactus Courts* at the Other Stage of the Public Theater. So when Dee and I graduated from Yale, we moved back to New York, where she worked as the administrator of an off-Broadway theater group, I taught playwriting at Adelphi University, and we waited for my inevitable success.

Then Dee began suffering from abdominal pains and, a few days later, collapsed at work. Someone called me at Adelphi and told me she had been taken to Lenox Hill Hospital. I rode the subway there, found her unconscious and running a high fever, and held her hand for an hour. She was then taken to an operating room, where emergency surgery was performed.

Two days later, a doctor came to Dee's room and talked to us both. He spoke plainly, telling us that she suffered from a condition called endometriosis. I had never heard of it, but a thrill of fear went through me when I heard the term. "Her womb wants to get pregnant so badly it's producing too much tissue," he explained, "and it's messing up her whole system. If you want to have a child, you'd better have it now. In another year, it may be impossible."

Suddenly, everything was clear to me. It was true I had not loved

Dee when I married her, but I had learned to love her and had promised God I would be faithful to her forever if he would keep me free of the sickness. Then, at Yale, I had slept with an actress who was in *Cactus Courts*. Dee, of course, didn't know this.

Now God was showing me what happened when you didn't keep your promises. He wanted us to have a child as proof of our love, and he had given Dee endometriosis—so I could save her and myself.

Two months before my play went into rehearsal at the Public Theater, Dee and I started trying to have a child. The doctor soon told us that our efforts had been successful, and she was pregnant.

But God was not through with me yet.

Joe Papp sometimes took an interest in your play—it was the worst thing that could happen to you—and decided that he knew how to make it work. I wanted actors, but Joe insisted on the real thing. For the small but important role of Bobby Lee, Joe insisted we cast a guy who had been in Rikers and had then taken an acting class and starred in a play about child molesters. But this guy was not very good and afraid of his agent, who had ordered him to take the part, and on the night his agent came, he mumbled his lines inaudibly.

The play fell apart, and several important audience members walked out. God was still punishing me, and this time my punishment was to see my play performed badly, because I had not been strong enough to stand up for it.

Joe finally hated my play so much that he erased it from the official history of the Public Theater—if you look, you will not find it there. The only person who seemed to understand this was not my fault was Melissa, an actress in the play. Soon I was going down to her apartment in the Village, where we made love all afternoon and told each other all our secrets. It seemed I could not remain faithful to Dee, and I was stricken with guilt but could not give the affair up.

Dee finally guessed I was having an affair, and one day, when I came home, she said, "Will, I *know.*"

"Good," I told her, "because I'm tired of hiding it."

"And I want you to know that I understand—because I've been unfaithful myself."

I suppose she thought this would make everything all right; but when we told each other the names of our lovers, our shame and anger were so great that, afterward, we couldn't stand the sight of each other. We should never have had this conversation.

But we stayed married for the sake of our child, and Dee, now visibly pregnant, began saying I had failed as a writer. "You've had your chance," she told me one day. "Now it's my turn. I want you to get a *real* job for a change, so I can stop working when the baby comes."

So I bid a tearful goodbye to my lover, Melissa, and told her we could never see each other. Then I started looking for a job. But I had trouble finding even temp work.

At this time, I was still taking my acting class because I thought it helped my writing. Our teacher was a former child movie star, who called his technique "moment to moment" and encouraged you to hold back nothing. He was a very good teacher, and everybody who took that class got better.

Everybody except Chris, an actor from Denton, Texas. He was a little younger than me and had come to the city after I graduated from Yale. All the girls in the class liked him, but I thought his work was inferior; he often played rednecks with a strong regional accent he would never have used in Denton.

This happens to some Texans who come to New York—their

origin becomes a form of insecurity. New York threatens them, and they become what I call professional Texans. Finally their work is nothing but behavior and mannerisms, and they forget all about playing their real selves.

One night, Chris and I were talking after class, and he told me, "You know, I saw *Cactus Courts*. And I got to tell you, it was a failure."

He was being the professional Texan that night—a little rough with me, but honest.

"Go on."

"But I think I know why, and I'm gon' tell you honestly. Joe Papp did it because you went to Yale. But then you made some mistakes. For one thing, you didn't use real Texas actors."

"The casting was Joe's idea."

"Tell you what you oughta do now. You oughta let me direct a scene from it, with people from this class who know enough to go moment to moment, no bullshit. Then you ask Joe Papp to come see it."

"Joe has no interest in seeing me or this play ever again," I said.

"Always putting yourself down, aren't you? But I think he'll come. And when he does, he's gon' see the real play—the play you wrote—and he's gonna want to do it again."

"What part do you want to play?"

"Me? I thought I'd play Bobby Lee, the guy who talks about how he beat up that girl. That's the best writing in the play, and it's the right part for me, don't you think?"

He wasn't right for it, but I told him to go ahead and work on the scene. They rehearsed for a month. The performance was held in our classroom, the basement of a church on the Upper East Side, and I took Dee with me to see the results. Our child was due in two months.

The scene went just as badly as I had expected. The guy and the girl playing the leads were upstage, in bed. Chris sat downstage, drinking beer and delivering his monologue about the girl he had beaten up. He was indicating, as actors say—everything was delivered in his forced Texas accent, which wouldn't have fooled anyone back in Texas for a single minute—and to me he wasn't menacing at all.

At that moment I resolved never to write a play about Texas again. I was trying to do something that just couldn't be done. No actor would see I was trying to write like Chekhov, and no Texas actor would play the text at all—just smother it with his voice, like a chicken-fried steak in cream gravy.

But when the lights came up, everyone applauded, and our teacher congratulated the actors and talked to them for a long time. Then I stood up and told them that it had been very good work, but even before I finished, Chris was shaking his head. He knew what I was going to say next, which was that I was not going to ask Joe Papp to come see it.

So I told them once Joe had made up his mind, he wasn't going to change it. But I would ask a director friend to come see it, and maybe they'd get a job out of it.

"Oh, bullcorn," Chris said. "Truth is, you were never gon' ask Joe Papp."

Our acting teacher said it was getting late, and he was going home. But after he left, the argument got even more heated, until I finally stood and said Dee and I were leaving.

"Not before I tell you what I really think of you—what everybody thinks about you," Chris said, his face floating before me. "Yer a real New York asshole."

I had to do something irrevocable, change my life. So I will admit that I struck the first blow—even that I felt real satisfaction when I saw Chris falling to the floor. Then Chris jumped up and hit me in the face, but neither blow hurt at all. This time, it was I who had lost control and started a fight—repeated the past and finally *gotten it right*.

When they set my broken hand at Lenox Hill Hospital, Dee told me I had frightened her and said, "I don't know you anymore." But we stayed together for the birth of our daughter that summer and into the early fall.

Even after I left Dee—finally moving in with Melissa, of course—I still tried to be a father to my daughter. For years, I picked her up after daycare and school, made her supper, took her on weekends. I paid for my sins—I am still paying for them—but I have never been sorry that Dee and I had a child because, on the night she was conceived, I heard the music again.

27

For the next seven years, I was a great sinner. I had left my wife and infant daughter for another woman. Dee's friends hated me, my Yale friends hated me, and even my old Texas friends hated me. After a while, it made me happy to be that way. Melissa and I lived on the Lower East Side. Sometimes I even swam in the Hudson River, which was cold and full of shit. Writing was no longer a holy vocation, but a way of making money. I wrote articles about sex for *Cosmo*, listened to Billy Joel, grew a long beard, lived in a slum, and drank too much.

Divorced, I watched my daughter grow up from a distance, took her to movies in Times Square, and taught her how to shoot pool. People were afraid of me. I knew a little about everything practical—carpentry, cooking, sex, plumbing, and property law—and was happy in every way but one: I had not heard the crystalline music since the night my daughter was conceived, and my belief that there was a meaning to life was disappearing fast.

After Nixon's impeachment, the whole country wanted to forget the sixties and, for a while, took its character from Jimmy Carter, who was from Georgia and an entirely different person—simple, religious, and self-righteous. Country music became popular even in New York and Austin. My brother Ray's group split up, and he returned to Nortex, where he got married and went to work for the railroad. My father became a respected figure in AA, retired, and began collecting social security.

Then one day, in the first year of the eighties, I wrote a short story (I wanted no more of theater actors ruining my work) about oilfield roughnecks. Melissa thought it was funny, so I sent it to *Penthouse*, who published it. The story was then optioned by a producer at a big movie studio, who asked me to come out to Hollywood and write the screenplay.

To my surprise, I liked it out there very much. Los Angeles is nothing like San Francisco—it's more like Dallas, but with an ocean nearby. I bought a little Japanese sports car, learned to eat sushi, worked at the studio in Burbank, and swam in the great Pacific Ocean. The screenplay of my short story was never produced, but I made some money for a change and considered moving out there for good. Melissa and I had been living together for seven years, and now we could afford to get married and have a child. But something held me back; I was afraid my daughter would be angry with me if I remarried.

When Melissa and I returned to New York, my career took another strange turn. I met an old friend from Yale who wanted to produce a musical and asked me if I would be interested in writing the libretto. The score would be provided by a singer/songwriter who had been called the Jack Kerouac of country music, and the subject of his recent songs was the Civil War.

So I came up with a story about Walt Whitman, Abraham Lincoln, and the Negro troops who had fought for the Union, which I called *Song of Myself*. It was a great pleasure to work with a real singer/songwriter, and the libretto turned out well. We were offered a production at the American Repertory Theater in Boston, and my Yale friend began saying, if the show went well there, he might be able to raise enough money to take it to Broadway.

Then, in early September 1983, my mother called me at daybreak. "Will?"

"Yes, Mom," I said.

But I knew somehow, even before she told me, that my father had been taken to the hospital, found to have incurable cancer, and been told that he could only live another six months. What other reason could there be for my mother to call me at daybreak?

Not long after my father got out of the hospital, he went down to Aum-Sat-Tat to take Phase Five again and learn the last lessons of the On the Beam Society. By that time I was busy with the rehearsals of *Song of Myself*, but in October, I flew down to San Antonio to see my father.

As I drove through the steel-pipe gate of Aum-Sat-Tat in a rental car, I began to get nervous. My suspicions about what had really happened to my father here began to come back to me.

Lately, I had been reading in the *New York Times* about congressional investigations of CIA and army programs with strange names, like MKUltra. These programs—which had begun as early as the late forties and early fifties—had involved giving psychedelic drugs like LSD and mescaline to unwitting subjects and volunteers. The object of these programs was mind control, and according to these articles, some of the early experiments had been performed at Brooke Army Hospital in San Antonio, where Dr. Truman had his first cosmic illumination.

The only question remaining in my mind was not if this had happened, but how much had Dr. Truman known? It seemed to me that, at some point, he must have known a lot—not only that he had been given a psychedelic drug at Brooke Army Hospital but also that Aum-Sat-Tat was being used by the CIA or the army as a control group, giving subjects lysergic acid and mescaline, and observing their reactions.

I parked in a gravel lot and walked up the hill. Aum-Sat-Tat had changed in the more than twenty-five years since I had been there. The Big House, with its library of Dave Dawson books, had been torn down. But the pool was still there, and there my father was waiting for me, sitting under a big oak tree.

"Hello, Sonny," he said.

"Hello, Dad."

"I'm learning great truths here every day," he said. "And there was that night years ago, when I was able to see this world as the creator sees it."

"I was just thinking about that," I told him.

Then my father and I sat there in the shade of the oak for a while, smiling at each other, but I was thinking it was time my father knew what had really happened to him here.

The first of my proofs was the preparation. Dr. Truman had told my father he was going to have a cosmic illumination that very night as he sat by the pool during the SLUMP. Then he had hypnotized him and given him a suggestion that the experience would be a good one.

"Can we still take the old paths that used to lead up the hill?" I asked my father.

"No, Sonny," he said. "They've all been closed down."

I was sorry to hear this, because the paths and the signs along them were the second part of my proof. In the fifties, Dr. Truman had turned the hill behind Aum-Sat-Tat into an environment for Beamers who were having a cosmic illumination—playing Beethoven on hidden loudspeakers; lighting up the woods with colored lights; putting up the signs that had so fascinated me when I was a child, with arrows pointing to Heaven and Hell and Phase Five; and the telephone booth for calling God.

Ken Kesey, with the money he made from the sale of *One Flew Over the Cuckoo's Nest*, had bought a ranch near La Honda, California, and used the surrounding woods for the same purpose. When I was living in the Haight-Ashbury, everybody was talking about this. Tom Wolfe, in his book *The Electric Kool-Aid Acid Test*, described how Kesey put up loudspeakers and colored lights in the redwood grove, turning them into a sort of psychedelic theme park. Or perhaps one of Kesey's followers got the idea from Dr. Truman.

Third, there was the character of my father's experience—hallucinations, flashing lights, intricate patterns, a slight sense of struggle—which were like my own psychedelic experiences on peyote and LSD but unlike my "natural" mystical experiences, which were pure, effortless bliss and completely without discomfort.

None of this, of course, was proof in the legal sense—and CIA Director Richard Helms had ordered the documents that might have mentioned Aum-Sat-Tat destroyed in 1973, after Watergate. But it was proof enough for me.

"A lot of years have gone by since you were first here," I said.

"Oh yes," my father said. "It's still a beautiful place, but it's not what it used to be. Now Aum-Sat-Tat is just a retirement home for old Beamers."

He explained that the On the Beam Society, although its members once numbered in the thousands, had never chosen the path of Scientology—had never gone public or declared itself a religion—and had faded almost out of existence. But old Beamers still lived in the remaining cabins.

"And Dr. Truman's still around," my father told me.

"Is that so?"

"Would you like to walk up the hill and see him?"

"All right," I said, my nervousness returning.

Dr. Truman lived in a limestone house at the top of the hill. He was an old man now, but his hair was still black—although dyed, I think— and he still sounded almost exactly like Kern Tipps, the Mutual Radio Network sportscaster who had announced the Southwest Conference football games when I was a child.

"You are well on your way to another cosmic illumination," I heard him tell my father as they stood there on his porch.

Lost in sudden anger, I looked away from them and found myself staring at a ball of daddy long-legs spiders beneath the gutters of the house, which sickened me.

Dr. Truman must have sensed my anger, because he said quietly, "I don't bother them, and they don't bother me. To me, all forms of life are sacred."

It was a reprimand, and my father nodded in agreement. Dr. Truman was a con man—there was a tradition in India of holy con men—who had achieved nirvana, probably with the help of a drug, and was now being self-righteous. I stared angrily at him, but he didn't smile. Just stared back at me until I had to look away.

As my father and I walked down the hill, I felt strangely sad and empty. It was the end of the long mystery, the end of the Journey.

My father put his hand on my shoulder and said, "There goes a great man."

"I hope you're right, Dad."

At the bottom of the hill, we sat again by the pool. After a while, my anger passed, and I was able to think clearly.

I had wanted to tell my father he had been made a fool of. His cosmic illumination had been produced by a drug, and my own mystical experiences had not. He might have had natural mystical experiences in his youth, but his drug trip replaced them in his mind—it was much more impressive—and so he forgot them. Finally he had become an alcoholic, hating himself for not having another cosmic illumination.

But what was the difference after all? Both kinds of experience were real enough—and both faded away. I had almost stopped thinking about God, and it had been years since I had heard the music. What good was enlightenment, chemical or natural, if the memory of it was lost?

The answer was all around me. It was unfortunate that Dr. Truman had never told my father the whole truth about his cosmic illumination, but he had opened the door for him. Aum-Sat-Tat was still my father's favorite place in the whole world, the place of his greatest discoveries— and here he had finally come to rest, at the end of his days.

"What are you thinking about, Sonny?" my father asked me.

"Nothing," I said. "I'd like to hear a story again."

"About Beethoven?"

"No," I told him, "but a story about music. I mean your own story, the one about the time you were in Germany and played Liszt's piano."

So we sat there by the pool, and my father, the original Dharma Bum, told me his greatest war story one more time.

Dr. Truman died that year, and my father died only a month or so later. So my father never lived to see *Song of Myself* open on Broadway, and I never told him of my conviction that Dr. Truman had given him acid, probably as part of a government program. Nor have I ever written about it until now. I cannot prove it, and as my agent always says, if you have no proof, there is no money in it.

28

Winning a Tony award for *Song of Myself* was like an near-death experience: There was a flash of light, and I found myself meeting people it seemed I had known all my life—famous Broadway and film stars from my childhood, including old Van Johnson, who gave me the award and was still very positive and youthful.

Melissa and I were married in Los Angeles at the home of friends and, on our honeymoon, drove up the coast to San Francisco. There I stood on the front porch of the house where had I lived in a closet during the Summer of Love. We drove on as far north as Gualala, where we stayed in an old hotel surrounded by redwoods and swam in the great Pacific Ocean.

When we returned to New York, I took a job teaching playwriting at Brooklyn College. The other faculty members didn't think much of me—success in New York is always temporary, and writers are a dime a dozen—but I had some good students and enjoyed teaching. *Song of Myself* ran for two years on Broadway, and I found great satisfaction in the idea that my work, although it was thoroughly disliked by some critics, was making money, and it still is.

Some of this money I spent on a psychiatrist. Yes, I had sworn I would never do this again, but perhaps every writer in New York has to see a psychiatrist sooner or later. He told me that I suffered from bipolar depression (the latest version of despair) and prescribed Prozac, a new drug at that time. Prozac prevents the absorption of serotonin, a natural chemical that gives one feelings of safety, and soon I felt much better.

Finally I told him all my secrets—my encounters with love, sin, despair; my mystical experiences; and the horrors of the Sickness Unto Death. But ironically, my psychiatrist had never read William James or taken psychedelic drugs and had no religious or political beliefs of any kind. He explained that my mystical experiences had obviously been the product of my bipolar depression and told me the only important thing in life was to be happy. He also advised me never to write about my father or the On the Beam Society.

For two years, I was a complete believer in Prozac, which I associated with a feeling of both calm and quiet excitement, as if it was a full moon night. But one day, I realized that not only was I not writing; the Prozac had made me impotent.

So I stopped taking Prozac and stopped seeing Dr. Irwin. Melissa had decided he was a waste of money long before, and I have only one explanation for seeing him in the first place: Nobody shares all of themselves with anyone, not even their wife, but they will tell a total stranger anything. You might say I needed a stranger to talk to.

Then I bought a cabin on a lake in Texas—not on Lake Travis, but a smaller lake, which had the same limestone cliffs and ink-blue water, and was just upstream from an old dam on the Brazos River. It was also ideally located, north of Austin, west of Dallas, and south of Nortex. I could easily drive to any of these towns, and both my mother and my brother still lived in Nortex. Ray had married, adopted three boys, was playing in local bars, and told me he was happier than he had ever been in his whole life.

I had decided to write a novel instead of a play or a movie script, because Texas was my home, and there were many memories here I wanted to revisit. But when we first went to the cabin for the months of April and May, I had difficulty writing, and there was nothing for Melissa to do but lie on the end of the dock in the sun.

To stop seeing a psychiatrist had been easy, but when I stopped taking Prozac, I couldn't sleep or dream for months and still could not make love to my wife.

Then I began having a series of vivid dreams—about Jody Brown. In one of them, she was buried up to her neck in dirt, and I thought, *She's dead.*

When we returned to New York, I went back to my storage vault to look for her letters, which I had kept in a green, metal, fireproof box. In my dreams, I found those letters in various places—in closets, in Eastwoods Park, in the cemetery near my home in Nortex where I had grown up—but I could never find that green metal fireproof box, although I searched the storage vault from top to bottom.

Finally I went down to Houston to meet the author of a script I was writing for television and looked for Jody's home. But I could no longer remember the name of the street she lived on, and when I drove around the neighborhood looking for the house itself, everything had changed. I even thought about hiring a detective, but at the last minute, it seemed this might threaten my marriage. I have never seen Jody again.

By the end of that winter, I had been off Prozac a year. I was sleeping through the night but still impotent. Then I took a job writing the screenplay of a novel by another writer, which finally involved going out to Los Angeles, where I lived at a hotel in Hollywood and worked at the movie studio in Burbank.

Melissa came out and stayed with me for a week. It was a strangely warm week of rain, lightning, and mudslides, and a large sinkhole appeared in the street across from my hotel one night. For some reason, all this chaos was highly erotic, and Melissa and I rediscovered our longing for each other. So it is true that good fortune, bad weather, and strange hotel rooms can lead a man and a woman to fall back in love with each other, but I think it was the earthquake that finally did it.

We woke after midnight to the rocking of our room, the cracking of the walls, and bright green flashes outside as the power lines went down. There was a long silence, broken only by the barking of dogs, and then we were overtaken by the earthquake lust, which Mary Renault has described so well in her novel *The King Must Die*. When it passed, Melissa fell asleep, but I lay in the moonlight, which seemed to grow brighter and brighter until I found myself thinking about my life in a way I never had before. Then I realized that, for the first time in years, I was hearing the crystalline ringing of the music.

When we returned to New York, Melissa said she thought she was pregnant. A visit to her doctor confirmed this, and for the second time, I felt the youthful happiness of knowing my wife was going to have a child, of starting over—and again, of losing control of my life. A few months, later she went for a sonogram, and there was our child, its head a silver bubble on the television screen. The nurse said, "I can see the sex. Do you want to know what it is?"

Melissa and I looked each other, nodded, and said, "Yes."

Then the nurse told us, "It's a boy."

In May, we flew down to Dallas and drove to our cabin, where I went back to work on my novel. It was turning into a story about the sixties, and I decided I needed to drive to Dallas and see Lutz, to ask him some questions.

After spending a great deal of his life in and out of mental institutions, Lutz was now living in a Jewish nursing home in North Dallas. His parents had been dead for several years.

I had seen him here before, but today it took me a long time to get used to his appearance. He wore gray sweatpants, a University of Oklahoma sweatshirt, and sneakers and weighed almost fifty pounds more than he had three years ago. When he got in my car, he was trembling uncontrollably as he struggled to light a Saratoga—a nonfiltered cigarette favored by bikers and mental patients.

His condition was not his fault—not the product of the illegal substances he had taken—but of a neuroleptic drug called Prolixin. In his first year at Rusk, he had been given Prolixin to prevent him from committing suicide. It had ruined his central nervous system and produced something called tardive dyskinesia—a sort of Parkinson's disease. Lutz had never gotten over the symptoms, which for some people were irreversible, and now they had gotten much worse. He looked like a man being continually frightened by flashes of lightning. The hardest part was knowing he would be this way for the rest of his life.

But his first question was, "What kind of drugs have you brought me?"

"None," I said, and he groaned.

"You didn't bring me *anything?*"

"What did you expect?"

"Cocaine, codeine, acid, pot. They would have been so easy for you to get, and it's so impossible for me."

"I don't do drugs anymore."

"All right," he said. "But you've got to buy me a Frisco Burger. The food in this place is terrible."

"Let's go, then."

We went to the nearest hamburger stand, where we sat inside, and I ordered him a double Frisco Burger with a large order of cheese fries. It was disturbing to watch him eat because he chewed with his mouth open—pieces of hamburger meat and bun falling out of his mouth and dripping on his sweatshirt—always staring right at me. For a long time, he held a French fry between his lips, pointing it directly at my face as if I were responsible for his condition.

"How's it going?" I finally asked him.

"Same old shit," he said. "I'm on Haldol. Breakfast is two pieces of French toast and a glass of orange juice. I smoke a pack of Saratogas a day, and I can beat anyone on the floor at Ping-Pong." (Lutz had always excelled at Ping-Pong, the sport of the clinically insane.) "I don't know how Jesus Christ got into the act, but every Saturday, this Lesbian minister comes here and plays hymns on her accordion. She praises Jesus Christ and makes us sing along."

"How did it start this time?"

"One of my voices told me to put salt instead of sugar into my coffee. When I stirred it, my coffee turned into a talking galaxy, like the scene in Go Dar's *Week-End,* and told me to stop taking my medication. So I did."

The other customers were staring at us.

"You're sure you haven't got any drugs?" he asked me.

"No."

"And you can't get me some?"

"No."

"Then what are we going to do now?" he asked me.

"Let's go to Fair Park."

Lutz and I had been to Fair Park before. I had recently discovered the buildings were designed by the writer Donald Barthelme's father, an architect back in the thirties. Now they had been restored and were considered one of the outstanding examples of Art Deco architecture in the United States—the world of tomorrow made material.

Together Lutz and I walked across the plaza toward the Automobile Building, the Science Building, and the Great Hall of Texas, where there was a throne room with a seat for every county in the state.

"Would you like to see the Cotton Bowl?" I asked him. "Or go to the Health Museum and see the giant beating human heart?"

"No, I want to go to the Midway."

The Midway was running on a reduced schedule because it was summer, but we went anyway. Many of the rides were closed, but the Midway still smelled of spilled mustard and overheated machinery. In a roller-coaster car, we rode through a fun house, skeletons appearing and flying toward us. I couldn't stop thinking that this was Lutz's life—a thrill ride that had lasted forever.

After a while, we walked back to the plaza and sat on a bench beneath Big Tex, the cowboy statue who wore the largest pair of Levi's in the world. It was a summer day of the sort I am fond of—big white cumulus clouds sailed overhead, and thunderstorms were possible.

"Well, I guess this is the last time we will see each other," Lutz said suddenly.

"Why do you say that?"

Instead of answering, he said reflectively, "You were all right, until you started hanging around with your drama friends. Then you started thinking you could become another person."

"You're forgetting I'm a writer—not an actor."

"Whatever you are, you're a phony."

"All I was ever trying to do was get more immediate. Get up there into the light."

But he still refused to look at me.

"Who are we doing this all for?" he finally said.

"Our children, maybe."

"I shall never have them."

I said nothing.

"There used to be a baseball throw here," he said. "When you were a child, you probably spent all your time throwing baseballs at the Negros, dumping them into the water."

I had to think hard to remember this, but I finally said, "I'm ashamed to admit it, but you're right."

"So you have always been a racist."

"And you have always been the real Kinky Friedman."

"That asshole," Lutz said. "He got everything from me."

More clouds sailed over, and for a long time, nothing more was said. I felt pity for Lutz—because he had suffered so many dreadful mishaps, because of his disfiguring tremor, because he was fixed forever at the point when he had lost his mind and his self, and because he was still back there in the sixties.

"Did we ever find it?" I asked him.

"What's that?"

"The meaning of it all, the great truth, the secret of life."

"Did you?"

"Maybe once or twice—but I keep forgetting it."

He thought about this for a moment and then smiled and said, "I think I have also found it."

Now a strange thing happened. From that moment on, I begin to think of Lutz as Danny again—my old friend, the first of my companions—still bearing the scars of the Journey, but beneath them, courageous, true, forever the same.

"Tell me more," I said.

"It all goes back to the Order of DeMolay and the Gnostic Gospels," he said. "Jacques de Molay, the leader of the Knights Templar, was not burned at the stake for concealing his treasure—but for refusing to reveal the secrets of the Gnostic Gospels."

"I remember Jacques de Molay," I said.

"Yes, you played him in the DeMolay degree. You were terrible, by the way—worse than Victor Mature in *Samson and Delilah*."

"I did the best I could."

"The Knights Templar," Danny went on, "lived in the ruins of the temple after they took Jerusalem. There, Jacques de Molay found the Gnostic Gospels and was converted. For this, he was burned at the stake by the Catholic Inquisition. But the secret faith of Jacques de Molay became the faith of the Masonic order—Gnosticism, the belief of the early Jews who valued knowledge above all things. Knowledge, and the love of all that is natural—including the love of Jesus for Mary Magdalene, even the love of one man for another."

"I've heard something like that."

"But the Catholic Church suppressed the Templars, which is why nobody in the Order of DeMolay could be a Catholic. You, of course, never questioned this."

"No," I said. "You're wrong. I have never stopped wondering about this."

"As to where I found my faith," Danny said, "it was in a place that you would never dare to look."

"You mean at the hospital?"

"Yes," Danny said. "I've had friends at the hospital who taught me much. Some are gay, and of course you hate gays. But they have helped me find a moment. It comes to me when I am not on drugs. And it feels as if a strong light is shining on me ..."

"I know that feeling," I said. "I know exactly what you're talking about."

"The mind is clear; it is simple and pure and strong."

"It has to do with love, doesn't it? The big secret is for everybody. And it has to do with love, all the people you've loved."

But something I said had disappointed him. He looked away and shook his head. "You will never find the big secret," he said sadly, "because you have forgotten what we were looking for in the first place."

"I have *not* forgotten," I insisted. "Just say the word, and I will follow you."

Danny stood suddenly. "I have to get back to the home," he said. "But I'll tell you a few more things along the way."

So I followed him toward the distant streamlined buildings of the world of tomorrow.

EPILOGUE

This, then, has been my account of the Journey to the West, the journey of the sixties, when the old ideas were remembered and then forgotten again. At first it seemed it would be a boring decade, but overnight the world turned upside down, and it was everyone for himself.

We have learned again what we have always known—that work and freedom are more important than money and that love is the best thing in life. Then there are the mysteries I solved, the secrets I once thought were so important. This was only one aspect of the sixties, but it was the part I knew best, and I have tried to write about it honestly.

Inequality and misfortune are bad, and war is worse. But worst of all things is despair, because in the end, you lose your self, or your soul. Despair is the enemy of life and seems to have been around since the beginning, although what the Greeks thought about it is hard to say. Sometimes I think of despair as the first principle of Buddhism—that all of life is suffering—but Buddhists believe we get another incarnation. Christians believe we have only one life in which to find Christ, after which it is heaven or hell.

My mother was a Christian, and my father was a mystic. My tastes ran to Zen Buddhism and the early Greeks. But I believe it was Danny who first taught me that that despair was the enemy and had to be defeated.

According to William James in *The Varieties of Religious Experience*, there are three antidotes to despair. Alcohol is the least powerful, and it soon becomes addictive. Psychedelic drugs are far more powerful and allow us to reach true mystical states but also produce hallucinations, disorientation, and discomfort. Strongest of all are natural mystical experiences, which are very much like the moments of clarity and serenity we knew in childhood, but are the most easily forgotten.

It is true that, in the fifties, the government gave psychedelic drugs to unsuspecting people at places like Aum-Sat-Tat—the government may have done more to bring on the sixties than Timothy Leary ever did—and this ruined some people's lives. But I no longer think about it much. In fact, all mystical states are natural. There is only one problem--all are forgotten. This can be as frustrating as being given information about the fate of the earth by alien visitors and then being told you will not remember it.

Now that I am old, life becomes more accidental and inexplicable every day. But somewhere along the way I have learned not to feel sorry for myself or profess I am an expert in these matters or even choose a faith. I find that refusing this choice makes me strangely happy.

I live in Brooklyn because, for all its faults, I like it better than the town where I was born. My days are calm and predetermined. I watch my children grow up and hope they will do well. I have two of them, and the one thing I have done for them is teach them how to swim—I have noticed people who can swim are at ease in the world. On my shelves are a few books that are important to me. I work and accept the fact that, as I grow older, the music grows fainter and is finally gone. We are lucky if we know it more than two or three times in a lifetime, and these moments always seem to come in our youth.

There may be an afterlife of some sort, but I have never been much on reincarnation. One life has been enough for me. When this life is over, there may be nothing else for us, and we may never meet again. In any event, it is best not to hope.

But I know there is another world that sometimes sheds its light on us. For me it has something to do with time, with having children, and with the music that is heard at various times in our lives. Lovers who are ready to reproduce seem to hear this music. It draws them on, and after this, there may be no other time that is exactly right. There have obviously been plenty of children born whose parents never heard or have forgotten the music, but the gift persists.

Just as I know that my mother and father must have heard the music on the night they made me or the night I was born. And I hope to hear it once more on the last day of my life, when I start my own final Journey to the West.

ABOUT THE AUTHOR

BORN IN TEXAS, William Hauptman first traveled to California and New York in the sixties. A graduate of the Yale School of Drama, he is the author of both plays and fiction. *Domino Courts* won an Obie Award. *Big River*, an adaptation of *Huckleberry Finn*, written in collaboration with composer Roger Miller, won seven Tony awards when it opened on Broadway. His fiction has appeared in the *Best American Short Stories* anthology, and he has published a collection of stories, *Good Rockin' Tonight*, and a novel, *Storm Season*. Hauptman has also contributed journalism to the *Atlantic Monthly*, *Texas Monthly*, and the *New York Times Magazine* and written several screenplays for the studios. He has taught at the James A. Michener Center for Wrriters at the University of Texas, and his work is part of the Southwest Writer's collection at Texas State University in San Marcos. His daughter, Sarah, is employed by the State Department, and his son, Max, is a captain in the United States Army.

Printed in the United States
By Bookmasters